THE HAPPY HOLIDAYS CRIME COLLECTION

JACQUELINE VICK

Classical Reads

ISBN 978-1-945403-31-6 (ebook)

ISBN 978-1-945403-48-4 (hardbound)

ISBN 978-1-945403-56-9 (paperback

Frankie Chandler

I'd like to introduce you to Frankie Chandler, unwilling Pet Psychic. Frankie's "gift" is an unwelcome pain in the butt. She still hasn't gotten used to receiving messages from animals, and she's constantly— and often inconveniently—surprised by the methods they use to get through to her. It doesn't help that animals obfuscate like seasoned politicians, only animals have the excuse that they're, well, animals.

Trouble with Turkeys

I stared at the pasty white, twenty-nine-pound turkey defrosting in my kitchen sink and broke into tears. How did I get myself into this mess? Was I insane?

Taking a deep, tremulous breath and turning my thoughts to the night I issued Detective Martin Bowers the invitation to Thanksgiving dinner, I decided it was his fault.

We were sitting on the cushy leather couch in his living room watching a holiday film on his flat screen television… Okay. It was *Night of the Living Dead,* and I'm not sure if Halloween counts as a holiday.

Anyway, while Helen Cooper was being murdered by her beloved but now zombified daughter, Karen, Bowers grabbed me and shouted. "Brains!"

I screamed, which only encouraged him. He started gnawing on my neck. I responded with shrieks of laughter, my hands pushing at his shoulders to get him to stop because it tickled. He tapered off into nibbles, worked his way to my earlobe, and went in for a long, slow kiss.

After a long period of non-dating, we had finally taken the plunge six weeks ago at the end of my best friend

Penny's wedding on an Alaskan cruise. Before that, there had been an attraction, but we never made it to where we set a time, got together, and did something fun. A date. Then, after a minor mishap involving my accidentally transmitting to him the image of a screaming cat, Bowers declined to pursue a relationship. His excuse? He wanted to remain sane. Baby.

That all changed when shipboard entertainer Marvelous Marv was murdered on the cruise. Sneaky Penny told Bowers what happened, exaggerating my state of hysteria, and he used his vacation time to join us. At the end of the cruise, which included the successful capture of the killer, Bowers pulled me outside onto a cabin balcony and confessed that he longed to see me outside of a murder investigation.

These past weeks I had discovered a playful side to the usually serious detective that surprised me, though I didn't get to see it often due to his hectic schedule with the Wolf Creek Police Department. When we managed to snatch a moment for a classic film like *Night*, we enjoyed each other's company.

Bowers, exercising his incredible self-control, broke off from our kiss before it became too heated. He leaned back and wrapped his arm around my shoulder. I've heard of people cooling things down with a cold shower. Bowers delivered the equivalent when he said:

"Have you thought any more about Thanksgiving?"

The other thing Martin Bowers had said as we stood alone on the ship's balcony on that last day of our Alaskan cruise was he wanted me to meet his sisters.

After his mother died, Bowers was raised by a gazillion older sisters. I knew it was important to him that I meet them—or they meet me. However, the idea of being surrounded by a gaggle of protective women forming a barrier around their baby brother, women who probably expected him to remain chaste, single, and devoted to them for life. Or else join the priesthood. I was intimidated.

He backed off after that first mention and gave me time to consider his proposition. I ignored the request and hoped he would forget about it. Then, about a week ago, he suggested we drive up to his eldest sister June's house for Thanksgiving, where I could meet the entire Bowers clan.

Therefore, it was desperation and a healthy dose of fear that prompted my next move. I put on what I thought was a sexy pout—without a mirror I couldn't be sure it didn't look like I had gas—and I said, "But I thought we could have our first Thanksgiving as a couple right here in Wolf Creek."

He frowned and removed his arm. Then he rested his elbows on his knees, folded his hands, and tapped his thumbs together, a habit I noticed he fell into when pondering unpleasant thoughts. "You mean heat up one of those pre-cooked dinners from the grocery store?"

He made it sound as if that option was only available for the elderly, infirm, and people with no hope, so I swallowed my "yes" and said, "No, silly. I'll cook."

Both brows shot up. "You want to cook for me?"

I suppressed my irritation. What did he think I did with those frozen egg rolls we had snacked on earlier? "Sure. Why not?"

"There's a lot involved." His clear blue eyes clouded over with doubt. "Are you sure you know how to prepare a turkey dinner?"

"Of course." How hard could it be? I'd watched my mother do it for years.

A slow grin spread across his face, and then he pulled me close and kissed me with enthusiasm. Too late, I realized the enormity of what I had just agreed to do. Flashbacks raced through my head. The way my mother and aunts would describe a newlywed's first holiday meal with a reverence usually reserved for Grandma's pot roast recipe and anything involving Erma Bombeck. The successful woman had the respect of her man, her peers, and all extended family members. The failure...it didn't bear thinking about.

Bowers lifted his head and stared down at me. "I'm not boring you, am I?"

My preoccupation must have shown in my tepid response to his kisses.

"You got me thinking about the menu," I lied.

He gave me an affectionate peck on the forehead and scooted back to his spot on the couch.

"Well, are you going to roast the turkey or broil it? Frying is a pain in the rear end."

There was more than one way to cook a turkey? Mom just popped it in the oven. I knew there was a broil setting on the dial, but—no. I said roast.

"Good choice. That's my favorite. Do you have a stuffing recipe?"

"Boxed?" I giggled at his expression. Fortunately, he thought I was joking. "I'll use my mother's, of course."

He raised one brow. "Sausage?"

Did we need sausage *and* turkey? "Why don't you let me surprise you."

He nodded. "Okay. I just need to warn you that I like my mashed potatoes lumpy. That's what I grew up with, and it stuck."

Did powdered mashed potatoes come in a lumpy version? I'd have to check.

"Why don't you let me make the pie?"

I clutched his shirtfront in both hands. "You bake?" Maybe he cooked, too.

He pried my hands away and kissed my fingertips. "You just worry about the meal and I'll handle dessert." He wiggled his eyebrows at me. I gave him a weak laugh in response.

"Frankie, this isn't too much for you, is it? Be honest."

His voice held real concern. I couldn't disappoint him.

"Everything will be great."

___

"Teach me how to cook."

I was in my usual booth in the Prickly Pear Bistro. Penny, the proprietress, was seated across from me. Normally an extreme optimist, Penny had the additional patina of a newlywed. She reeked of joy.

"I can help you with that. Lasagna is a good recipe to start with. It looks complicated, but it's not."

"I need to start with Thanksgiving dinner."

Her smile trembled at the edges and her left eye twitched.

"You mean a turkey?"

I nodded. "And stuffing, mashed potatoes, and something to do with sausage."

"The sausage is for the stuffing," she mumbled.

"So, come on, Pen. Oh. I know. We could do a trial run and I can use that turkey for Chauncey and Emily's food." My dog and my cat.

Penny folded her hands on the table. "Frances, how many times have you seen an actual turkey dinner on the menu here?"

"You have turkey sandwiches," I argued. "And there's turkey in the club sandwich."

"I said *actual turkey dinner.*"

I met Penny's serious gaze.

"Never," I whispered.

She nodded. "It haunts me. I've been thinking that I should have married Kemper right after Christmas. Then I would have had more time to grow on him before Thanksgiving came around." She held her head in her hands. "What was I thinking?"

"Pen, you grew up on a farm. How could you not know how to cook a turkey?"

She shrugged her slumped shoulders. "I oversaw the mashed potatoes and the cranberries. I never paid attention to what Mom was doing. Or Grandma. They worked so hard. I was afraid they'd ask me to help, and I wanted to get back outside and shoot skeet with Grandpa and my brother." She smacked her forehead. "Selfish, selfish, selfish!"

It might throw off the balance of nature, but this situation called for a role reversal. Since Penny had turned pessimistic, it was time to dust off Optimistic Frankie. Poor thing hadn't seen daylight since I was eleven years old.

"For Pete's sake. It's a turkey. Someone must know how to cook it. I mean, where do all the Thanksgiving dinners come from?"

Ann, the Prickly Pear's seasoned waitress, came to the table with the coffee pot. I grabbed the wrist of her free hand.

"Have you ever cooked Thanksgiving dinner?"

She grinned as she refreshed our cups. "Every year."

"See, Pen? It can't be that bad."

"I order it from Momma Mia's Restaurant and Deli. All I have to do is reheat it. I used to make it all from scratch, but…" She shuddered.

Penny rested her forehead on the table. "I'm doomed. Kemper's mom has been calling him to find out all the details. I know she's secretly hoping I crash and burn. And I will."

"No." I made my tone firm. "We are not going down without a fight."

She reached across the table and grabbed my hand. "Do you think we can do this?"

And like Thelma and Louise about to drive over the cliff to their deaths, we smiled at each other and took the leap.

———

"Why are you suddenly interested in my recipes?"

My mother was incapable of answering a question without a full investigation. I hadn't told her that Bowers and I were dating. Not that I thought she would hate him. She immensely enjoyed their conversation the time he called Loon Lake, Wisconsin, to question her about my Aunt Gertrude when that lady was a suspect in his murder investigation. She asked after *Martin* during our twice-weekly phone calls.

If I revealed that I wouldn't be the only one sitting down to enjoy the results of my efforts, the pressure to succeed would be unbearable…for her. She would probably fly out to oversee the operation. So, I lied.

"Because I can't make it home for the holidays. It would make me feel like I was there if I knew we were eating the same thing."

After ten seconds of silence, my mother quietly said, "We could send you a plane ticket."

Just about to point out I couldn't very well cook my own Thanksgiving dinner in Wolf Creek if I was in Loon Lake, I realized that *I couldn't very well cook my own Thanksgiving dinner in Wolf Creek if I was in Loon Lake!*

If I slipped a note under Bowers' door saying that there was an emergency back home, my mom and dad would pick me up at the airport with smiling faces. I sniffed. I missed those faces. All the usual Thanksgiving delights would appear on the dinner table as if by yummy magic, with no effort on my part. I could fall into a trypto-phan-induced coma and not worry about drooling. I could pretend I was a kid again and leave my responsibilities behind for a week. Adulthood is overrated.

I shook myself just like Chauncey after he's had a bath. No, no, no. I could not abandon Bowers. I had to woman up and face this fear or it would defeat me.

"I wish I could, but business picks up around the holidays."

Mom would never suggest I walk away from business, not after watching me struggle so long to make ends meet.

She sighed. "There's always next year. Got a pen?"

I did.

"We'll start with the stuffing since that's the most complicated. You want a half a cup of chopped leeks—"

"Leeks. Those are the small onions, right?"

"You're thinking of shallots. Leeks are long, green stalks with a bulb."

I'd look up a photo online later. "Right."

"You want to make sure you wash between the layers to get the dirt out and don't use the green part. It's too tough."

"Shouldn't the green part be the tasty part?"

She paused. "Why don't you use yellow onions instead?"

"Check. Brown onions."

"Yellow."

It went on in that vein for some time. When we got to

the candied yams, which I hate, I told her I had enough to go on for now.

In the background, my father called out, "Tell her to take a picture and email it."

After I hung up, I called Penny. "I have the goods. My mom spilled all her recipes except the one for candied yams."

Penny made a shuddering noise. "Yams."

"Now, all we have to do is grocery shop and do a trial run."

"Maybe we should each cook our own and then compare notes."

She sounded vague. Shifty.

"I thought this was a team effort?"

"The thing is, I got *my* mom's recipes from her. You know what a great cook she is."

"And my mom's not?"

She tittered. "Of course she is, for a city folk."

The addition of a cutesy drawl did not make me appreciate the humor more.

"Admittedly, Mom has never killed her dinner with her bare hands, but I think she did pretty well. For *city* folk."

Penny giggled. "I suppose you'll get a frozen turkey from the grocery store."

"Why? Are you going to shoot your own? Not many turkeys hanging around in Arizona." I didn't know if that was true, but it made sense to me.

"No, silly. I'm going to pick one out at Frazier's Farms. Why don't you come with me?"

It sounded like a challenge, so I agreed to pick her up in twenty minutes.

⸺

11

"Narragansetts." Penny breathed the word as if it were a prayer.

Normally when I'm going to be surrounded by animals, I close my mental doorway to keep out the white noise and other sounds—and images—that animals send me. With the turkeys at Frazier Farms, I didn't bother. There wasn't a solid thought floating amid the entire bunch.

"I see you're admiring my flock." Farmer Frazier approached us with a smile on his middle-aged, handsome face. His arm and chest muscles pushed against the red-and-black flannel shirt he wore out over a pair of jeans. He reached down and tickled the closest turkey under the chin.

"They're beautiful," Penny said.

He grinned like a pleased parent.

And they were. Their feathers were a pattern of white and black with touches of brown, offset by red, white, and blue heads.

"It seems a shame to eat them," I said.

Both Penny and Farmer Frazier gasped in horror. His voice trembling, the turkey farmer explained.

"If people don't eat them, then there's no call to breed them. Farmers stop raising them, the turkey breed disappears."

Penny nodded, somber. "The White Holland."

He took off his baseball cap in a show of reverence. "The Beltsville Small White."

I broke into their moment of silence. "Where are the small ones?"

Farmer Frazier put his cap back on and winked at me. "You want a hen."

"I do?"

"These are toms. The hens are kept separate, so the

guys don't fight over them. Why don't the two of you ladies wander and pick out one you like?"

The turkeys were pasturing on several acres of fenced-in land patrolled by mixed-breed dogs. I told Penny to go ahead because I had a question for the farmer.

"I'm just curious. How much are your turkeys per pound?"

"Ten dollars."

"Oh. Do you have any three-pound turkeys?"

He laughed until he saw I was serious. "Tell you what. You're the lady that talks to animals."

I hadn't realized my reputation had made it past Wolf Creek.

"Your friend told me when she called to check our hours." He looked over his shoulder at a single turkey sitting by itself next to a wooden fencepost. "I don't know what's wrong with Matilda. Normally, she's the first one out the barn door to snatch up the snails and worms on the move from the morning dew. Lately, she just sits in the same spot and mopes. She's not sick, but I can't get her excited. I even offered her a nice, juicy grasshopper, but she turned her beak up at it. If you can, er, talk to her and find out what's happening, I'll give you a twelve- or four-teen-pound hen for thirty dollars."

"Deal."

Considering how uncommunicative the turkeys had been so far, I didn't have much confidence that I could hold up my end of the bargain, but it was worth a shot.

Matilda looked up on my approach, the skin under her chin flapping. Smaller than the turkeys I had seen so far, her prominent colors were white with black markings. She wasn't disturbed by my movements, so I crouched down close to her and tickled her under the chin as I had seen Farmer Frazier do.

A tremor of fear ran through me, projected to me by Matilda. Okay. Turkeys could communicate. So far, so good.

It seemed obvious to me what a turkey would fear most. Farmer Frazier stood behind me to my left. I turned my head and asked, "Are you planning to eat her?"

He stared as if not sure he heard right. "Miss, I don't name my food. Matilda's a pet."

"But you said she stays in the barn with the rest of them."

"She doesn't *sleep* there. She's got a bed in the house. I bring her down in the morning to lead them out. She's like a cheerleader who gets them all eating. If anyone lags, she herds them outside. She's a *working* turkey."

"Gotcha."

She was smart enough to have a job. My thirty-dollar hen was in the bag.

I cleared my mind and then thought of a large, slimy grub. She clucked. Then an image of Farmer Frazier. A rush of warmth filled my chest. I peeked over at the object of her affection. He watched our interaction closely and seemed pretty concerned about her, so her feelings weren't misplaced.

Next, I pictured the open field. Another tremor of fear lasted until I looked at the fencepost next to her. The fear went down a notch.

"I think she's staying next to the fence because she feels safe here."

"Matilda? Afraid? Impossible. I'd put my money on her against any tom, even without spurs."

Spurs? As in jingle-jangle spurs? Game over. I stood and put my hands on my hips. "Spurs? As in cock-fighting?"

He swooped down and grabbed the closest tom, who had been happily munching on a beetle. As the bird squawked out a protest, the farmer held out its skinny leg. A long, sharp claw stuck out on the backside above the feet. "A spur. Only toms have them. Matilda is a hen."

Maybe I was being sensitive, but Farmer Frazier seemed disgusted with me. I rubbed my hands together and searched the yard for more clues. A wave of malevolence passed over me. I tried to pin down the source. My gaze stopped on the open door of the barn where I had seen a flash of black.

"Be right back."

I trotted to the barn doors and peered inside. A shadow darted behind an empty trough.

"That's Pierre."

I jumped and spun around. Farmer Frazier obviously didn't trust me to run loose on his turkey farm.

"Pierre?"

"He keeps the mice under control."

"Pierre is a cat? Huh."

I walked back to Matilda, projected an image of Pierre, and got an immediate response. She flapped her wings and squawked.

"Are you sure that mice are the only things your cat hunts?"

"Positive. If he ever went after the turkeys, that would be the end of him."

Matilda was afraid of Pierre. No wonder. Pierre sent off vibes that should not come from a nice kitty. The farmer seemed confident that the cat knew better than to hurt the turkeys, so it wasn't a case of hunter's instinct gone wrong. Anyway, why would he focus his dislike on this one bird? The other turkeys weren't afraid. I had an idea.

"Does Pierre sleep in the house?"

"In the barn." He added, in case I needed it spelled out, "With the mice."

"I think it's possible Pierre is jealous of Matilda and has been messing with her." He moved to examine his pet turkey, but I held up a hand. "Psychological torture. Cats excel at it. You should give Pierre a nice kitty bed in the barn, someplace high where he feels important. And maybe you should scratch his ears sometime, especially when Matilda's around. It will let him know you love them both equally."

"But I don't. He's just a cat."

I rolled my eyes. "Fake it. For Matilda's sake."

Instead of thanking me, he said, "Step away from Matilda nice and slow."

"But—"

He wasn't looking at me. I followed his line of sight to a turkey on full display.

"How pretty!"

The bird's feathers stretched out, and it flapped its wings, proud to be a turkey. What a natural beauty. My excitement receded.

"Is he growling?" I asked as the tom lowered its head.

When the turkey charged, Farmer Frazier made a grab for me, but my scrambling feet moved me out of reach. A gigantic wing slammed against me. That turkey could pack a punch. I fell back against the fence. As the bird jumped in the air and reached for me with his spurs, the farmer hoisted me over his shoulder and deposited me on the other side of the fence. With wings flapping and feet flying, the bird didn't look as cute. It stopped at the fence, satisfied that I was no longer a threat, and snorted. It sounded like a victory snort.

Farmer Frazier leaned on the fence and looked down at the tom turkey, who was now innocently snatching up bugs. "Sorry about that. He's been protective of Matilda since he was a jake. Had to use a broom to teach him not to go after me."

Penny returned just then, holding a dandelion and chewing on the stem. "I found a bird. It's the one with the extra-large gobbler."

He grinned. "I would have picked that one myself."

"He's a beaut alright. Reminds me of one my grandpa had."

"Your family raises turkeys?"

She nodded, obnoxiously casual. "Among other things. There's no better way to get your meat than straight from the source."

When I thought back to her family's farm, I only remembered the cows.

He raised his brows. "That's a refreshing attitude. Some people are squeamish." He turned to me. "What about you? Have you picked out one you like?"

"You pick it for me," I said. I had no problem eating meat, and all these turkeys would be going to market anyway, but I didn't want to pass the death sentence on a particular bird.

"Do you want the turkey dressed or undressed?"

The question was for Penny. "Undressed."

"Right you are. I'll deliver them both on Tuesday next week, freshly slaughtered so you can keep them until Thursday."

I handed over my thirty dollars and thought about how pleased Bowers would be.

―

Bowers had a brief break in an investigation on Sunday afternoon, so he picked up Chinese and dropped by my house for a quick dinner. I couldn't offer him television, since my small TV was in my bedroom, but the conversation was just as entertaining…for him.

"And the turkey attacked."

He tossed a piece of teriyaki chicken to Chauncey to make up for the three pieces he'd already given Emily. Unlike Farmer Frazier, Bowers liked cats.

"I mean really attacked. Not just," he waved his hands in the air, "the mind-thing?"

If possible, he avoided mentioning the word psychic in any form.

I rubbed the back of my shoulder where it had connected with the fence. "This was definitely a real attack. If Farmer Frazier hadn't picked me up—"

Bowers stopped chewing. "He picked you up?"

"Only to throw me over the fence."

"I'm surprised he could do that, seeing as he was probably—what—sixty and decrepit?"

"Early fifties, handsome, and he had more muscles than you do. You should try throwing around your suspects for exercise." I kissed his cheek. "But I like you better."

He held up a fist and mock growled. "If I got ahold of that turkey, you'd see some real muscle. Why I'd—"

He didn't have to finish the thought because I was laughing hard at the image of *Bowers versus Turkey, coming to a theater near you.* I stopped laughing when I noticed he was texting on his cell phone. He'd done that several times since he got here.

"You don't have an addiction we need to discuss, do you?"

He hit send and set the phone down.

"You're acting like a dopamine addicted teenager." I picked up his phone and looked at the last address texted. "JuneBug60?" I narrowed my eyes. "Are you texting your sister?"

He gave me a sheepish grin. Bowers sheepish? Not in his DNA. Of course, when dealing with family, the rules go out the window.

"I mentioned that you were making me Thanksgiving dinner and—"

"You what?!"

Chauncey hid behind the couch and Emily hissed.

He set down his fork and wiped his fingers on a napkin. "If I had known it was a national secret, I wouldn't have."

"Sorry. I didn't mean—it took me by surprise. That's all."

He moved closer. "No one has ever offered to do something so special for me before. I guess I was bragging."

"Bragging?"

"Just a little."

My face felt warm. "You were bragging about me?"

"I do that all the time," he said, as if he hadn't just made me melt.

"Like what?" I know, I know. A needy move.

He brushed my auburn hair back over my ear. "How beautiful you are." He brushed his lips against mine. "How kind." He kissed me again. "Funny." He tapped my nose. "Sexy." That kiss lasted longer than the others.

"You tell your sister I'm sexy?"

"Well, maybe not that."

When his phone buzzed, I dove for it and held up my prize.

"Let's see what she has to say."

Bowers' text had been to tell her I was getting a fresh

turkey straight from the farm. His tone sounded suspiciously reassuring, especially as his message began with *No worries.*

I glanced at him and scrolled up to see the whole conversation.

Bowers: *Sorry, June. Can't come. Frankie making me dinner.* A symbol of a turkey followed this.

JuneBug60: *Frank? U prefer eating at station with guys???*

Bowers: *Frankie. FEMALE. Told you about her.*

JuneBug60: *Animal trainer, right? Does she train turkeys to jump on the plate? HA! B careful U don't get a tofu turkey.*

Bowers: *Carnivore.*

JuneBug60: *Relief. What's the menu?*

Bowers: *Surprise*

JuneBug60: *Uh-oh.*

Bowers: *Frankie excellent cook.*

JuneBug60: *Better B Mr. Finicky.*

Bowers: *Am not.*

JuneBug60: *Are so.*

Bowers: *Not.*

JuneBug60: *So.*

Bowers: *Not. To infinity. Frankie can out-cook you any day. No need to worry.*

JuneBug60: *Really. BTW, thx for asking after Ed.*

Bowers: *Sorry. How's Ed?*

JuneBug60: *Lost toe in fight but feisty as ever.*

Then he told her I had picked out a farm fresh turkey.

Her response was *Artificially inseminated commercial breed, probably. Broad-Breasted White. Not much flavor.*

My cheeks flushed, and I quickly texted back. *Narragansett. Bred the old-fashioned way. Sex.*

"What did you say to her?" He took the phone from me. After he read my text, his face registered shock. "You used the S word with my sister?"

"Give me a break. She's been around long enough that she's probably heard the word before."

"Not from me."

I picked at my fried rice with a chopstick. "Who's Ed?"

"June's Rhode Island Red. He got into a fight with another rooster."

"Wait. Your sister has a rooster?"

He chuckled. "I hope so. She raises chickens."

"She has a chicken farm?"

"She has a farm, and she has chickens. I don't know that I'd call it a chicken farm. Certainly not in a commercial sense."

I gaped at him. "You set me up. You told her I could out cook her. Cooking fowl. Pitting me against an expert. And how would you know? I've never cooked for you before if we don't count popcorn and egg rolls."

"I trust you."

"Do you know what kind of pressure that puts me under?"

"You're getting worked up over nothing. A friendly sibling verbal sparring match. Frankie, you have to understand. I'm the baby."

"I got that from your texts. To infinity."

He grinned. "The baby *brother*. My sisters are bound to fuss over me."

That didn't fit into my image of Detective Martin Bowers. Serious, efficient cop. Handsome grown man with crinkles around his eyes when he laughed and bags under his eyes when he was working a case. He was too old to be anyone's baby brother.

The phone buzzed again. This time Bowers got to it first and held it out of reach. He read it and sucked in his breath. I read over his shoulder.

Doesn't sound like you Marty. Who is this?

"Give it to me."

"Okay. Maybe I was insensitive. I'm out of practice. Still, I don't think you want to get into it with—"

"Give—it—to—me."

He held out his phone. I snatched it from him and typed. *Frankie. Straight from the source.*

Bowers stopped breathing. The cursor blinked. Silence.

Suddenly, a laughing emoji, tears spilling out of its eyes, flashed on the screen along with the words *Give me your number.*

Which meant she wanted to talk to me. About Thanksgiving dinner. The one I was supposed to be whipping up for her baby brother. I shoved the phone back in his hands. "You're right. I don't want to do this."

He sighed. "I tried to warn you." He stood and shoved the phone in his pocket. "It's too late now. If I don't give her your number, one of us is going to have to explain why when you eventually meet her."

"Then I won't meet her."

"Ever?"

"Let's see. She's your oldest sister. How old is she?"

"Frankie!" He crossed himself.

"Fine," I mumbled. "Give her my number."

He patted me on the shoulder. "You will regret your impulsiveness."

Then he kissed me on the top of my head and left.

He hadn't been gone five minutes before I received my first text from Bowers' oldest sister.

JuneBug60: *Got everything you need for the big day?*

I texted back that I was set on ingredients.

JuneBug60: *Timing is everything. Pre-cook what you can. Saves trouble. No surprises. BTW, Marty loves candied yams. Hope you got a good recipe.*

I noticed she didn't offer me hers. Candied yams.

Blech. That would be one item I would be buying from the grocery store pre-made.

———

On Monday, I spent fifty dollars on a trial run of the side dishes, not including the original ingredients.

I had set out the bread, spices, sausage, onions, and celery for the stuffing on the counter and double checked them with the recipe. I didn't want to have to interrupt the process with a trip to the store. Chauncey lay on the kitchen rug, his paws folded under his chin, his eyes focused on the food on the counter. Probably the sausage.

One onion, chopped.

I pulled an onion out of the bag and got the big knife from the chopping block. When I pushed down, the knife slipped. I gripped it tighter and sawed, but it only made a dent. My little-used knife was so dull that it wouldn't cut an onion. I ran to the grocery store and got a sharpening mandrel.

The instructions said to swipe the knife down the mandrel moving away from your body. I positioned everything and then let her rip. The edge of the knife stuck and then slipped off to the right with a jerk. I had been pulling up on the mandrel to give the knife some resistance to work against. As soon as the knife passed the end and it no longer provided opposing pressure, the metal rod flipped back and hit me on the forehead.

Chauncey left the room.

I ran to the store and bought a bag of chopped onions from the freezer section.

One cup of chopped celery.

The knife sliced through the edges of the celery, but it left a stringy, unpleasant skin attached. I knew there wasn't any frozen celery—I checked when I was there for the onions—so I decided that fresh celery was overrated, found some celery salt with an expiration date of 2008, and tossed some in the bowl.

I tore up some slices of bread. The recipe called for dried bread cubes, but I figured the bread would dry out in the oven, anyway. Then I sliced open two packages of ground maple sausage. The store had been sold out of the sage sausage.

Then I poured in a box of chicken broth and mixed it all with my hands. It was disturbingly runny. I set the oven timer, piled the stuffing into a metal pan, and popped it into the oven.

"That wasn't so bad."

The cranberries I had down pat, since my mother always let me stir and pop the softened barriers into a sauce. Those didn't need practice.

The bags of rolls and corn waited in the freezer for the special day, so I set the timer for an hour and took a nap.

"Frankie."

I heard my name from far away and rolled onto my side.

"Frankie, honey. I think something's burning."

"Turn the oven off," I mumbled, wrapping my arms around my pillow. My pillow had shrunk. I must be on the couch. Wait. What would be in my oven in the middle of the day? And who woke me up?

Too late, I shot off the couch and ran to the kitchen. Bowers pulled a smoking pan of stuffing from the oven and dropped it in the sink. When he turned on the faucet, the pan sizzled.

"Whatever you were making, I think it's ruined."

It was a small thread, but I grabbed it. He couldn't tell it was stuffing. I looked down at the pan of glop in my sink, burnt beyond recognition.

"Dog food. I was making dog food."

Chauncey whined as if on cue and I made a note to give him a treat after Bowers left.

"It smells like burnt pancakes."

"I really shouldn't, but I add a touch of maple syrup to Chauncey's food. He likes it."

With both hands around his bicep, I steered Bowers back into the living room.

"What are you doing here? And how did you get in?"

He put on his official cop frown. "I've told you before that you should keep your doors locked, even when you're at home."

Still sleepy, I leaned my forehead against his chest and yawned. "I unlocked it when I went for the mail. Sorry."

He put his hands on my shoulders and backed me up so he could look down at me. His expression showed a level of concern that seemed disproportionate to the offense.

"You know the Good Morning Bakery?"

"Bob Davenport's place. Why?"

"He's had some—unusual—occurrences lately. It seems that someone is getting in at night."

"Oh, my gosh. Is Scoots alright?" Scoots was the inappropriately named German short-haired pointer that Bob used as a watchdog for his shop after a few local burglaries. Bob had hired me to find out why Scoots was chewing through the drywall in the shop's storeroom, and I had to explain that dogs are social animals. Scoots was probably frustrated being alone all night, especially since he had enjoyed his role as the family pet up until now.

"The dog is fine. So is Bob. It's more odd than dangerous. He locks up for the night and leaves Scoots free to roam. When he returns in the morning, things are still locked up, but there is a pastry gone and money on the counter. Nothing else is out of place."

"That doesn't sound so bad."

His lips thinned out into a disapproving line. "It's still entering without permission. Bob feels violated. And if there's someone breaking into locked buildings, I don't want you here alone with your door unlocked giving criminals an extra incentive."

He kissed my forehead to take the edge off his lecture on home safety. "That's why I stopped by."

"To tell me to lock my doors?"

"I need to work tonight, so I won't be able to drop by later."

His long goodbye kiss made up for any disappointment I was feeling.

I didn't call him the next morning since he had a late night. Besides, I was up and dressed by seven to wait for my turkey delivery. It didn't come until ten.

A scruffy-looking, older man in blue jeans and a wrinkled sweatshirt held out my turkey.

"Here you are, ma'am."

"That can't be mine."

He checked the tag. "Frances Chandler? Fourteen-pound hen?"

"That's right, but…it's still dressed."

He looked at the turkey to see if he missed something. "This is undressed. Feathers on and everything inside."

I looked closer. "The feet are still attached."

He held out a clipboard. "I need you to sign here that I delivered it."

It wasn't this man's fault that my bird was fully feathered. I signed. He shoved the turkey into my arms and left.

Once I kicked the door shut behind me, I looked around for some place to put it. As I stepped forward, I nearly did a face-plant when I tripped over Chauncey. He hadn't shown me this much attention since…never. He pranced so close to me as I moved into the kitchen it felt like I had three legs.

I dumped the bird in the sink and yelped when I saw the head was still attached. Then I yelped again when a black blur streaked over the counter and skid to a stop next to the sink. Emily gazed down with awe, her tail twitching. When she made chirping noises—the same noise she makes to attract helpless robins—I picked her up and deposited her on the floor. Like a magnet, she was back at the sink before I had time to straighten up.

My refrigerator had an empty shelf—all three were pretty empty—so I opened the door and hauled the turkey over. It took three shoves to make it fit, but I finally got the door closed.

Then I was on the phone to Penny.

"My bird still has feathers."

Penny tittered. "Of *course* it does, silly."

"I thought undressed meant they would take its clothes off, meaning feathers. Why would you want feathers? What possible advantage could feathers be to a dead bird? You told Farmer Frazier to deliver them to us this way. *You* might be an expert, but why would you do this to *me*?"

"Calm down. Have you got a large pot?"

"No."

"Well, *get* a large pot, heat some water to about one hundred forty-five degrees, and let it soak until it's cool enough to touch. The feathers will come right out."

"I didn't realize I was going to have to skin it."

"You're not skinning it silly; you're plucking it. Oh. Do you have one of those kitchen blow torches?"

"Do you think that's something I would own?"

"Right. You can borrow mine."

"Pen, I'm not handy with open flames. I was planning to cook my turkey in the oven."

She shrieked with laughter. "You want to burn off the pin feathers, not cook the darn thing. I suppose a fireplace lighter would work. That sounds less dangerous, since, you know—"

"I'm completely inept? Thanks, Pen."

I went to the store and purchased a large, aluminum stock pot and a kitchen blow torch. Then I went back to the store for the fuel, since I had assumed the torch ran on batteries. Wwhile I was there, I purchased the ingredients to redo the stuffing.

Thanksgiving was tomorrow, so I had to get moving on the turkey. I pulled it out of the refrigerator and crammed it into the pot. Those feathers took up a lot of room. Before I got the water going, my doorbell rang.

I peered through the glass and saw Farmer Frazier standing on my stoop, his arms crossed over his chest in a posture of discomfiture. I opened the door.

He squinted his eyes at me. It must have been a habit from working in the sun without sunglasses.

"I need help with Tom the Terror."

"Pardon me?"

"Tom the Terror. He attacked you."

"He's not on the chopping block?" I said hopefully.

"Not for sale. See, he's the dominant tom. He keeps the rest of them in line. Organized."

"And he's missing?"

"Nope."

I bit my lip. "Maybe I'm missing something, but I don't see where you need help."

He took off his ball cap and scratched his cheek. "After

our talk about Matilda and Pierre, I did what you said. I got the cat a nice bed and placed it in the rafters, so he could look down his whiskers at everybody. He does. And I even tickled him under the chin, just like I do the turkeys."

"Does he like the changes?"

"Seems pleased as punch."

"And is Matilda still hiding by the fence?"

"She's her old self again."

I turned my ear toward him, as if I hadn't heard right. "Again, what is the problem?"

He laughed self-consciously. "I'm not sure. Matilda told off Tom yesterday. Since then, he's been…well, he's been courting the ducks. Spends all his time by the pond trying to, well, get himself a girlfriend."

"Oh." My eyes opened wide. "Oh, my."

"Right." He gestured toward a red pickup truck parked at the curb. "I thought you might talk to Tom for me. I'll pay your going rate."

My going rate would cover some of the extras I'd had to buy for Thanksgiving.

"Let me lock up."

It would have been an impressive sight, but the pathetic aspects got in the way. Tom the Terror was in the zone. His gobbler was bright red, infused with blood, and his feathers were fanned out in full display. The problem was the beneficiary of his attention—an angry and confused Mallard duck.

"See what I mean?"

Tom danced tight circles around his chosen recipient, rattling his wing feathers and whispering sweet nothings. She, in turn, hissed for all she was worth.

"Has he, um, been attracted to ducks before this?"

Farmer Frazier, mesmerized by the bizarre behavior of his head tom, took a minute to respond. "I certainly hope not."

Maybe a reminder of his favorite hen would do the trick. I conjured up an image of Matilda and threw it at him. In response, he amped up his fancy footwork and his tail feathers, if possible, spread even farther apart.

Tom the Terror, rejected by Matilda, had found a substitute. I'd known people who, right after a breakup, had tried to make their former partners jealous. The turkey seemed to be practicing the same behavior. If those same people had seen their former love while in the company of their substitute girlfriend or boyfriend, the response would naturally be to ramp up the attention given to the substitute to show they didn't care. Continued images of Matilda might cause a duck molestation. I needed a diversion.

"What does Tom hate most?" I asked. "I mean, what would get his attention?"

Farmer Frazier stood with his hands on his hips, watching Tom with open embarrassment. "Back when he was in his right mind, if anything threatened the flock, he would have been right there defending them."

I sent an image of Pierre, but Tom didn't lose a step.

"Like what? Give me an example."

"A coyote or bobcat."

I wasn't taking any chances. Coyotes and bobcats wouldn't normally hunt together, but in the little movie I put together, they were side-by-side, sneaking through the tall grass and ready to pounce on a sweet, unsuspecting hen. Then I crossed my fingers and played it for him.

Tom froze.

"Quick. Where are most of the turkeys right now?"

He looked at his watch. "Probably headed for the barnyard."

I gave Tom a wide-angle shot of the hen, the coyote, and the bobcat that included the fence and the barn door. Tom did a quick U-turn and loped past us, headed for the barn.

The poor duck didn't know what to make of it. She fluffed her feathers and slipped into the pond.

I explained to Farmer Frazier that I wasn't sure if my solution would stick, and he could call me any time for a refresher. No charge. When he dropped me off in front of my house, I was fifty bucks richer. At least I thought I was.

I pushed the front door open and immediately yelled, "Drop it, drop it, drop it!"

Chauncey had my turkey by the neck and was dragging it around the living room. Emily clutched the back of the corpse and rode it, growling with her back arched. There were feathers everywhere.

Emily hissed at me when I swatted her away. Chauncey thought I wanted to play tug with the turkey. I finally rapped him on the snout and yanked the bird away.

My Thanksgiving dinner. Shredded and covered in dog spit. Uneatable.

I smiled. "Good doggie."

———

I didn't have to work up any actual tears, because the conversation took place over the phone, but I made my voice all high-pitched and whiney and added lots of sniffs. To my ears, I sounded like Ralphie from *A Christmas Story* when he tried to fake an icicle attack for his mom after almost shooting his eye out with his new BB gun, something she warned him against.

As soon as he heard my voice, Bowers went into protective mode, snapping out questions in a sharp voice.

"What's happened? Are you alright?"

"Farmer Frazier picked me up—"

"*Again?* What's with this guy? Do I need to talk to him?"

"In his truck," I clarified.

"What did he do?" Bowers' voice had gone so deadly cold that I hurried to clarify.

"Nothing. I read his bird for him. But when I got back —" I sobbed.

"I'll be right there."

"No! It's too late. My turkey is ruined."

"We're talking about your turkey? Ruined how?" he added, cautiously.

I explained how I had forgotten to put the turkey back into the refrigerator before leaving with Farmer Frazier and Chauncey and Emily had coordinated their efforts to maul my Thanksgiving dinner.

"And there were feathers everywhere!" My voice caught for real as I thought about how much cleaning I was going to have to do.

His response? Not calming words or comforting coos. He laughed. Literally shouted with laughter.

"I'm sorry," he wheezed. "I just—" and off he went again. Muffled noises came, like someone covering the phone with their hand. They were followed by a voice akin to the Teacher in *The Peanuts* cartoons. Then additional shouts of laughter.

"I'm sorry. I just had to—"

"Tell your friends what a joke I am?"

That sobered him up.

"It was a relief. I thought something had happened to you, and, and, and—" He choked back another laugh and took a deep breath. "Frankie, I think it's wonderful that you were willing to go through all that trouble for me, but don't stress out about it. A turkey from the grocery store will do just fine. In fact, let me make a call and have one delivered to you. Okay, sweetie?"

The thought of not paying for another turkey mollified me. When a voice in the background called out something, Bowers said, "I've got to go," and hung up.

When the phone rang less than a minute later, I thought he was calling back. Instead, it was Penny.

"How is your turkey coming along, Frances?"

"Fine. Just fine." I lied because I'm petty and I didn't want Ms. Farmer lording it over me with tales of how her turkey had practically unzipped its feathers and stepped out of them.

"That's great! Wonderful!" Too heavy on the joy, even for Penny.

"What's wrong?"

"Well, I got my water heated to one hundred forty-five degrees on the thermometer, and then I put my big boy in."

Her voice was too strained for this to be a happy story.

"And?"

"Well, Kemper got home early for the holiday, ha-ha, and, well, he was feeling frisky.

"Ew. Skip this part."

"I forgot all about the turkey with—stuff—and my turkey boiled."

"That should make it easy to pluck."

"No. Boiled whole, with the feathers on. Without being cleaned. As in not a good thing. It looks disgusting. I mean, I kept it going so I could give you the meat for your pets, but I can't serve that abomination for Thanksgiving dinner." She gave a big, heaving sigh. "Kemper's mom will be delighted."

"I met Christina Mohr on your wedding cruise. She was a pleasant woman. Not the type to crow over someone else's turkey tragedy."

"You don't get it. When a woman's son is being cooked for by another woman, it triggers a psychotic reaction. It's embedded in female DNA. I'm sure our ancestors probably had a name for it."

"And I'm sure you're imagining things." I made a noise of disgust. "Good grief. You've been married for over two months. Shouldn't you have a little self-control by now?"

There were sounds of sniffling, followed by a hiccup.

"Are you crying?" Penny never cried. "I didn't mean it. You can have all the sex you want."

She choked out a laugh. "Thanks. I'll let Kemper know we have your blessing."

"Why did you order the darn thing with feathers anyway?"

"I got the terms mixed up," she said, meek as a plucked turkey. "We were a *dairy* farm, not a turkey farm. Grandpa only had a few turkeys around for the holidays. I just— when we got to Frazier's, being in that environment made me miss Wisconsin. I wanted to show that I hadn't lost Penny the farm girl."

I remembered the turkey Bowers said he would order. Surely, there would be plenty for four. Although Penny had been a little snotty about her turkey knowledge, she was still my best friend. "Why don't you come here for dinner?"

She gasped. "Really? You would do that for me?"

"You're right. That is a little much. Forget I offered."

Silence.

"I'm kidding, Pen. Of course, you can come."

I hit the end call button on my cell phone and set it on

the kitchen counter, but I picked it back up when I heard a tiny voice calling out, "Hello? Hello?"

"Hello, Mother."

"Oh. You're home."

"You don't know that for sure. This is a cell phone. I could be anywhere."

She chortled into the phone. "Where would you go? I called to see how *things* are going."

"Going fine. I had a client today."

"I mean important things. Did you pick up everything you need from the store? You know, most stores are closed on Thanksgiving in normal places."

She meant small towns where people were recognized as individuals with families.

"I have everything I need, thanks for asking."

"Did you get the onion?"

"Yes."

"The sage sausage for the stuffing?"

Should I explain that the only flavor left was the maple?

"I got sausage, yes."

"The bread cubes?"

"I have bread. I'll cube it."

"You should buy it already dried. It works better."

I had no idea I could buy dried bread cubes. What will they think of next?

"I have everything."

"Did you remember the celery?"

"That's part of the everything I have."

"What size turkey did you get?"

I had no idea what Bowers had ordered. "I think it's twelve or fourteen pounds."

"You *think*? Check the label."

"Ah. Thirteen pounds. There was, um, blood on the

35

label that made it hard to read."

"You'll have plenty of leftovers…since you're only cooking for one."

"There's someone at the door. Gotta go. Love you!"

I hung up before she backed me into a lie. It wasn't just that I didn't want the pressure that would come once my mother knew I was cooking for Bowers. It was the *Frances is dating someone…again,* and all that went with it.

My parents were my biggest supporters when Jeff, the boyfriend I had moved in with against their express wishes, turned out to be a jerk. *Why buy the cow when the milk is free?* Grandma always said. The humiliation of discovering that an old-fashioned and rather disturbing statement was true—and the public way Jeff betrayed me—sent me fleeing to Wolf Creek, Arizona. If I mentioned that I was dating again…and if it didn't work out… I shuddered. I would have to join a convent. For now, Bowers was my secret.

Unfortunately, Bowers didn't share my desire to keep things quiet. My cell phone buzzed.

JuneBug60: *Heard about the turkey. Left my first turkey leftovers on enclosed porch overnight. Dog got at it. Ate the whole thing, then barfed. HA!*

———

By seven o'clock that night, the turkey still hadn't arrived. I texted Bowers to ask when I should expect it. The answer came at eight-thirty, when he returned my call.

"Oh, Frankie. I am so sorry. I got caught up in a riot and forgot about the turkey."

It was a sign of my growing affection for him that I first asked how he was before I told him there would be no Thanksgiving dinner. Ever.

"I'm fine. I'll go to the store right after I stop at home and shower off the blood."

"Blood?"

I swallowed hard. I knew the police risked their lives every day, but in Wolf Creek, Arizona, how much danger could there be? Then I remembered the two murders that I had been involved in—the solving, not the killing. Modesty wouldn't allow me to think a murder couldn't take place without my involvement, so there had to be others.

"There's a lot of blood, but it's not a big deal. Head wounds bleed."

I closed my eyes to stop the room from spinning. Bowers could have been seriously hurt. Even killed. My imagination kicked into overdrive. Fanged gunmen ambushing him. What if he had been killed? My stomach did a flip, and my knees went weak. *Stop it*, I told myself. It was time to pull on my big girl panties.

"You go home and stay home. I mean it. I'll get the turkey. Why don't I stop by first and make sure you're alright?"

"I—you don't have to."

"I'll be there in twenty minutes."

It was more like thirty since I hadn't taken a shower myself that day. When I rang his front doorbell, my hair was still wet, so my red turtleneck was suffering from soggy shoulders. He opened the door wearing grey sweats and a t-shirt. When I saw the stitches above his left temple and the purple area under his eye, I gave a little cry, grabbed his middle and hugged him tight.

He patted my shoulder. "I'm fine. Really."

I tried to let go, but my arms wouldn't let me, so he shuffled back into the house with me still attached and swung the door closed.

"Frankie. It's okay."

He stroked my wet hair and then wiped his hand on his sweats. After he peeled me away from him, he led me to the couch. That's when I realized we weren't alone.

Seated on that same couch and looking as cool and gorgeous as ever was Detective Juanita Gutierrez. She looked different somehow. She wore a stylish pink pantsuit and had pulled her thick, brown, luxurious locks into a ponytail. If I hadn't known her nickname at the station was The Python, I would have said she was a perky housewife.

The corners of her mouth curved into a smirk. My hackles went up in response.

"If I had known you had someone looking after you, I wouldn't have bothered you."

"We were working together undercover."

"Sounds cozy."

Gutierrez stood. "Call me later, Marty."

Marty?

Bowers sat down, put his left foot on the coffee table, leaned back and closed his eyes. He patted the couch next to him. I sat on the next cushion over, so he wrapped a hand around my shoulder and pulled me into the crook of his arm.

"It's been a long day."

"I thought you were working on the bakery break-ins."

"That, too. In fact, I have to go out again tonight."

I took his hand in mine and played a silent game of *this little piggy* with his fingers. When I got to the index finger, his hand jerked.

I let go. "Sorry."

He took my hand and squeezed it tight. "I think that knuckle is going to be pretty swollen by tomorrow morning."

"So, what kind of undercover operation? Can you say? Or is it still ongoing?"

"We've had our eye on an anarchist group. FOPS. Freedom from Oppressive Prices Syndicate. We got word that they were going to show up at Kidland."

"A toy store? Why would they terrorize kids?"

"Kidland got the bright idea to get in early on the Black Friday business. They were offering free Ho Dolls to the first hundred shoppers."

Ho Dolls. Some genius had come up with dolly prostitutes, though I couldn't see much difference between the outfits the dolls wore and the ones I saw on teenage girls. When some parents became outraged and deemed the toy inappropriate for minors, the makers claimed they were anti-feminist, since most prostitutes are girls. They also claimed that, since the dolls came with changemakers, they were educational toys. Schmolastic Books proposed to feature them in a series for school children.

While many parents steered clear of the dolls, there was that segment eager to appear open minded. They scrambled to grab up the questionable toys, including the limited-edition Teasey.

"What did the anarchists want with Ho Dolls?"

He shrugged. "What do anarchists always want? Violence. Confusion. They knew there would be a lot of people there. They announced over a megaphone that capitalist pigs should provide free Ho Dolls for everyone and provoked a riot. Gutierrez and I were pretending to be a couple shopping for Christmas presents. We were in the superhero section when all hell broke loose."

"I noticed she didn't look roughed up."

He opened one eye to see if I was serious.

"Thank God she was there."

"What do you mean?"

"Most of the rioters were women. No matter how justified, when a male cop takes down a woman, someone is bound to videotape it, post it on the internet, and claim police brutality. It's difficult to wrangle a raging, screaming woman with kid gloves."

"Is that how you got that cut above your eye?"

"We identified ourselves as police and were making our way toward the front of the store when the crowd surged. An entire bicycle display came down on me. Then a woman kicked me in the face. Gutierrez took her out." He grinned at the memory. "While she was cuffing the woman, the woman's friend came charging like a rhino. I was still trying to get out from under the bikes and thought I was a goner, but the Python blocked her approach and cold-cocked her. Dropped her like a sack of potatoes."

"Well, I'm glad you're alright." Since his eyes were closed again, I kissed the tip of his nose.

"Right as rain," he mumbled.

With great reluctance, I told him I would thank Gutierrez next time I saw her. "What time do you have to go back out?"

He rubbed his eyes and sat up. "What time is it?"

When I told him, he said he had another hour.

"Why don't I set your kitchen timer for thirty minutes so you can get some sleep?"

He didn't argue, so I set the alarm and left him to take a quick nap.

As I stood in the entrance of Dickenson's grocery store and gaped at the half-empty shelves, I imagined this was what it would be like when the zombie apocalypse hit, and people took to their shelters.

Please, please, please let there be turkeys left I prayed as I made my way to the meat section. *Just one turkey. That's all I need, God.*

And there was one turkey remaining, but it was in the hands of a gray-haired man who was standing next to an employee and chatting. A sob slipped out, and both men looked my way.

"Can I help you?" The employee addressed me in that friendly manner that comes when there is only fifteen minutes left until closing.

I responded with a weak smile. "Only if that turkey is being held for me."

The guy with the turkey laughed. "This baby is going to make a few families at the homeless shelter happy."

Homeless people. I couldn't even pull out the pity card.

"Why'd you wait so long?" the employee asked.

"Well…" I poured out my tale of woe, which sounded more comic than tragic when repeated to strangers. They certainly had a good laugh at my expense.

When he finished wiping the tears out of his eyes, the employee reached into the box on his cart and pulled out a gigantic bird.

"I was saving this one for my dinner."

"I couldn't take your dinner," I said as I reached for the bird. He waved off his sacrifice.

"The in-laws are coming over. All seventeen of them. We already have one turkey at home. I can get a ham just to mix things up."

It's possible I kissed him. I know he blushed after my profuse thanks. The turkey was on sale, but it wasn't the price that made me do a double-take.

"Twenty-nine-pounds? How long will it take to get the inside cooked? It's as hard as a rock."

Both men stared. "You want to defrost it first, young lady," the shelter volunteer said.

"Before tomorrow? With what? A hair dryer?"

"Put it in a sink of water with some ice."

"Gotcha."

I already had the stock pot, but I didn't know how much ice I had at home. After grabbing a cart to relieve my sore arms, I picked up a bag of ice and went through the checkout.

Half an hour later, I had a stockpot full of turkey, water, and ice on the stove, far out of the reach of my furry companions. Besides, that bird was too heavy for my pets to move, even if they teamed up.

That night, I slept like a rock.

———

Someone was watching me. I was in danger. My subconscious understood this even as I struggled to open my eyes. And my chest felt heavy, probably suffering under the burden of preparing Thanksgiving dinner.

Thanksgiving!

My eyes snapped open to find Emily seated on my chest, her face inches from mine. I shooed her off and shuffled to the kitchen, half-dreading what I would find, but the turkey was still in the pot submerged in water.

I heaved the pot over to the sink and let the water drain, took a break to feed my furry charges, and then grabbed a pair of scissors to cut away the wrapper. If memory served me right, there were slimy things inside the turkey that needed to come out before I cooked it. That meant I had to reach into the gaping hole between its legs. Not only was that going to be embarrassing for the turkey, but I had a fear of reaching into dark places ever since I had been scarred at a haunted house. We had to reach inside the hole in a sealed box. The big kids told me the cold spaghetti that oozed through my fingers was intestines. I freaked.

After searching under the sink and through the drawers, I went into the garage and found, to my great surprise, that I owned gardening gloves. I slipped these on and returned to the kitchen to violate the turkey.

I thought I had a hold of something, but it wouldn't budge. I yanked and pulled without results. Disgusted, I tore off my glove, squeezed my eyes shut, and reached inside. The innards were there, but they were frozen to the inside of the turkey.

My cell phone rang. When I saw it was Bowers, I snatched it up with my clean hand.

"Happy Thanksgiving, sweetheart."

Despite my frustration, I smiled.

"You too." I hadn't yet thought of a nickname that didn't sound stupid. *Big fella. Pooh bear.* Even *darling* sounded pretentious when I said it.

"Did you find a turkey?"

"Sure did. Are you feeling better today?"

"Tired and sore, but I'm looking forward to dinner with you."

"Me too." I'm so clever with the sweet-talk.

"I have a favor to ask."

"Anything." I swear it slipped out before my brain could engage.

"Are you able to handle a few more for dinner?"

"A few more what?"

He laughed. "Dinner guests."

Dinner guests. That sounded so formal. Something that demanded good silver, crystal, and china. My coffee cups didn't even match.

"How many? Because Kemper and Penny are coming. Penny had a turkey mishap, too."

"Great. The more the merrier."

I couldn't think of anyone Bowers knew around here, at least not anyone who wouldn't be with their own families. Maybe some of the single guys he worked with.

"Who is it?"

"You've never met one of them. The other is Gutierrez."

Gutierrez. The woman so gorgeous that clothing designers begged her to wear their trifles. The woman whose personality was so strong that I could pick up her vibrations, just like I did with animals. The woman who didn't like me.

"Are you there?"

"Sorry. I got distracted."

"I'm the one who is sorry. I shouldn't interrupt you in the middle of cooking. So, it is okay?"

To be petty or generous. Which would Bowers find more attractive?

"Of course it's fine. I'll see you—"

I hadn't yet told him what time to come. Twenty-nine pounds times twenty minutes a pound divided by sixty minutes per hour was...ten hours? It was eight a.m. now.

"The only turkey they had was pretty big. It's going to be a little later than I had expected."

"How late?"

"You might want to eat a big lunch."

He laughed. "Make sure you don't stuff the bird, or it will take even longer. We'll be there around four and I'll bring some hors d'oeuvres."

I turned the oven to 350 degrees and realized I didn't have a pan big enough to hold the monstrous bird. And that's when I looked at the frozen turkey in my kitchen sink and cried.

Not only would I present my new boyfriend with the worst Thanksgiving dinner since the pilgrims butchered that first tough, wild bird, but my best friend, her husband, and a beautiful, evil woman would be there to witness my fall. And a stranger.

On the bright side, I might kill them all with under-cooked fowl and they'd never be able to gossip about the event. I wondered if I could talk Bowers into skipping the turkey to keep him safe.

"You will *not* be my downfall, mammoth bird."

That malicious, dead fowl's response was to present me with the most dastardly device ever created by man. Nuclear weapons were no match for the small, thick plastic thingy that held the legs together. First, I tried my scissors. Pumping them open and closed, open and closed, they merely made a mark on the plastic strip. I pulled a steak knife from my silverware drawer and sawed. Ten minutes later, with more maneuvering than a brain surgeon working in the dark, blindfolded, I had set the legs free.

Grasping at the theory that the turkey would defrost faster from the inside out, I turned the tap to the hottest setting and blasted the main cavity of that bird with steaming water. After five minutes, the ice melted enough that I could pull out the giblets and neck and set them on the counter. My confidence rose a notch.

After ten minutes, I turned off the water, wiped the sweat from my face, and headed out in search of a foil pan.

My luck was changing. Dickenson's had opened for the morning with a skeleton crew. The checker glared at me as she rang up my purchase, but I didn't care. I had my pan.

Back home, I hoisted the bird from the sink into the pan. That sucker flattened the foil, so I shoved a baking sheet underneath. After rearranging the oven racks to make room, I hauled the bird across the kitchen and shoved it into the oven. It was nine a.m.

Something was missing. The neck was still on the counter, but where had the giblets gone? I checked the floor, looked inside the sink, and was about to have myself certified insane when I caught sight of Emily sprawled on her back in her bed, legs outstretched and an expression of ecstasy on her furry face. Since I didn't know what to do with turkey guts anyway, I shrugged off the loss.

Now for the stuffing. I froze. My turkey took up every centimeter of space in my oven. How was I going to cook the stuffing?

I bit down on my trembling lower lip. The sign of a mature person is his or her ability to ask for help. It was time to call in the reinforcements.

"I was just going to call you," Penny said, sounding gay since she didn't have to cook a turkey. "What time do you want us there?"

"Now. I need your help."

I explained the situation to her. Instead of trying to ward me off with a crucifix and garlic, Penny said it wasn't a problem. In fact, she didn't even need my ingredients.

"I can make the stuffing. You make the cranberries. Those get done on the stovetop. Besides. I'm already wearing my good sweater. White."

I gasped. "Oh—my—"

"Gobstoppers," Penny interjected. She didn't like swearing.

I shrieked. "I forgot the mashed potatoes."

"Is that all? I got it covered. In fact, I made green bean casserole already just because I like it. I planned to bring it with me."

"And rolls. How will I get the rolls done?"

"You can bake those while the turkey rests."

I started to breathe normally again until I remembered the gravy.

"All I have is a jar," Penny said.

"Sold! Bring it with you. Bowers is handling dessert."

I hung up, relieved. Chauncey sauntered into the room with something hanging from his mouth. I snatched the feather away. Good grief. I was going to have to speed clean. Maybe if I shoved everything into my bedroom...

Bowers was the first to arrive. I answered the door in a royal-blue sweater and black slacks, my auburn hair in loose waves, and pink, fuzzy slippers on my feet.

"The others are coming on their own."

He handed me a covered pie plate and returned to his car for the hors d'oeuvres. After I set the plate on the counter, I lifted the lid for a peek. A perfectly latticed apple pie with sparkling sugar on the golden crust. I was in big trouble.

He came into the kitchen and handed me a carton of vanilla ice cream. I popped it into the freezer and eyed the trays he set on the counter, covered with foil.

"I figured you would be using your oven, so I made stuff we could serve at room temperature. He took off the foil and waited for my reaction.

"Is that baked brie?"

"I skipped the cranberry sauce, since we'll have that with dinner." He rifled through a bag. "Here are the crackers. Do you have a plate?"

Every plate I owned was on the table. My mother had given me a set of dishes for my high school graduation. What I initially thought of as a bummer gift had served me well over the years. Today was the first time I'd have the entire set laid out.

I dug through the lower cabinets until I came up with a couple of pie tins leftover from restaurant takeout orders. I lined them with paper napkins and handed them over.

"Do you have wine glasses? I brought a bottle of pinot."

"We can rinse out the water glasses when we're through," I suggested. "Or use coffee cups, unless someone wants coffee."

The doorbell rang, and I ran to get it. Penny grinned at me and swept into the room carrying a serving dish. Kemper trailed behind with several more, each wrapped in a quilted warmer to keep the dishes hot. She arranged them on the table.

"Hey there," Bowers said from the kitchen. "How are the honeymooners?"

Penny blushed a deep shade of pink. "You told him!"

Bowers raised one brow. "Told me what?"

"I haven't said a thing."

When Bowers came out of the kitchen, Penny changed the subject by asking about his black eye and stitches. While he explained, I moved to the kitchen and pulled the rolls and the corn out of the freezer.

Penny joined me, leaving Kemper and Bowers to discuss boring man-stuff, like what chance the Arizona Cardinals had of making the playoffs. "So, who are the other two places for?"

I rolled my eyes. "Gutierrez and a mystery guest."

Penny gasped. "Gorgeous Gutierrez?"

"Yes. Invited by Bowers." I tried to keep my tone light. Bowers had never shown any interest in Gutierrez to my knowledge, but his feelings might have changed after she saved his skin yesterday. It was odd of him to invite her.

"That was nice of him." Penny had returned to her typically optimistic self. "Oh! I forgot the flowers in the car."

She sent Kemper out to retrieve a Thanksgiving arrangement she had purchased. On his way out, he ran into our remaining guests.

Gutierrez looked fabulous in fawn-colored, soft, knit pants and a sweater of gold and black in a diamond pattern. I tried not to compare us, but really. Next to her, Catherine Zeta Jones would look frumpy.

She seemed slightly uncomfortable without her holster. Of course, she was probably carrying in her purse. She stayed near the entrance and scanned the faces without moving to greet them. Having been a social misfit many times, I recognized the signs. I had pity and went to welcome her.

Gutierrez wasn't the type to inspire hugs, so I shook her hand. "You look great. Very festive."

"Thanks."

I noticed she didn't return the compliment. She handed Bowers a bottle of wine. He made a noise of appreciation when he read the label.

"We'll save this for dinner."

I peered over his arm. Reserve St. Croix from Minnesota.

When the second guest stepped out from behind Gutierrez, I recognized him immediately.

"It's the turkey delivery man," I said before I could edit myself, but he took it as a compliment and grinned. He had shaved off the whiskers and put on an old but presentable brown suit. He wasn't bad looking when he cleaned up, and I put him at closer to fifty than sixty.

Bowers introduced him to everyone as Michael, though he didn't explain how they knew each other. Then everyone moved toward the snacks Bowers had prepared. I knew about the brie, but I hadn't seen him bring out the stuffed mushrooms.

"You made stuffed mushrooms from scratch?" I whispered as he popped one in his mouth.

"Frozen section at The Food Warehouse. I have my limits." When he winked at me, I felt a goofy rush of awkward excitement that faded when I saw Gutierrez watching us. Her expression was neutral—the female version of Bowers' cop face—but she had always projected her emotions in a way I could pick up on. This time, it was sadness mixed with envy. Flustered, I looked away.

In the time I had known them both, Bowers and Gutierrez seemed more like competitors than friends. They had professional respect for each other, but they didn't seem particularly warm and fuzzy together. She might have taken that relationship for granted, hoping it would grow into something more intimate. Then, along comes some red-headed pet psychic to spoil it all. Was it possible she saw me as a threat? I didn't want to be a threat to the lady with the gun.

Bowers had already opened the wine to let it breathe. Now he asked if anyone would like a glass. My guests were charmed—or pretended to be charmed—to be drinking their wine from beverage glasses featuring superheroes. It had taken me years to collect them all. When I handed Gutierrez a glass featuring Wonder Woman primed for battle, she raised one brow at me.

"Different." She nodded and took a sip.

I left her to check on the turkey.

Maybe it was because I hadn't stuffed it, or maybe it was because I had par-boiled it in the sink in my attempt to defrost it, but the turkey looked done. The deep golden-brown skin promised to crackle, and clear juices skirted the edges of the baking pan. Now, how to get it out of the oven without spilling.

Bowers was at my side and peering over my shoulder. "What's the thermometer say?"

"I don't have a thermometer, but the red thing they stuck in the breast popped up. That means it's done, right?"

"Let's have a look."

With the care of one diffusing a bomb, he slid the pan off the rack and placed it on a trivet I had set on the countertop. He jiggled the legs and almost pulled one off.

"I'd say it's done. Do you have a dish towel?"

I retrieved one from the drawer and he draped it over the bird while I adjusted the oven temperature for the rolls.

He frowned at the turkey. "Do you have a serving tray?"

"I have another baking pan. Oh. I need that for the rolls." I dug around and found a metal platter that was more suited for Bowers' brie and crackers than a twenty-nine-pound turkey, but Bowers said it would do. He maneuvered the bird onto the platter, sighed at the site of the crushed aluminum pan, and asked me for a saucepan.

I handed him the largest, and while I put on the corn and cranberries, he tipped the drippings from the baking pan into the saucepan.

"Are you saving that for something?"

He looked at me, surprised. "It's for the gravy."

"Oh. Penny brought..." I picked up her jar of store bought.

Bowers took hold of my shoulders and turned me toward the living room. "You entertain our guests and I'll make the gravy. Bring me the leftover wine."

"So that's how you work your magic in the kitchen. You drink."

"It's for the gravy."

Bowers was cooking in my kitchen. I felt a tingle of wonder at Bowers performing such a domestic act in my home. It moved him from an uber-professional, extremely attractive cop to a human being. It didn't seem real.

Before long, Bowers announced dinner was ready. I rushed to the kitchen to take back the duties he had assumed, but he shooed me out and told me to sit down.

Penny had added the flower arrangement to the table —a burst of orange, red, and yellow flowers pouring out of a cornucopia. She also made a few imperceptible changes to each setting that made the table look more inviting.

She took a seat with Kemper at her side. Gutierrez and Michael sat in the chairs opposite. Bowers marched out with the turkey and set it next to the head of the table which left me all the way at the other end. He returned with a basket of rolls and a bowl of corn and made one last trip for the mashed potatoes and cranberries. The butter, salt, and pepper were already out, and Penny had removed the warmers from her dishes.

It was showtime.

"Michael, could you say grace?" Bowers asked.

The older man seemed pleased at the prospect. He made it an impromptu prayer.

"I won't ask you to bless us, Lord, because you already have. Good food. Good people. It truly is a day for Thanksgiving."

We responded with an enthusiastic *Amen.*

Everyone passed their plates around the table and each person doled out a serving of whatever item was closest. I handed out the rolls.

I took a deep breath, cut into my slice of turkey, and popped the first bite into my mouth. I chewed. And I chewed. After a hard swallow, I said, "Could you please pass the gravy?"

My bird had gotten a bit dehydrated.

The gravy made the rounds. Twice.

Bowers raised his glass of wine. "To friends, our families, and our hostess, Frankie."

Gutierrez was the last to leave. Even then, she seemed reluctant to go. Finally, when I offered to pack up some leftover turkey for her, she scooted. I closed the door behind her and gave my smile a rest. My cheeks hurt. Being a hostess required social skills I didn't have.

Penny had insisted on helping me wash up, so I had nothing left to do except relax.

Bowers handed me my glass of wine—a Scooby-Doo glass. Yes, Scooby-Doo is a superhero. We sat back on the couch. Chauncey and Emily, freed from my bedroom, immediately joined us.

"That went well." He wrapped an arm around my shoulder, but I scooted forward and set my glass on the coffee table.

"I have a confession to make."

He sipped his wine. "You've never made a Thanksgiving dinner before."

I cringed. "Was it that obvious?"

"Only to me because I know you so well."

I dropped my face onto my open hands. "I'm sorry. You wanted to go up to your sister's and dine on a delicious meal. Instead, I forced you to stay here and eat leather. I served most of the food out of pie tins, except what Penny brought. If it weren't for you and Penny, everyone would have starved. Maybe that would have been better."

"Hey, hey, hey." He lifted my chin. "You jumped in there and tried something new, something that would intimidate most people, and you did it for me. That means a lot."

"Oh my gosh. I forgot candied yams. June said they're your favorite."

He cleared his throat. "I hate them, but I don't want to hurt my sister's feelings, so I feed them to the dog under the table."

That should have made me laugh, but I was inconsolable.

"And I didn't just poison *you*. Penny is my friend, so she'll forgive me and force Kemper to do so as well, but what about Gutierrez and Michael?"

He sighed and gave up on cheering me up. "Michael is damn glad to have a holiday meal outside of the shelter."

"Shelter? He's homeless? But he has a job delivering turkeys."

"And that's not enough to live on. He's actually been spending his nights at Good Morning Bakery."

I gaped. "*He's* the criminal?"

I could see from the changes in his expression that Bowers, the upholder of law and order, was struggling against his compassionate side.

"Technically, yes. But he always paid for the pastry he ate."

"How on earth did he get in?"

Bowers grinned at me. "Scoots."

"What. The dog strolled over and opened the door?"

"Yes."

I lowered my voice. "Is Michael psychic?"

"No! He's an animal trainer."

Oh, my gosh. Is that what my future held?

"He got to know Scoots when he would drop by the

bakery for lunch as a regular customer, and he taught him a few tricks."

"Like how to grow opposable thumbs and turn a doorknob?"

When Bowers laughed, his eyes crinkled. He stopped laughing and rubbed the cheek under his black eye. "I thought I was the sceptic. The back door locks from the outside, but there's a bar so that anyone inside can get out. Michael taught him to—"

"Target." Chauncey sat up and looked for the bullseye. I held out my palm so he could press his nose against it and then rewarded him with a piece of brie.

"Exactly. Except he didn't use his hand. He used a signal. Three raps in succession. He would rap on the back door, and the dog would target the bar and open the door. Scoots was happy to have the company, and Michael had a warm place to spend the night. In the morning, he would pick his breakfast from the discounted day-old stock in the refrigerator and leave the money on the counter."

"Scoots wasn't a very good guard dog."

"Bob relieved him of duty and is getting an alarm system instead."

The story stopped being funny when I realized Michael had lost his temporary shelter.

"I talked to Johnathon Frazier. He didn't realize his employee was so bad off. He's happy to have an extra hand on the turkey farm. He has an old bunkhouse Michael can live in."

"How do you do that?"

He cocked his head. "Do what?"

"Read my mind."

I saw the twitch when I mentioned psychic possibilities, but he covered it with a grin.

"Great minds think alike."

I hesitate before asking my next question. I didn't want to seem petty, but I wanted to know why Bowers had invited Gutierrez for dinner.

He took my hand and gave me a repeat performance on the mind-reading thing.

"Thank you for being nice to Juanita. She's going through a rough patch."

And turning to you for sympathy? I didn't say it out loud. Definitely petty.

"Her boyfriend said he needed space. Apparently, he wanted to spend Thanksgiving with another woman and her family."

Been there; done that. The most emotionally debilitating experience I'd ever had was finding out the man who said he loved me, the man to whom I had given everything, had moved on to graze in other pastures. I no longer had feelings for Jeff, but the memory stung.

"I'm so sorry to hear that. It stinks."

"She only told me after the job yesterday. I'm sorry I sprung her on you last minute, but her family lives in Maine, so she couldn't make other plans after she found out. And she's taking it hard."

"She hid it well."

"It's hard for her to express herself. Comes with the job."

He took my hands in his. "It's difficult being a cop's wife. I've seen the toll it has taken on my friends' marriages. It's a lot of work. Are you sure you want to keep seeing me? It won't be all laughs."

My face felt warm, and I looked down, self-conscious. "We're just dating, so I can always dump you."

He tipped my chin up, so I had to meet his eyes. "Frankie, there's only one reason a grown man dates a woman, and that's to discover if they would make a good team. A permanent team. I'm not playing with you."

Bowers couldn't know how much his words meant to me. I was speechless, which was just as well. He lowered his head and kissed me. After a while, he stretched out on the couch and pulled me down so my head was resting under his chin. In a few minutes, I felt a rumbling in his chest and heard soft snores.

His phone buzzed to say a message had arrived. I glanced up, but his eyes were closed. Should I? I really shouldn't, but I did. Moving slowly, I reached over his head and took his phone from the end table.

JuneBug60: *Best TG ever???? Wow, Marty. She must be some cook. Love and kisses. Junie*

Kitty Christmas Caper

I flicked on the light switch and held my breath with the hopes that two rows of cheap multi-colored lights could turn the barren, colorless interior of U Behave, my animal behavior business, into a cheery Christmas wonderland. It wasn't happening, at least not for me.

"Oh, Frances," cooed my best friend Penny, better known as she-who-is-perennially-cheerful. "Doesn't it remind you of home?" Penny is one of the few people who gets away with calling me Frances. To everyone else, I'm Frankie.

By home, I assumed she meant Wisconsin where we grew up rather than Arizona, where we lived now. Arizona didn't have a Christmas season. As proof, on the other side of the windowpane, a pink, flowering bush provided a resting place for a contented bird. Not a hungry, shivering, freezing bird. A decidedly happy, warm bird.

"Considering that Wisconsin is under three feet of snow right now, no. Arizona is nothing like home. If this were home," I said, pointing to the floor inside the entrance, "there would be a soppy mat and the tile would be dirty and wet from people stomping the snow from their feet."

"Then you should be happy you don't have to mop every five seconds." Penny took in the glow of lights and sighed a happy sigh. Then she grabbed a handful of tinsel and a sprig of holly and headed for the entrance.

Her happiness routine didn't stand a chance against my holiday depression. "My shop looks like squatters have tried to decorate an abandoned warehouse."

Penny nestled the holly into the tinsel over the door, and after stepping back to review her touches, she added another piece of tape. "You're exaggerating, as usual."

She stepped behind the counter with me to get the full effect. "This looks like Christmas."

I dug my heels in. "Christmas looks like pine trees and gingerbread men and Uncle Tim dressed up in a Santa suit that stopped fitting him fifty pounds ago. Christmas looks like roast turkey and cheese sticks and a punch bowl filled with enough grog to drop a platoon of soldiers."

Penny put an arm around my shoulder and squeezed. "Believe me, I know how hard it is the first year away from family, but it's time to start your own traditions here in Wolf Creek. And this," she swept her arm to include my pitiful display, "is a nice start."

"You're just happy because The Prickly Pear looks amazing."

This morning, we'd met at Penny's bistro, which connects to U Behave through my back door. When she'd taken over an old bakery, there had been an extra room with a separate entrance they had used to sell their day-old goods. She rented me the space (for free) because she insisted clients would only take me seriously if I had a walk-in storefront.

Usually, The Prickly Pear popped with colors from the namesake cactus—sweet yellows, hot pinks, and warm purples. This morning, the restaurant touted an old-fashioned Christmas. Felt bows in deep red decorated the end of each booth like church pews reserved for a wedding. Silver bells hung from the light fixtures, large bulbs glowed warm in red, green, and orange from the edge of the counter where the customers paid, and around the windows, she'd spray-painted frost and stenciled Christmas trees on the glass in washable paint. She'd even made green aprons with cheerful snowmen and frolicking elves for her staff, and she had lined the pockets with candy canes to hand out to patrons. Everyone was required to smile.

"I miss snow," I whined. "I miss Mom and Dad. I miss cheese curds.

"We have—"

"The real kind that squeak on your teeth."

"Don't be a grumpy pants. Christmas is about more than temperatures and decorations. It's about those we love."

"Most of whom are still back in Wisconsin," I reminded her.

"It's about the birth of Jesus."

I wasn't about to take on the Christ Child. Instead, I glowered at my decorations. A renegade red light rebelled against the senselessness of an Arizona Christmas and flickered.

Penny tipped her head and grinned. "You can get just as many presents in Arizona. Maybe more because your parents miss you."

"Now you sound like Mrs. Claus doing publicity for Santa," I grumbled.

"Don't be silly. She wears those little spectacles. I've got twenty-twenty vision."

Dear, sweet Penny. I don't know how we became best friends in our childhood. She is preternaturally perky. Me? The queen of cynicism. Penny keeps telling me it's all just a facade and deep down I'm really a kind person. She points out the animals I've helped, and she's right. I do like animals. It's people I can't stand most of the time.

Maybe she was right. Maybe this first year away from family would make me appreciate them more when I went back for Christmas next year...if I could afford it.

I'd been making a name for myself as a pet psychic— all bells and whistles, if you know what I mean. I'd cold read people, watching their reactions to my dropped hints and suggestions to guide my readings. Then I'd added a touch of common sense for realism. Nothing psychic about it.

Then a dog named Sandy broke through my mental barrier and I wound up with real abilities, which sounds exciting, but not when you're surrounded by corpses in the middle of a murder investigation. After that experience, I started blocking out the images and thoughts I got from animals through a technique I'd learned via a psychiatrist who thought we were discussing a hypothetical psychotic case. I'd re-billed myself as an animal behaviorist which wasn't as attractive to clients as a person who could read their pooch's mind and channel dead Aunt Dora. I wasn't making any money. Maybe I could put that on my Christmas cards and generate a few sympathy donations from Mom and Dad.

Just as I was warming up to the whole presents-in-the-mail idea, I heard a fizzle and a pop, and the lights went out.

"Stupid, piece-of-crap lights. I should just close for the holidays and be done with it."

Penny fluttered over to the bulbs. "One of the red ones went out. This one, I think. Just replace it and you'll be good as new." She checked her watch. "I've got to go."

She hesitated, and her brow creased with a rare expression of uncertainty. "You're coming to rehearsals, right?"

Penny had won the role of the Ghost of Christmas Past in the community production of Scrooge. With her blonde good looks and a disposition that made Doris Day come across as a shrew, she did have an other-worldly quality about her. Today was her first time reading from the stage while the crew practiced with the spotlight, and she was suffering from a case of stage fright.

"I wouldn't miss it," I said with a grin plastered on my face. I would if I could, but sometimes one must suffer in the name of friendship.

U Behave was on the corner of Maricopa and Main. The theater was only a five-minute walk down Maricopa, so I moved to unlock the front door so we could leave without passing through The Prickly Pear.

"Who rehearses at eight in the morning, anyway? Don't actors usually sleep in?" I wouldn't even be awake if Penny hadn't guilted me into meeting her at the crack of dawn to decorate my place. She had bribed me with a latte and a side of bacon and eggs from her café.

"The director, Mrs. Glen, is retired. She likes to get an early start to her day. Since everyone in the cast and crew is either retired, a student, a homemaker, or owns their own business, it works out."

As I led the way outside, my toe connected with something solid and I lost my footing. Penny caught my arm before I hit the pavement. A large cardboard box blocked my entry way.

Penny unfolded the tabs and squealed. She pulled out the occupant and hugged him to her chest.

Fine, long gray hairs stood on end like the down from a baby bird, and from this angle, I could see a white spot on the kitten's bottom, as if he had backed into a freshly painted wall. After a few hugs, Penny handed the bundle over.

He was incredibly soft—until he dug razor-sharp claws into my shoulder. I tried to pull him off, but he renewed his efforts and clung to me like a little remora.

Oblivious to my pain, Penny said, "Kemper would kill me if I brought it home." She referred to her long-time boyfriend. "He's allergic, and he'd never be able to drop by, and that would be a problem. My television is bigger than his, and it is football season. Go Packers."

Kitty had moved on to my shoulder-length, auburn hair. While he limited himself to chewing on it, I was fine, but then his paws became tangled and he declared open war on my roots.

"I wonder what time the pound opens?" I mused aloud.

"Frances!" Penny shrieked. "You wouldn't!"

"Emily—ouch—wouldn't appreciate the competition." I lied. My black-and-white cat would probably train the kitten to be her slave. I was more concerned about my position in the food chain. I was already third in line behind Emily and my mutt, Chauncey. Fourth place didn't sound any better.

Penny took hold of the struggling kitten and gave a few yanks.

"Ow, ow, ow!"

She freed the kitten from my hair and handed him back to me. "If you don't want to take it home, you'll just have to find the owner." After one last tickle for Kitty, Penny took off for her stage debut.

I held the kitten up to face me and looked into a large pair of crystal-blue eyes. He had white around his mouth, clown-style. He broke the stare down by licking my nose.

I carried my furry cargo around the corner, past the entrance to The Prickly Pear, and into Canine Camp, the doggie daycare owned by Seamus McGuire. His clientele consisted of dogs, but he might know something about kittens. I'd adopted Emily when she was an adult, and I hadn't a clue how to care for a baby cat.

The bell above the door jingled as I entered the daycare, raising a cacophony of barks. The last time I'd been in here, I had an unsolved murder on my hands and the key witness was one of Canine Camp's clients.

Seamus' part-time bookkeeper, a Goth college student named Charlie, stepped out of the office and squealed, a girly reaction that didn't quite go with her purple-streaked hair and nose ring. "What a cutie! Can I hold it?"

Seamus, followed by his barking charges, wandered over to the fence that separated the lobby from the play area to see what all the fuss was about. I hadn't seen him for a while, and he looked as boyishly cute as ever with his dark red hair—practically brown—his freckles, and his dimples.

"I found this little fur ball outside my front door," I began. "I'm not sure what to do with him—"

"Her," Charlie said, holding up Kitty's tail end so I could verify it for myself.

"She can't be more than eight weeks old," Seamus said. "She should be with her mother, at least until her twelfth week."

"Don't blame me. I just found her."

He came through the gate, first nudging aside a few

curious hounds, and then went into his office, talking while he dug through drawers. "I'm guessing at the age. She might not be on solid food yet, but you'll still have to feed her." He held up an eye dropper.

I gaped. "With that? It'll take forever!"

"Babies take patience." He handed over the dropper with an expression that said it was probably a good thing I was single and without maternity prospects.

"How often do I feed her?"

Seamus grinned. "She'll let you know."

And she did let me know in tiny screeches the entire ride home. My pets are usually indifferent to my arrival, but they smelled something enticing today. My large ginger mutt ambled off the couch—the one he's forbidden to sleep on—and nudged my purse. I'd dropped Kitty in there while I unlocked the front door.

When her head popped out, Chauncey took a step back and growled, while Emily leapt on top of the bookcase and hissed. The competition for cutest-in-the-land had begun, and my grown cat didn't like the odds.

Once I'd settled onto the couch with a dropper full of milk that had been warmed on the stove, Kitty seemed to sense a potentially unpleasant experience. Not that I blamed her. I could imagine someone shoving a plastic nipple in my face. Not good. She squirmed and twisted. Holding onto her with one hand was proving more than I could handle, but then Chauncey grabbed her by the scruff.

"Drop it—drop it—drop it!" I yelled, as if he would suddenly respond to a command he'd ignored since the day I'd picked him up from the pound.

He scooted onto the couch and, laying Sphinx-style, dropped Kitty between his front paws. It was as if she was his bargaining chip. You want her on the couch, you gotta take me.

About to order him off, my words stuck in my throat. Kitty had landed on her back between Chauncey's paws, and she now kneaded his chest and searched for teats. I moved the dropper to her mouth, and she wrapped her paws around it and started to feed. Incredible. Five minutes later, she was asleep.

I hated to move her, but Penny would be onstage shortly. Uncertain what my pets would do if left alone with a new toy, I scooped Kitty up and propped her in the same belly-up position in between two pillows on my bed. Hoping not to wake her, I tiptoed out of the room. She looked like such a little angel. Maybe a kitten around the house wouldn't be so bad.

Even though I was running late, I swung by U Behave first to check for clues. I hoped the person who'd dropped Kitty off had left a note taped to the box that had somehow come loose, but after a ten-minute search that included picking through scraps of soggy paper from the street gutter, I had to conclude she'd been abandoned sans note.

When the perpetrator selected a box, at least he or she had shown enough compassion to choose one large enough to allow Kitty to move around in comfort. It must have held something large. Or a whole bunch of small items. At this rate of clever deduction, I'd have the mystery solved in...never.

Across the top flap remained the residue of a torn mailing label. The right-hand edge of the return address was legible, but the four letters there didn't make any sense. UMES.

Perfumes? It was an awfully big box. That would have been a lifetime supply of scent. What about fumes? Had the box been part of a delivery to an exterminator? Eww.

It was interesting how the air holes had been cut into one side of the cardboard box, almost in the pattern of a smiley face. Half an hour of research and the only clue I had was the perpetrator was happy.

Half an hour! I ran all the way to the theater.

The Wolf Creek Players had access to the Dynamite Theater, named so because the building had once ware-housed—you guessed it—dynamite back in the good old days before Arizona joined the union. I understand they used explosives to help flatten out areas for roads or railway lines or anything that required a flat surface. I thought the name sounded like some smarmy playboy from the eighties: That's one dynamite theater!

The white mission-style building had modern glass front doors, and I swept through the tiny lobby and into the main theater. I couldn't hide my entrance, as the floors were wooden and creaked. A lot. Every head turned my way, but they immediately lost interest and returned their attention to the stage.

An actress stood under the spotlight, her fists clenched tightly and her shoulders hunched from the tension of a good fight. I took a closer look. Penny???? What a good actress! Who knew? I didn't remember a fight scene from Scrooge, but then I hadn't watched the movie in a while.

Her voice rang out clear. "Don't you think it would be better if I entered from stage left so it doesn't look like I'm sneaking up behind Mister Scrooge?"

Penny pointed to my right, so stage left must have been

her left. She was using her reasonable voice—even and calm—which would have struck fear into anyone who knew her. You just don't want to anger sweet people. They're like baby rattlesnakes who haven't learned to control their venom.

It wasn't influencing the short troll who looked up at my friend from the orchestra pit. As I got closer, I could make out spiked orange hair that matched the woman's outfit and, when she turned in profile, I could see it matched her thick, tangerine lips as well. And her glasses, though they had sparkly rhinestones in the corners to distract from the eyeball-burning effect of the rest of her toilette.

"Penny, dear, I want you to enter from the right because Marley just exited stage left. I don't want it to look like a traffic pattern." Mrs. Glen must have been a gin drinker because she sounded like Harvey Fierstein.

"But, and I know it's an assumption, don't Marley and I come from the same place? Wouldn't it make sense if we entered from the same direction?" Penny's voice climbed steadily in pitch, so that direction ended in a squeak.

Mrs. Glen tossed her script down on the nearby piano. "For criminy sakes! You're a ghost. You can enter from any flipping place you please!"

She took a deep breath and straightened her glasses with the palms of both hands, probably to spare her bright orange talons. "Penny. Sweetheart. Try it once from the right. For me?"

Penny was a sucker for pleading, though she paused long enough that I could tell she was struggling to find a polite way to refuse. She finally bowed her head and wandered behind the appropriate curtain, while Scrooge pulled his nightcap over his eyes, tiptoed across the stage, and amused the crew with an imitation of Harpo Marx from Duck Soup.

"That's enough, Danvers!"

At this barked out order, Danvers settled into his miserly role. The players ran through it one more time, with Penny delivering her lines in a monotone voice that suggested she was playing the Ghost of I-Don't-Give-a-Damn. Finally, the director called for a break.

Everyone, including those watching from the audience, filed up the stairs to the left of the stage—my left—and disappeared behind the curtain. I followed. A table had been laid out with coffee and snacks to recharge the troupe. Packaged cookies were stacked into a precarious pyramid. The tip consisted of oatmeal cookies, but my attention zoomed in on the chocolate chip package halfway down. I jimmied my prize out. In the process, I sent the entire arrangement tumbling down onto the table and floor. I stepped back and pretended it hadn't been my fault.

"Got it!" squeaked out an excited voice. A head of brown hair nudged my leg aside, and a girl around eight years old swept the cookies into her arms and dumped them on the table.

"You didn't have to do that but thank you."

She grinned up at me. "That's okay. I didn't like the triangle anymore. I want to try a tower." She proceeded to suit actions to words.

A middle-aged woman handed me another package of chocolate chip cookies, and I absently tore them open and ate while she talked.

"Heather loves neatening things up. I swear she's part brownie. The kind that visit shoemakers in the night, not the scouts." She held out a hand. "I'm her mother, Andrea Saunders."

"Do you have a part in the play?"

Andrea looked down at Heather. "Nope. She's the little star. She's playing Timothia." Off my look, she burst out laughing. "They couldn't find a boy suitable to play Tiny Tim. One little guy showed promise, but he was a ham. Instead of just limping, he kept tipping over and dragging himself around the stage. Mrs. Glen couldn't trust him not to do it during the performance."

The tower collapsed, and Heather gamely started over.

"So, she's keeping the stage in tip-top shape?" I smiled. "Is she for hire?"

"She's just bored. At home, her bedroom's a disaster."

"Mom!" Heather wailed.

"It is."

Heather grinned, showing a missing front tooth. "But only because I like my stuff where I can find it."

Mrs. Glen wandered up and selected a Styrofoam cup filled with coffee from in front of the urn. Heather frowned at the coffee ring the cup left behind on the table and promptly snatched up a napkin and wiped the spot clean.

Andrea dropped her voice. "They really shouldn't make a child come until they're going to use her. It's boring for Heather to hang around. And me. At least she fills her time straightening up the snack table and fetching things for the crew. She's explored every inch of this building. She could give tours."

Just then Penny slid up to us. Her breathing was faster than usual, and when she grabbed my arm, I winced. "Thank you so much for coming."

"You seemed to handle yourself just fine." I grinned. "So, did you win the argument?"

Penny blushed. "That woman is determined to light my bad side."

"You have a bad side?"

"Don't be stupid. Everyone has a bad side."

My eyebrows shot up. Stupid counted as swearing in Penny's vocabulary. She blew her bangs out of her eyes.

"Any luck with the kitten?"

"I got her fed. I'm going to have to put up notices around my shop and see if anyone answers."

"Answers?" The actor, Danvers, hopped into the conversation and wiggled his fingers and eyebrows. "I've got answers. Now what's the question?" He had moved his imitation from Harpo to Groucho.

Penny gave him a smile that barely bordered on tolerant, so he grabbed a bag of chips and said, in the voice of Snagglepuss, "Exit, stage right."

Andrea Saunders reached out for her daughter. "Heather. Time to go."

"But I haven't gotten to act yet!"

"We'll be back." Andrea didn't sound happy at the prospect. "They take so long to get her onstage that I spend half my day running her back and forth. She may be eight, but she does have a life."

The little girl put the finishing touches on her tower and reviewed the results with pleasure. Then she abruptly turned to me and said, "I have a guitar lesson."

"You don't have school?"

"I don't bother with that."

Andrea took her hand. "She's homeschooled. She was acting up in class, and it turned out that she was bored with her lessons." She squeezed her daughter's hand and gave a proud-parent smile. "She's working at a fourth-grade level."

Heather looked up at this praise. "Can we stop and get an ice cream on the way home?"

Andrea gave us the indulgent-parent smile, the one that said Aren't kids a riot? "We'll see." The smile was wasted on me. I'm the one who usually wants to stop for ice cream.

Penny frowned. "Speaking of hungry children, when's the last time you fed..."

"Kitty. I went for an unusual name. Before I came here. About an hour or so ago."

"She's probably hungry again."

"So soon?"

"That's what babies do. Eat and sleep and poop."

My eyes popped open. "Poop? Will she know to use a little box?"

And since there wasn't a litter box in my bedroom, I rushed home.

Though I called out, "I'm home," as I walked in, my pets didn't come to greet me. I found Chauncey outside my bedroom, his nose pressed to the space under the door and a deep wine in his throat. I'd been smart to lock up Kitty. He might have eaten her.

I shooed him away and swung open the door. All was quiet, at least until I shrieked, which brought Chauncey running. Vertical streaks of light shone through the holes in my beautiful floral curtains. Wriggling and jerking from the top of one panel drew my gaze to Kitty, who was ready make her next mark. The curtains began to tear, and she stilled herself to enjoy the ride down to the bottom. Chauncey raised a racket, but he made no move to grab her. I did.

Tiny demon in hand, I noted the small stain in the center of my bedspread. I set her down and leaned over, praying that it was a fur ball. Do kittens get fur balls? If it wasn't a fur ball, what was it? Did I have any bleach in the house? Would I ever sleep in my bed again? When I reached for her, Kitty was gone.

I found her in the living room climbing Mount

Chauncey. He didn't seem to mind. My dog held still as she situated her furry bottom on his head, and he gave me a look that said he expected extra kibble as payment.

I had to find this kitten's mother, and that meant tuning in to her tiny head. Ever since my involvement with a murder, I'd managed to keep the thoughts of animals from invading my brain by using imagery and closing the door, literally, on their brainwaves. I didn't look forward to opening that barrier, but I took a chance.

Focusing on her blue eyes, I zoned in on her energy signature, which is how animals communicate with me. Sometimes I feel something, sometimes I hear things, and sometimes I see images.

A pleasurable tickle started in my ears and spread into a feeling of lightness and joy in my chest. Just when I thought this reading wouldn't be so bad, a loud moan rose and in a crescendo of volume and pitch, followed by the tinkle of breaking glass.

Repeat that, I thought, trying to impress my request on Kitty. She didn't comply. With the limited attention span of a toddler, she sent me an image of a tawny playmate, her mother's fur-lined belly, and a frightened mouse running for its life. The effort tuckered her out, and she slid down Chauncey's nose until she plopped, belly up, between his paws. Asking a few times more for specifics on the heart-wrenching moans didn't get me anywhere, so I took the hint and prepared warm milk.

While she drank her fill, I considered the noises. Moaning and a crash of glass. It couldn't possibly be another murder, right? How many murders could there be in a small town like Wolf Creek? Maybe the crash of glass had been from a car accident. Was Kitty traveling in the family vehicle, enjoying the ride, when her people parents met with a terrible end? Was she an orphan? I admit I panicked. I called Detective Martin Bowers.

"Wolf Creek Police Department."

I asked the receptionist to put me through to him. We'd met during the murder investigation when he'd popped round to grill me about the death of a maid. A traffic accident might not fall under homicide, but I figured he would know anything bad that had happened in Wolf Creek in the last few days.

"Bowers." His voice had that detached, calm professionalism that I knew went with a poker face. It made him good at interrogations.

"It's Frankie."

I accepted the pause with good grace. The murder investigation had ended with me reading an animal's mind in order to save two lives. Bowers had been an unwilling participant in the event. He probably had me labeled in his neat little notebook under Freak and spent nights trying to find a plausible explanation for what he'd witnessed.

"Can you tell me if there have been any domestic violence calls in the last two days? Or car accidents?" I hesitated before adding, "Or murders?"

Another pause. "Why?"

Fair enough question. I voiced my suspicions about Kitty's strange appearance at U Behave—leaving out the parts about the moaning and the glass—and he let out a sigh which I assumed was infused with the relief that there wasn't anything allegedly supernatural involved.

"Frankie, do you really think a person would get into a car accident and, in the middle of bleeding, find a box for the kitten and drop it off at your front door?"

"What about murders?"

"There haven't been any."

I detected triumphant undertones, so I said, "That

have been reported." That didn't go over well. He lost his cool facade, which happened often when he dealt with me.

"Don't you think you're getting worked up over nothing? You tend to be a bit...imaginative. So, unless there was blood on the box..." His tone sharpened. "Was there?"

"No-o-o-o."

"Well then."

Okay. I was going to have to tell him about the moaning and the glass. That didn't go over well, either.

"What do you mean, moaning?"

"Just what I said." I did a fair imitation of what I'd heard. "And then I heard broken glass."

As much as he hated to acknowledge my abilities, he had seen firsthand what I was capable of, which made him testy. "For cripe's sake, the cat probably tripped his owner up and he broke a wine glass or a coffee cup."

"Her. It's a girl cat. And it wasn't that kind of moan."

"There are kinds?"

"If I tripped, I'd be surprised, and it would be more of a yelp. This was a moan of anguish and pain. The kind of an agonized, soulless cry that sends you under your covers and praying until morning." Okay. That did sound theatrical, but it described it.

"You're not going to find the owner. Just accept that you have a new pet."

As I hung up, I thought Bowers had a point. I might not be able to find the owner, but that didn't mean the owner couldn't find me. And what if it hadn't been the owner who left Kitty by my door? Maybe a good Samaritan had found her and left her outside U Behave because I dealt with animals and they assumed I would know what to do with her. She was my responsibility. I grabbed my camera, woke Kitty up from her nap, and set her on the coffee table.

First, I took a shot from the front, making sure I captured those crystal-blue eyes and clownish mouth. Then I spun her around to take a shot of the white patch on her bottom. I had just zoomed in to get the details when I paused. I wanted to make anyone responding to the ad prove that Kitty was theirs, and the white patch would be my test.

After transferring the photos to my laptop and printing off some flyers with basic contact information, I returned to U Behave and taped the notices to every light post and sign around the block, adding the last one to my store window. I returned home feeling I had done my good deed for the day. I only hoped someone would respond. As it turned out, I didn't have long to wait.

The next morning, a bulky man covered in tattoos waited outside U Behave with a large brindle pit bull. He looked a little scary—the guy, that is—so I took my time opening the door. When I finally let him in, he immediately asked about the kitten.

"It's yours?"

"Sure is."

"What's its name?" I used it because I wanted to know if he even knew Kitty's gender.

He paused. "Kitty."

Coincidence? Or did he just lack imagination, like me?

"What's Kitty look like?"

He held up my flyer. "Like this."

"I mean, are there any distinguishing marks on her...or him?"

He failed the test. He didn't know about the white spot

on her haunches. He gave up gracefully, setting the flyer on the counter so I could reuse it.

"She's a cute little one." He scratched his ear. "I don't suppose you know of anyone else with a kitten that needs a home. It would have to be free."

I took in his shaved head, his muscle shirt, and his many tattoos—especially the bright pink Gina on his neck —and then peered over the counter into the impassive face of his burly friend. The dog was missing the tip of one ear. Definitely a gangbanger type who probably engaged in dog fights.

"If you think I'm going to help you train that dog to kill using innocent kittens—"

He stepped back with a horrified gasp. "Petey loves cats!"

I crossed my arms in front of my chest. "I bet he does. You want to tell me where he lost the ear?"

"I have no idea. It was missing when I adopted him, poor thing." Tattoo Guy rubbed the ear between his fingers and Petey's tongue lolled, while his eyes clearly said *I adore you*.

"Right. And I bet Gina and you are just friends."

"Hey! Watch your mouth. Gina's my mother."

I bit my lip. "Seriously?"

"Seriously. And Petey does too love cats. His best friend was our Calico, Duchess. She died of old age last week, and Petey's been inconsolable."

I had to admit that was a big word for a gangbanger.

"I want to find him a new friend, but I can't afford much."

Oh. "I'm so sorry. I have to be careful." I finished with a half-hearted smile.

He glared at me, his distaste apparent. "You've got a sick mind." He looked down at Petey. "Doesn't she?"

Petey barked, and with that final pronouncement, Tattoo Guy and Petey wiped the dust of U Behave off their feet just as Penny skipped in through the back door.

"You found the owner!"

"Not yet."

"But you took down all the flyers."

I hurried to the street and made a quick circuit around the block. Penny was right. All that remained of my Kitty campaign were a few remnants of paper still taped to sign posts. On my return, I slipped into The Prickly Pear and joined Penny in a booth for a conference.

"I don't get it," I said. "Who would take down the flyers?" I thought of Tattoo Guy and Petey. He had a flyer. Could he have made a move to eliminate the competition? I couldn't imagine he would have gone around the entire block, though. And how could he be sure where exactly I had posted my notices? For all he knew, Kitty's picture was plastered throughout downtown Wolf Creek.

"Isn't it against the law to put signs up on city property?" Penny asked. "Maybe a government employee took them down."

"Give me a break. People do it for garage sales all the time. And I can't imagine a meter maid taking the time to remove them all."

"It's too early in the day for the meter maids," Penny agreed.

"Speaking of early, why aren't you at practice?"

Penny's face clouded over. "Mrs. Glen had a dentist appointment. I have to be at the theater at eleven. Are you going to stop by again? It really helped, having you there. I don't expect to go onstage until around eleven-thirty, so you don't have to hurry to get there."

That last bit was added to make the offer more attractive. My presence hadn't had any impact on Penny that I could see. It's not as if I leapt to her defense against the perils of entering from stage right, but since she had asked, I knew I'd go.

"Why don't you bring some flyers to the theater?" Penny suggested.

It didn't sound promising, but why not? But first, I had an appointment.

———

The Doberman Pinscher cocked his pointy ears at me and gave a healthy growl.

"It's alright, Romeo," said the fluffy woman who had called for my help. "He's so protective of me." She tittered.

"So, Mrs. Tucker," I said, letting the dog sniff the back of my hand. "You said something about your husband sleeping on the couch?"

"Call me Dorinda." She sighed. "Romeo just loves to sleep on our bed, but he does take up a teensy-weensy bit of room." She affectionately rubbed his muzzle. "You silly goose."

"This couch?" Eyeing her purple plush couch as if it were a problem to solve, which it was, I dropped down on it and yelped when I encountered the pointy edge of a spring. Did they still make cushions with springs? The plush purple covering was pristine—no tears or faded spots —so I had to assume this couch existed before I was born, and Dorinda was an excellent seamstress. Or else she paid someone to have it re-covered.

Changing positions didn't make the furniture more comfortable, and I started to notice the fabric wasn't as plush as it appeared. The fibers were stiff, not soft and smooth. If I tossed and turned overnight on this thing, I'd probably wind up with rug burns. Mr. Tucker had my sympathy.

"Close the door," I said, standing.

Mrs. Tucker's eyes went to the already closed front door. She hesitated. "Which door?" She sounded as if she were being tested and wanted to make certain she'd pass.

"The bedroom door. Time to mark out which territory is yours and which areas Romeo is allowed to access. I'd also start the TANSTAAFL program." I pronounced the word Tänstoffle.

"That sounds complicated."

"It's an acronym. There ain't no such thing as a free lunch. Get it? Let's say you want to let Romeo on the couch."

"But the couch is so uncomfortable! The dog would hate it! Wouldn't you, sweetie?"

The dog whined.

Funny how she didn't consider whether her husband would like it or not. "If you want to allow Romeo on the couch," I repeated, "make him do a trick first and have the couch be his reward. Make him sit before you feed him dinner. Anything you give him is a reward for requested behavior."

Dorinda gasped. "That's just mean."

"It's actually healthier than spoiling him. Healthier for you, healthier for Romeo, and healthier for your husband's back. When it's time for bed, just say goodnight and close the door behind you."

She shot a panicked look at her dog. "But what if Romeo needs to get in at night?"

"He's a dog. What can he possibly need from your bedroom?"

"I don't know. A hug?" Apparently, Dorinda wasn't

ready to give up her big, toothy security blanket. Time for the direct approach.

"Have you tried lying on that couch? Trust me. Your husband's not going to put up with it for long. Right now, you're making him play second fiddle to a dog. If you want him to stick around, your husband needs to be king of the castle."

Dorinda's lower lip trembled. She seemed to be having a tough time choosing between her pet and her mate, so I helped her out. I jotted down a few websites and handed her the paper. "Get the dog his own bed. Make it a good one and he won't care. Let him feel like top dog. Just make sure your husband feels like top man."

She didn't like the advice any more than she liked writing out the check, but I finally got out of there fifty bucks richer.

There was still time to run home before Penny's play practice. Actually, there wasn't, but I wanted to be late so I wouldn't have to stand around waiting for Penny to go onstage. I checked in on Kitty. The curtains couldn't have gotten any worse, so I'd left her in the bedroom. Hoping to fix the misperception that my bed was the potty, I'd moved Emily's litter box into a corner.

My cat shoved past me as soon as the door was opened and relieved herself, glaring at me the whole time. As for Kitty, she had enjoyed a good romp in the sand—as evidenced by the litter scattered around my rug—but she didn't poop.

Emily put extra effort into her final kicks, spraying my wall with a healthy dose of sand, and strutted past me, nose in the air and distinctly out of joint. I'd have to get her a catnip mouse for Christmas to make it up to her.

In the kitchen, my answering machine blinked at me, letting me know that a telemarketer, computerized system, or bill collector had called. I was wrong. The message was from Bowers.

"Frankie, Bowers. Call me." What a warm greeting. Would my girlish ego ever recover? I figured I should stop being sarcastic and just be grateful he called, so I phoned him back.

"Just checking in on the, um, kitten thing. I'm sure you were putting me on about noises and moaning and all that. Heh-heh." His fake laugh showed he had taken me seriously.

"I wasn't kidding."

Silence. "Well, at least it's just a lost kitten and not anything more serious."

"It is a serious problem," I said, irritated at being dismissed. "The animal rescues are overloaded this time of year, and, well..." I didn't have it in me to make a lost kitten sound as important as a burglary or a homicide.

"Don't worry about it. You'll find it a home."

"I hope so."

"Well...just don't do anything stupid. Bye."

As I dropped the phone back onto its cradle, my Official Christmas Gift List caught my eye. Mom and Dad were always hard to buy for, but I thought every woman could use a Snuggie, and Dad, an avid golfer, would appreciate a club cleaning kit. I had written the list in a financially optimistic mood, but now my budget had me reevaluating what I could afford. Maybe my parents could split something, instead...like a roll of mints.

Kemper was practically family, so I had to keep him on the list. Since Penny had been dating him for over a year, I figured I could give them a joint couple present as well. I'd just have to come up with something they could both use and share, a difficulty since they lived in separate apartments. A popcorn machine for movie nights sounded cool, but with my budget, I'd have to settle for one of those humongous popcorn tins that came with a selection of cheddar, caramel, and plain.

My thoughts wandered to Seamus McGuire of Canine Camp and Bowers. I had liked them both before things went terribly wrong at the end of the murder investigation. Seamus, too, had been present for my big communication with Sandy the dog. It hadn't turned out well. The murderer was caught, and Sandy walked away unscathed, but I'd lost any hope for potential dates.

Maybe I should scratch them both off my list. At least Bowers, after that phone call. As if I would ever do anything stupid.

All this Christmas-type activity was starting to depress me, but there was one holiday tradition that never failed to lift my spirits. But first, I had to perform friendship duty at the theater.

———

Andrea Saunders and a cheerful old woman who was playing various walk-on parts had done the snack table proud. There were slices of cheese in various cutout shapes, crackers, bowls of nuts, and chocolates in Christmas-themed wrappers.

It wasn't as if I spent all my time hovering over the food, but I did have a good view of the stage if I peeked through the curtain. Penny calmly stood under the glare of spotlights while a young man played around with various settings.

His voice called out from above, behind the spotlight. "Your hair is such a nice white-gold that I want to catch the highlights without washing you out."

Penny preened a little and responded, "Take your time."

At the same time Mrs. Glen shouted, "Hurry it up. This isn't a beauty pageant!"

Though Penny stiffened up, it didn't look like there would be an ensuing fight. It wasn't much fun to watch a spotlight shift hue, so I wandered around backstage.

My time in theaters had been limited to a view from the audience, and I found behind the curtain both interesting and...dangerous. Thick cables snaked across the floor, and when I tripped, I almost careened headfirst through the backdrop and joined Penny onstage. A crew member grabbed my arm and yanked me back just in time, but the hanging depiction of Scrooge's fireplace swayed from the ceiling.

"Scenery!" Mrs. Glen shouted. "Are we having a problem?"

The stagehand—probably a mere college Freshman judging from his desperate attempts to grow a mustache—called back. "Sorry! It's under control!" To me he hissed, "You need to be more careful."

"Maybe you should tape these chords down before someone breaks their neck." I snapped at him out of embarrassment, and though he took it in stride, a few other faces peered up from their work with disapproving frowns. I did an about face and looked for a place where I could safely and unobtrusively wait for Penny. A small staircase in the corner, partially blocked by equipment, seemed to promise solitude.

The wooden steps headed down into an underground passage. At the bottom, the temperature dropped ten degrees and I stood in a stone-walled tunnel, enveloped in darkness.

It was kind of creepy, but since scurrying back up the

stairs like a frightened ninny in front of the crew wasn't high on my list, I took the only course possible and proceeded—very slowly—down the passage. The air smelled damp, like when I've forgotten a soggy towel in the bottom of my laundry basket. Or like a tomb.

Forcing my thoughts to brighter places, I focused on the chill. This would be a nice, cool place to hang out in the heat of summer. Hey, gang! Let's head on over to the Dynamite Theater and stand in the tunnels!

Because I couldn't see two inches in front of my face, my feet had gone off course, and I bumped into the stone wall. Bits of it crumbled at my touch. I wiped my hands on my jeans and adjusted my course, but I froze at the sound of light footsteps behind me.

"Who's there?" I hissed. Receiving no response, I waited a moment and listened. Nothing. After two quick steps forward, I stopped. My tracker didn't check his steps fast enough. I was being followed.

Logically, the crew would have noticed if a drooling psychopath wielding a large sword had passed backstage, so I spun on my heels and headed with purpose back toward the illuminated stairs. In the strains of light coming from the theater, I could make out a small form as it skittered back up to the stage. Heather. Either that or a killer midget.

Backstage wasn't turning out to be my cup of tea, so I took a seat in the theater and waited for Penny to take the stage again. Then I realized she was onstage, only she lay flat on her back.

Danvers danced around her, shaking and waving his hands. "Who, or what are you?"

"I am the Ghost of Christmas Past," Penny mumbled.

"Project, Penny, dear!" Mrs. Glen commanded.

"I *am* projecting, but I'm talking to the ceiling!" Penny shot a finger up toward the rafters to make her point.

Mrs. Glen's sigh filled the theater. "Marc Foster's ultra-modern production was a huge success with audiences. His vision is a proven success, so I don't think you should turn your nose up at it, young lady."

"I'm on my back, for Pete's sake! And this floor is dirty."

"You're a ghost, Penny dear, which means you're a corpse. Corpses don't move. We're going for gritty reality."

"The audience is going to strain their necks to try to see me." Penny lifted her head and squinted into the theater. "Frances? Are you straining to see me?"

From my angle, it was obvious there was a body on the floor, but my loyalty and Penny's wrath were too much for me. "I do feel a slight crick in my neck."

"Fine. Fine!" Mrs. Glen motioned Penny up.

Danvers held out a hand and pulled Penny to her feet. She looked a little dazed. Maybe acting wasn't her thing.

"We'll have to think of some other way to spice this show up," Mrs. Glen said, pacing in front of the stage.

Danvers pulled his nightcap down. "I could base my performance on an interpretation by the Marx Brothers." He pointed a shaky finger at Penny. "Who-a are-a you-a? And wachu a-want?" he said in a bad Italian accent. Chico Marx, I supposed.

Mrs. Glen put her hands over her ears. "Danvers, you're going to drive me batty!"

Fingers and eyebrows wiggling, he said, "It will be a short drive."

"Everybody go on break!" she screeched.

I hit the Safeway on my way home. Nothing could cheer me up like decorating a batch of Christmas cookies. At the last minute, I decided to make my favorite holiday tradition as simple as possible and bought one of those pre-made rolls of sugar cookies from the refrigerator section. Then, on impulse, I stopped at a roadside stand and purchased a four-foot balsam, which was half-naked by the time I untied it from the roof of my car. I hoped a bucket of water would bring it back to life.

Sticky with sap, I proudly righted my first Arizona Christmas tree in a plastic bucket filled with water. A few rags stuffed around the base—okay, every summer outfit I owned—helped prop the tree upright. Then I found a beach towel and wrapped it around the base for a skirt. When Chauncey approached in sniffing mode, I said, "Don't even think about tinkling in the house."

My search for ornaments didn't go as planned. Maybe I'd left the box behind in Wisconsin. Determined to make Christmas work, I dug through my sock drawer until I found some red tights decorated with snowflakes. My mother is under the impression that a girl should have stockings for every season. I pulled out the Easter and Halloween pairs as well and snipped off the feet. At least they were festive. A few binder clips to hold them in place and my tree had decorations.

Next, I emptied my grocery purchases on the countertop and set the stage for some Christmas fun, determined not to dwell on my faraway family and the lack of snowfall.

My Christmas CD was buried behind some Andrew Manze and a Steven Curtis Chapman greatest hits I'd forgotten I owned. As I listened to the crooning of Andy Williams, I peeled the wrapper from my roll of pre-made sugar cookie dough, complete with a colored Santa center.

I set the oven to preheat and sliced the world's least creative holiday cookies.

Once they were in the oven, I mixed powdered sugar and milk with a drop of vanilla and a dash of salt and stirred red food coloring into sugar to use for sprinkles.

Look at me. Making my own Christmas cheer.

While the cookies cooled on the rack, I poured out food for Chauncey and Emily. The sound of the kibble hitting their bowls brought them running.

Chauncey entered the room wearing a hat of sorts. Kitty had fallen asleep between his ears, her legs hanging down on either side of his massive head. As the dog leaned into his bowl, she started to slide. I grabbed her just in time. This woke her up, which meant more heated milk and another fight with the dropper. It was time to find Kitty's home.

Perhaps the recent fright in the theater's tunnel had dampened my mood but I decided that Kitty's owner was probably dead. The moans and cries and shattering glass had to mean something, so I booted up my computer to pour over the most recent news offered by The Wolf Creek Gazette.

There was a fender bender on Beeline Highway, and some woman had fallen off the curb in front of the ACE Hardware store and fractured her ankle and her pride. She'd had her face buried in her telephone screen at the time of the fall, probably texting her nearest and dearest with the fascinating information that she was...leaving the hardware store.

Maybe Kitty's owner died in more nefarious circumstances. Perhaps a slip off the ladder through the picture window had been facilitated with a light push. Nobody would suspect, and the poor person would be written off as a clumsy oaf instead of a victim.

The noise I'd heard from Kitty could have been an Ooooooh. Maybe it wasn't a groan. Maybe it was some-one's name, calling out for vengeance. Like...Ula? I didn't come up with Ula on my own. The obits listed Ula Kinder-gaard, age seventy-two. It didn't say how she died, but the point was that Ula had departed from this world and might have left a dear, sweet kitten behind.

A quick check of the phone book listed one Kinder-gaard. The woman who answered the phone seemed surprised that anyone would inquire about the deceased.

"Ula was my mother," she confirmed. "Did you know her? I mean," she paused as if searching for the right phrase. "She didn't have many friends show up for her funeral."

"I have a question that might seem a bit odd."

Her friendly tone went gently into the night. "Please tell me you're not selling headstones."

"Do they make telemarketing calls?" I asked, surprised.

"I've had three. Now, please tell me what you want."

I cleared my throat, hesitant to jump to the point because it seemed heartless to move from dead mother to kittens but finding Kitty's owner was the purpose of the call. "Did your mother have a kitten?"

There was a pause. "You are kidding, right? Is this some kind of joke? Because it's not funny."

"It's no joke."

The woman's temperature had risen from ice cool to raging flame. "Which one of her lousy neighbors put you up to this—this call? Just because my mother put down red pepper to keep that stupid cat from pooping in her yard—I mean, it's not as if she tortured it. She didn't throw it in a toilet and close the lid or tie its feet together. Why should she have to put up with someone else's cat pooping in her yard?"

"She shouldn't."

"And it's not as if she could catch the thing. She was ninety-years-old for cripe's sake!"

"The paper said seventy-two."

"She didn't feel it necessary to tell anyone her real age, and I honored her decision."

"But seventy-two? Wasn't that pushing your luck? That's almost a twenty-year difference!"

She hung up.

Leaning back on the couch, the phone in my lap, I considered my next move. There was the clue on the box —UMES. I wondered what kind of delivery system chemical suppliers used. I could contact Excel Exterminations and ask. The owner, Carlos Rodriguez, wasn't a friend, but he was a nice guy. He'd even forgiven me for thinking he had been the murderer in my recent foray into crime. His wife, Martha, wasn't as forgiving, as her tone indicated once she found out who was calling.

"What do you want with Carlos?"

"It's just a quick question about his business."

"You're not going to accuse him of anything, are you?"

I heard the struggle as Carlos took control of the phone. He answered with his usual cheerfulness.

"Frankie. It's good to hear from you." I guess Carlos remembered how I had cleared his name. After I'd suspected him, of course.

"When chemicals are delivered to your business, do they come in a regular cardboard box?"

"Chemicals?" His voice shot up two octaves. "I don't use chemicals. Who's been saying I use chemicals?"

"What's she saying now?" That was Martha in the background.

"I phrased it badly," I soothed. "I have a box with, possibly, fumes in the name of the return address, and I'm trying to figure out where it came from. Do you know any suppliers—not that you would ever use them—who use fumes in the name?

"Fumes? Heck no. First, that would be a turn off. Second and most important, I only use natural techniques that aren't harmful to the environment or family pets."

"So, no companies you can think of?" I pressed, as if he might suddenly remember.

"Nada. I'm sorry I can't help you."

And I think he was. Like I said, Carlos is a nice guy.

———

Penny said rehearsals were at eight a.m., so the next morning, I gathered up some Christmas cookies to bring with me so the cast wouldn't think I was a mooch.

There was a light indentation in one cookie. Then another. And another. I held one up and recognized the pattern of a kitten footsie. Kitty must have liked the feel of frosting as it squished between her toes. It took a minute to pick through and find some without the extra decoration, but I still managed to arrive early.

Next to my anemic plate of cookies, I placed a stack of flyers advertising for Kitty's owner. It pleased me to be doing something proactive this early in the morning, but when my best friend shuffled up, all my happy thoughts disappeared, sucked into the thundercloud that hovered over her head.

Penny had dark circles under her cornflower-blue eyes, and her hair was thrown into a half-hearted braid. She grunted a greeting at me and stuffed a Christmas cookie in her mouth.

"What on earth?" I cried. "Penny. You need to get a grip. This is a play. It's supposed to be fun."

She brushed crumbs from her lips and wiped her hand on her jeans. "The evil one is still trying to force us to do the modern production."

I took her by the shoulders and gave her a shake. "Remember Christmas? Candy canes and kittens and all the other favorite things Julie Andrews sang about? And speaking of kittens..."

Penny didn't look like she cared, but I chattered on in a false-cheery voice hoping to snap her out of her dark mood.

"You wouldn't believe what the little bugger has been up to." I pointed at the cookies. "These are the only survivors. She walked on the rest. And I've been investigating like mad. Yesterday, I even called Carlos at Excel Exterminators."

A spark of interest lit in her eyes. "He took your call? I'm surprised his wife let him."

"She gave it the old college try. Remember the box outside my door? It had UMES on the return label, and I thought it might be FUMES, as in exterminator fumes."

"Don't waste money on those toxins." The creaky voice belonged to an old man in jeans and a blue shirt with Ted Proctor embroidered above the pocket. He must have been the janitor, or is the correct term maintenance man?

"Bert takes care of us real good around here," he continued.

"Is that your exterminator?"

He cackled. "You could say that."

Hoping to do a good deed, I mentioned Carlos's company, should Ted ever find himself dissatisfied with Bert's services.

He scratched the bristle on his cheek. "She has been slacking off lately. I'll keep your feller in mind."

An infusion of sugar had perked Penny up. "Did you

bring your flyers? We could post one up over the coffee. That way everyone would be sure to see it."

"They're right here." Or they were. "Where——?" I rummaged through the abandoned plates and Styrofoam cups and even peeked under the table. "They're gone!"

"Christmas Past! You're up!"

Penny winced at the gravelly voice of Mrs. Glen

"I had Geoffrey mop up your spot, so the floor is nice and clean," Mrs. Glen added.

"Just bring more flyers tomorrow when you come...if I'm still part of this fiasco." And then Penny, lower lip trembling, returned to the center stage floor.

———

It took me ten minutes to find Kitty that night. Maybe it was my own fault. If I'd bought lights for the Christmas tree, they might have reflected off her furry face, the only part of her that was sticking out of the snowflake stocking on the tree.

It might have been cute. Really, it was cute in hindsight. I must have been distracted by the little present she left me under the tree. On closer inspection, the entire skirt was soggy.

I glared at Chauncey. He'd responded to Kitty's challenge and marked his territory. I gathered up the beach towel, deposited it in the trash, and kneeled with a soapy rag to scrub the rug.

When the phone rang, I wasn't at my best, but the despondent voice that greeted me made me forget all about my troubles. Unfortunately, I tend to react to pathetic situations with calls to action instead of sympathy.

"Penny, are you still bummed about delivering your

lines in a prone position? Why don't you just tell Mrs. Glen it's undignified and refuse to do it?"

"Oh, that. Mrs. Glen decided Wolf Creek audiences weren't ready for modern theater."

"That's good, right?" Penny should have been ecstatic, but I wasn't detecting any ecstasy over the line.

"Frances! She's going to make me carry a sickle!"

"Don't they use sickles to chop through jungles? Or maybe they hoe fields with them. Isn't that farmer in American Gothic holding a sickle? Oh my gosh! She's going with Goth? She's not going to make you pierce your nose, is she?"

"It's not funny! Mrs. Glen decided that props really sell the story, so she wants me to carry a sickle."

"Why? You're not playing Death."

"It has something to do with the time period and symbolism. And why the hell do I care? It's just stupid."

Hell? Penny said hell? This was serious. "Honey, it might be awkward, but you'll think of something. Put flower decals on it to spruce it up."

"I was so looking forward to my costume. It's a beautiful dress, and I was going to look so pretty, floating around the stage in this wonderful, light fabric. Now I'm going to clump in with a sickle."

Something clicked. "Did you say your costume?"

"Of course we've got costumes. It's a play."

"Are they delivered in boxes?"

"I don't know, and why should I care?"

"Penny. Costumes ends with UMES."

"Oh." Penny got quiet, and I hoped I had taken her mind off her farm implement dilemma with my more important Kitty problem.

"So, Kitty might be from the Dynamite Theater? What would she be doing there?"

The idea was ridiculous. If one of the actors owned a mother cat, he or she would notice if they were missing a kitten. After another fifteen minutes spent consoling Penny, I made another sacrifice and offered to come to practice. Again.

"Frances, you are such a good friend," Penny said. "I'm supposed to be on at one-thirty tomorrow afternoon. They're doing a dress rehearsal." Then her voice dropped. "I'll be the one with a sickle."

―――

The lights were down when I arrived. Penny wasn't up yet, so I settled into a seat in the audience. Danvers cowered on his bed, while an actor I hadn't yet met loomed over him. It was the ghost of Marley, and he was in the middle of a tirade.

"It is doomed to wander through the world—oh, woe is me—and witness what it cannot share, but might have shared on earth, and turned to happiness! Oooooooh!"

Chains hung from each of the actor's arms, and when he threw back his head and howled out a long, drawn-out cry of anguish, shaking the chains with enthusiasm, I almost lost it.

I'd found my breaking glass. The chains, made of a lighter metal so as not to doom the actor to Marley's fate, tinkled rather than clanked—just like glass. And Marley's moans sounded just like the cries of agony I had heard in Kitty's head. That kitten had come from this theater.

Marley clanked off stage right, and lo-and-behold, Penny entered from...stage left. She floated in like a leaf caught up in a gentle breeze, her layered white gauze dress streaming behind her. The costumer had sewn crystals into the fabric, and she shimmered like an other-worldly specter...except for the giant sickle.

As soon as Penny was finished, Mrs. Glen called a timeout and scurried around adjusting the costumes, giving last minute pointers on the scenery, and conferring with the crew over changes.

I shot backstage, filled with excitement, and found Penny sucking down chocolate kisses like a Hoover, her sickle shoved up against the wall.

"Let me ask you something. Who's Bert? The janitor mentioned his exterminator was Bert."

"Bert? Do you mean Bertie? She's the theater's mouser."

"She's a cat." I wanted to clarify.

"Of course she's a cat. Duh."

Duh, indeed. Kitty came from the Dynamite Theater where even now a mouser named Bertie was probably prowling the halls, searching for her lost young. That didn't explain how Kitty wound up in a box outside my shop door, but at least I could return her to her real home.

"I'll be right back."

Kitty didn't want to leave my home. My own feline watched with enjoyment from atop the bookcase while I attempted to catch the kitten, first with simple bait, then with finesse.

I felt bad. She thought we were playing a game of catch the string. When she rounded the corner, I threw a bath towel over her, shoved her into a book bag and headed back to the theater.

By the time I got there, Kitty had fallen asleep, so I tiptoed backstage and searched for Ted Proctor, the janitor. Penny intercepted me with a huge hug, her sweet countenance restored.

"What happened to the farm implements?"

She sucked on her upper lip, holding back a giggle. "It was considered an insurance risk after I accidentally sliced through the scenery."

"Accidentally?"

"Honest."

I spied Mr. Proctor standing at the head of the tunnel stairs. "Then it looks like everyone's going to have a good day, including Kitty."

In response to my wave, Mr. Proctor sidled over. When I held up Kitty, he said, "Who have you got there?"

"I think she belongs to Bert."

He narrowed his eyes. "Kittens? That would explain why I haven't seen her around."

A small cry brought our attention to Heather. Her face was contorted in horror. "You were supposed to take care of her. Bert doesn't want her." And then the child began to sob.

Andrea put an arm around her daughter's shoulder and crouched down. "What do you mean?"

Heather pointed toward the stage. "All the noise scared Bert, and she moved the kittens. But she never came back for this one. She didn't want her." And then the sobbing started again.

"Maybe she got sidetracked," I said in my soothing voice. "Why don't we find out?"

"No!" Heather shrieked. "She'll kill her because all the humans have touched her."

"Um, I think that's only wild animals."

Andrea bowed her head. "I've got to stop letting her watch those nature shows."

"Heather," I asked. "Where is Bert?"

Though reluctant at first, Heather led us into the tunnel. It was lit now, as it served as a passage from the dressing rooms to the stage during performances. As we marched through, it didn't seem such a scary place, but I was still glad to emerge through the far staircase.

We entered a large room crammed with costumes on hangers. A short woman with a buzz cut mumbled over the pins pressed between her lips. "Need something?"

I spied the cardboard box before Heather pointed it out, the same size box as the one left outside my door, only this one was on its side. In the center of a pile of old rags lay the largest tabby I've ever seen. She let loose a threatening growl. As she had her yellow eyes focused on Kitty, I assume she thought I meant her baby harm.

"See?" Heather cried. "She's going to kill her!"

"No, kiddo," I sighed. "All those bad vibes are meant for me."

With caution, I held up the kitten and approached the mother, transmitting the warm, tingly feeling I'd gotten from Kitty when I first tried to read her mind. Mom wasn't buying it.

She stood, hackles up, and she shot me an image of what she'd do to my face if I didn't drop the kitten. NOW.

I set Kitty on the floor, scooted her forward, and took two gigantic steps back. Bert sauntered over, paused to give me a final glare, and then picked Kitty up by the scruff and carried her back to the box. The ungrateful kitten immediately swatted her tawny brother—or sister—on the head, and the two of them rolled around in a playful fight.

"We should leave her be," Ted said, and he herded us back to the stage.

"Why did you think I would take care of Kitty?" I asked Heather. "How did you even know about me?"

"Mommy said you were the stray pet lady."

Andrea blushed a deep crimson. "I might have said strange pet lady."

The cast and crew of Scrooge thought it was a hoot.

———

I wasn't the only one who missed Kitty's face. Chauncey lay on the living room floor. Every few minutes he sighed. Emily took the opportunity to murder her new catnip mouse on the couch.

My Christmas tree stank. My Christmas "stockings" were a joke. My cookies were covered in footprints. My business wasn't going well. I had overdue bills. And I still had to come up with affordable gifts for the holidays. Ho-ho-ho.

The doorbell rang. Probably the electric company coming in person to tell me they were shutting off my power.

Hiding my surprise, I invited Detective Bowers inside. He was, after all, bearing gifts. Or at least a paper bag that smelled good.

"They gave me the wrong takeout order at Silver Moon. Do you like pork fried rice?"

"I like food," I answered.

Chauncey gave his pant leg a half-hearted sniff and walked away. Emily, however, jumped on the armchair and preened for Bowers while he scratched her belly. My animals have distinct preferences, and Chauncey prefers Seamus.

I grabbed two clean plates and silverware from the kitchen, and we settled onto the couch with our dinner. Chauncey suddenly got more interested in Bowers, especially when he gave him some beef lo mein.

Bowers pointed his chopsticks at my one homage to the holidays. "Nice socks, but that tree needs lights."

"My Christmas decorations are crammed in a box at my parent's house. In Wisconsin."

Bowers grunted. "My first Christmas alone stank. After

growing up with umpteen sisters, it seemed strange to have a place to myself." He considered what he'd just said. "You'd think I would have appreciated the silence."

He took another mouthful of noodles. "How's the Case of the Missing Kitty going? Find any bodies?"

I set my plate down. "Make fun of me, but I did find the mother. The joyful reunion took place this afternoon."

His brows shot up. "You managed to trace the parents? I'm impressed." His eyes narrowed, and he waved his chopsticks around his head. "You didn't do any of that voodoo stuff."

"No, Holmes," I lied. "It was pure deduction."

His cell phone rang. After taking the call, he stood. "Never a dull moment." Instead of heading for the door, he fawned over Emily with too much focus."You wouldn't want to come to the station's Christmas party, would you? I mean, I figure you already know most of them from the, uh, other business."

"A Christmas party?" I held my breath. "You mean with cheese sticks and grog that's strong enough to embalm the entire precinct?"

"There will be refreshments, yes. As for the lethal punch, well, it depends on whether the captain makes it this year."

I clutched his shirt. "And a tree? And a Santa who is too fat for the suit?"

"Dray is playing Santa this year. You'll definitely get your wish."

"You're on."

His phone rang again. This time he waved and took the call outside on his way to the car, while I stood on my front stoop and watched.

The cheese straws might not be Mom's, and Santa wouldn't be Uncle Tim, but a girl's gotta adjust if she's going to tackle a new life, right? Maybe it was time to start new traditions. Maybe I could stand a long-distance holiday. Although my family was back in Wisconsin, my best friend was here...and some new friends. Maybe I could jump into the Christmas spirit right now.

My chest swelled with optimistic joy. I smiled for the first time this week. It didn't matter that my gifts would most likely come from the dime store sale aisle. Christmas was about love, and joy, and the birth of our Savior. Christmas was an attitude, and I planned to be the poster girl of holiday spirit, starting this minute.

I felt something wet on my face. Could there be snow? Would Arizona have a magical white Christmas? Looking up, I caught the tail end of a cactus wren as it flew into the night. I wiped my cheek. Bird poop.

Okay. It might take time. But at least I would get my cheese sticks. Now what would the drug store carry that would make a nice present for a homicide detective?

Collared

"Should I wear my hair up, or down?"

I didn't receive an answer to my question, as the person I had asked wasn't a person at all but my mutt, Chauncey. The interest reflected in the golden-brown eyes of my eighty-pound ginger rescue was solely food-based. As in *when are you going to stop fooling around and feed me?* Since I'd fed him ten minutes ago, I ignored him. He squeaked out some gas and jerked his head around to see who'd made the noise.

"Up it is."

I secured my shoulder-length, auburn hair on top of my head and let the curls hang loose, hoping it looked stylish rather than messy. I had less fashion sense than my dog, but I *did* have a fabulous dress my best friend, Penny, had picked out for me. It was ankle length, sapphire-blue, and fitted my curves without giving onlookers a detailed map of my anatomy, though there was a slit up one side to provide a flirtatious peek of my calf.

Once I stepped into the dress, I wiggled and twisted to get the zipper all the way up, and I was halfway there when the doorbell rang. I hopped to the door, slipping on my black high heels as I crossed the room.

Detective Martin Bowers of the Wolf Creek Police Department stood on my stoop holding a dozen roses, and when he saw me, he put on that expressionless cop face that hides what he's thinking. After almost five months of dating, I'd learned he couldn't control the emotions reflected in his dark blue eyes. They held my gaze with an intensity that made me nervous.

"You look beautiful." He gave me a quick kiss and moved past me to take the flowers to the kitchen table. "I bought them in a vase, because I didn't think you'd have one handy."

"You got me there," I said as I followed. I'm not known for my household management skills. I'd be lucky to find matching coffee cups let alone something as exotic as a flower vase. Once in the kitchen, I ran my fingertips along the soft petals of the closest fat red beauty. I couldn't stop staring. Roses. For me. I had a flashback of senior prom because that was the last time anyone who wasn't related to me had given me roses.

Now that he had put the flowers down, he pulled me close and gave me a proper kiss. When his hands slipped up my back, he encountered the half-done zipper and made a noise against my lips.

I pulled back. "I need help."

I turned my back to him, and after he pulled the zipper up, he brushed his warm knuckles across my neck. I shivered, and he took my hand and led me toward my bedroom. I stopped walking. After foolishly living with my last boyfriend, I had decided total intimacy was something I'd only share with a man who respected me enough to make a permanent commitment. Marriage. Bowers, who actually lived his Catholic faith, agreed. At least I thought so.

"That's not part of your Valentine's Day present."

He gave me one of his sardonic smiles. "I'm not planning to molest you."

Curious, I gave in and allowed him to lead on, surprised when he took me into the bathroom and positioned me in front of the mirror.

"Close your eyes."

I did so, and I felt his warmth when he leaned over my shoulder to make sure I wasn't cheating. He placed something cool around my neck and clasped it.

"Open them."

I gaped into the mirror. "Oh, Bowers."

A string of irregular, cream-colored pearls hung around my neck. First roses. Now pearls. Both gifts extremely romantic and so—adult.

I had trouble thinking of myself as a deserving recipient of a grown man's attention. My last boyfriend had never made it past the toddler stage, and he had gathered up my self-confidence and flushed it down the toilet. It wasn't his fault. He was a toad and therefore limited by his inability to attain human standards. It was my fault for putting up with his treatment. I still cringed when I remembered what a sap I'd been, though it came to mind less often as I discovered life beyond the lily pad.

I turned and wrapped my arms around Bowers' neck. "Thank you."

He lowered his head and kissed me. I could feel the warmth of his hands on my back through my dress, and as the kiss went on, the rest of me started heating up, too. He broke away first.

"If we don't get going, we're not going to make it."

That was not an acceptable scenario. We were headed

to La Hacienda Chop House, home of my absolute favorite mushroom and blue-cheese smothered filet mignon. I was sure it was my favorite, even though the times I'd had the chance to try it, something always thwarted my attempt to eat one. I forced myself to move away from him, grabbed my black evening bag, and led the way out the door.

The first and only time I had been inside La Hacienda Chop House was on a blind date. Penny's husband Kemper, at the time her boyfriend, had received a call from a college friend who was in town, and Penny convinced me to make it a foursome. It was an awkward time in my life. I'd just begun to receive messages from animals, and the constant assault of images and words and emotions was driving me mad. Though Dr. Robert Hayward got points for helping me find a way to control the noise in my head, he wound up in the debit column when he took it upon himself to order for me. When the waiter brought out a nicely broiled salmon instead of a steak, I almost cried. Bowers would not make such a horrendous error.

The maître d' led us through a restaurant dimly lit by miniature lamps placed at the center of each table. When he got to a private corner in the back of the room, he pulled back a plush, red velvet chair for me, and I took my place without tripping over my hemline. He handed us each a menu, and a waiter wearing a short, mustard-yellow jacket, black pants, and a black bow tie rushed up to serve us.

Bowers leaned forward. "Shall we force the man to recite the specials, or just order?"

He knew me so well. I giggled, and that made me reflect on the change that had come over me these past months. Like giggling. I was not a big giggler, but I seemed to do so often in Bowers' presence. I also took more time with my toilette, and the first thing my hand reached for when I got dressed in the morning had stopped being matching sweats. At the drugstore, I found myself pausing in the makeup aisle, though I had not yet been tempted enough to spend money on blush or foundation. The only concession I'd made to my routine was the mauve lipstick I wore tonight, but it wouldn't see daylight again until the next special occasion.

The waiter leaned forward attentively as Bowers ordered my magnificent filet mignon, a porterhouse for himself, and a bottle of pinot noir. We didn't mess around with appetizers, and the dessert tray would come later.

Bowers rested his forearms on the table. "I'm sorry our first St. Valentine's together has to be an early night."

He had to relieve another detective on a stakeout at the crack of dawn tomorrow.

"No problem. It's what you do."

"I'm glad you understand. It means a lot to me."

A squeal pierced the air, and everyone turned their attention to a table in the center of the room where a young man and his date, both in their mid twenties, were seated. Well, the young woman was sitting. The man kneeled on one knee at her side and held up an open jewelry box. Since she had one hand over her mouth to stop from hyperventilating, he took her other hand in his and slipped a ring on her finger. We all clapped as a waiter helped him to his feet.

Turning my attention back to my date, I found Bowers watching me.

"What?"

He gave me a brief smile. "Nothing."

I followed his glance back to the happy couple. "They're cute."

"And extremely happy."

His tone of voice and the way he stared reminded me of a satisfied Rottweiler trying to decide which end of the bone to gnaw on first. My insides fluttered, and I blurted out the first thing that came to mind.

"St. Valentine. Didn't he get his head chopped off?"

"Um, yes. Your catechism teacher would be proud."

The waiter showed up with the wine, Bowers approved the selection, and soon we both had a glass. Bowers raised his and said, "To the most beautiful woman here."

My cheeks grew warm. "You're not so bad yourself."

His navy-blue suit matched his eyes, and in honor of the holiday, he had on a rose-colored shirt and burgundy tie that set off his dark hair. Of course, Bowers looked handsome no matter what he wore. Men are lucky that way. Sweatpants and a t-shirt don't automatically make them look like slobs.

He took a long sip of wine—a fortifying sip, I thought —with his gaze on me the whole time. Then he lowered the glass and said, "Frankie, about my sisters."

We were about to argue, or at least have a conversation that would take the glow off the night.

"I want them to meet you, and I don't understand why you won't set a date to go up to my sister June's. You've already spoken to her on the phone, so it's not as if she's a stranger."

"What about the other dozen?"

He wrinkled his brow. "There's only seven of them, and none of them bite."

After Bowers' mother died, his older sisters had raised him. He was the baby of the family, and they watched over him like a team of Dobermans. They were important to him, and their opinions mattered.

"Won't you tell me what's bothering you?"

I toyed with the stem of my wine glass. "Bowers, what if they don't like me?"

He blinked, startled. "Not like you?"

I could see the idea had not occurred to him. "*You* like me. That doesn't mean they will, and if they decide I'm not worthy of their baby brother, it's going to affect our relationship."

"No. It won't."

"You say that, but it will. You'll wonder why they don't like me. You'll wonder what's wrong with me." I held up a hand to stop him from interrupting. "What *they* think is wrong with me, and then you'll start looking for the reason, and I'll know you're looking for the reason. When holidays come, you'll feel torn between visiting them and staying with me. Eventually, you'll resent me."

"You've got it all worked out."

I twisted my napkin in my hands. "I've given it a lot of thought."

His eyes narrowed. "You won't even give them a chance? That's pretty closed-minded."

About to retort it was safer that way, I winced and gasped.

"What's wrong?"

Bowers' eyes were still narrowed, but with concern. I'd just been slapped, not by a hand, but by a focused jolt of energy. I jerked my head and scanned the room. The maître de was leading a tall, thin man to his table, and his Valentine's date was a German shepherd wearing the blue vest of a service dog. The man wasn't blind, and he was speaking with his back to the maître de, so he wasn't deaf. I guessed the dog was there to help with post-traumatic stress disorder.

I turned back to Bowers, but he had his eyes trained on the service dog, his expression wary. He didn't like animals being around me because he had witnessed the chaos that sometimes follows. It was a good thing that he was preoccupied, because I couldn't have given him my full attention, anyway. The dog's vibrations were tense, like a rubber band ready to snap. I could feel the hairs on his back stand up in excitement because the hairs on the back of my neck did likewise, though I wasn't feeling excited. I was feeling sick.

The waiter placed our entrees in front of us, and Bowers gave his Porterhouse a distracted glance. I couldn't savor the smell of my filet, because my nostrils were being assaulted by every smell in the room via the dog. Steak sauce consisting of black peppercorns, merlot, vinegar, garlic, mushrooms, and rosemary. A twice-baked potato with cream, sharp cheddar, bacon and...cream cheese? Eww. I hated cream cheese.

Every odor in the room came to me. The lavender-rose perfume worn by the elderly woman dining with what I assumed was her son. The gel used to slick back the hair of the man who wasn't fooling anyone. We all knew he was bald on top. Sea salt. Cough drops. Parsley. Asparagus. Thyme. Aftershave. Dill. Carrots. Butter. I couldn't stand it.

"You're not eating your steak."

My eyes were watering when I looked up, and he sighed.

"I'm sorry. I wouldn't have brought it up if I'd known it would spoil your appetite." He smiled. "I didn't know anything could come between you and food."

"It's not that. It's the dog."

He glared at the dog.

I closed my eyes and imagined an enormous doorway. One tactic I used to get rid of animal interference was to close that door and trap all communications behind it. The door creaked shut, and the odors assaulting my senses dissipated. I sighed with relief and picked up my fork, ready to dig in.

"It's okay. I just—"

I jerked back and dropped my fork. It clattered on my plate as something slammed into my mental door and burst through. I heard a word that sounded like zoo-keh and saw an image of a gun, followed by a strangely salty smell. Without turning my head, I moved my eyes toward Skinny Guy. The dog got up and lumbered purposefully to the closest table. One by one, he sniffed the guests, oblivious of the woman's giggles and the man's disgusted snort.

"Zoo-keh." I tried it out several times.

"You mean *suche*?" Bowers said, though I thought he pronounced it the same way I did. "Now what made you say that?"

"I don't even know what it means."

"It's German for search."

Skinny Guy had told the dog to search. Search for a gun? I had to be mistaken. I tuned in to the dog again, and I got a sense of focus and purpose. Every muscle was tensed with concentration. He wasn't fooling around. In fact, he was looking forward to finding a gun so he could carry his search to a conclusion. Incapacitating the armed person. I had a sudden, horrible thought.

"Bowers," I whispered. "Are you carrying?"

"Carrying?" His brow cleared. "Is this a test?" Something in my expression told him I wasn't asking for the fun of it. He lowered his voice.

"Shoulder holster."

"Get rid of it."

"What?"

Behind him was a hallway marked with a sign for the restrooms.

"Get up, go to the bathroom, and get rid of your gun. Now. Right now." My voice cracked. "Please!"

"Not until you explain—"

I reached across the table and pushed his water glass onto his lap. He swore and jumped out of his seat, dabbing at his trousers with his napkin. He glanced around the room, probably from embarrassment, and then he saw the dog headed our way.

"Go. Now!"

To my surprise, he turned and left without further questions. The shepherd reached our table a few seconds later. I reached out and scratched his ears as he sniffed me. In response, he gave me a mental snarl. Not an *I-want-to-rip-you-to-pieces* snarl, but the kind of quick snap a parent dog might give to a puppy who is misbehaving. The dog was operating on automatic, and I was distracting him from his mission.

The canine patrol unit remained at attention until Bowers returned. My date paused when he saw the dog, and then he slid back into his chair. The animal's hackles went up, and he moved in for a sniff.

Not having up to one-hundred-and-fifty square centimeters of olfactory material in my human nose, I had no idea if the smell of the gun remained after the gun was gone. I assumed it was the powder that smelled, since guns could be made from steel, wood, plastic, and goodness knows what else. My human nose couldn't smell whatever it was they put in bullets, so there was no way I could tell if the scent lingered after the weapon had left the room.

Even as Bowers pushed the dog's snout away, it

continued to snuffle through his jacket. I created a mental highway between me and the back of the dog's head and prepared to send a message. I didn't have much time, because the shepherd's hackles suddenly stood taller, and it snorted in a breath through its nose, preparing to bark.

I threw out a brief film of Bowers at a firing range. After emptying his bullets into a floating target, he walked to a counter and handed his weapon over to an attendant. As he walked away, I said, "All gone."

The dog cocked its head, considering, and then the hair on his back smoothed down again.

"Is he bothering you?"

Skinny Guy patted the dog on the head. I could have sworn he made a motion with his hand before he said, "Come on, boy," and pulled at the handle on the back of the dog's vest. The dog held fast, and the man allegedly lost his balance, fell forward and landed on Bowers. As he struggled to disentangle himself, his hands swept over Bowers' jacket in a quick and efficient search. Bowers finally shoved him to his feet, and the man grinned down at him.

"You're the last one."

"Excuse me?"

The man walked back to his table with his dog at his side. Instead of sitting down, he turned and addressed the room, pulling his own handgun out from the back of his pants where it had been hidden by his jacket.

"Ladies and gentlemen, this is a holdup."

—

Skinny Guy stood over the elderly woman and her son and demanded she hand over her necklace. She did so silently and with as much dignity as a woman being robbed by an armed man and his dog could muster. The canine waited patiently, holding a bag that was half-filled with the jewelry and cash of other customers.

I'd have to give the guy an A+ for organization. As soon as he announced his intent to rob us, he made everyone raise their hands. While he and his gun kept an eye on us, he sent his canine counterpart into the kitchen to round up the employees, which the shepherd herded into the dining area like a small flock of sheep. Under Skinny Guy's direction, the staff of La Hacienda Chop House had relieved all customers of cell phones and steak knives before lining up against the wall as instructed.

Bowers wasn't talking. The way his jaw clenched and unclenched, he was barely holding it together. This might have been the natural disposition of a cop feeling just as helpless as everyone else without his gun. Since he wasn't making eye contact with me, he might have been feeling additional irritation at the person who had convinced him to get rid of that gun. I felt sorry for him, because it was in his nature to want to rescue people in this exact situation, not sit there and watch it happen.

But I was too busy to worry about Bowers' feelings. I had locked onto the dog and was listening. German shepherds can be anxious dogs, and this pup wasn't an exception. He gave off a wave of uncertainty, which he fought off every time the bad guy issued an order. Animals rarely think in words, but this one had something on his mind. I couldn't tell what because he wasn't speaking my language.

Halten. Halten. Halten.

Halten? Was that Skinny Guy's name? Bowers had mentioned German. A sudden memory washed over me. Sitting in Penny's kitchen as a sturdy farm woman served us Haferflockenkekse cookies. I couldn't pronounce it then, and I'm still not sure I'm getting it right, but one thing I knew. Penny's German grand-mother used to slip into her native language now and then, and *Halten* was German for *hold.* Or wait. Or hold still and stop fidgeting. At least, that's how Penny's Oma used it.

In a whisper, I said, "He's giving the dog commands in German."

Bowers looked skeptical and whispered back. "How can you be sure?"

We agreed without discussing it that Skinny Guy wouldn't be pleased to hear the victims chatting, so we kept our voices low.

"I'm not *sure.* There is one way to find out."

We both looked at the dog as I made a connection. In my sternest voice, which is the only way to speak German, I hissed, "Sitzen."

The shepherd's butt hit the floor, and Skinny Guy jerked his head toward him. I held my breath. But apparently, as long as the dog continued to hold the bag, everything was good, and he returned to ransacking the old woman's purse.

"You know German? I thought Chandler was an English name."

"It is, and I don't know much German. I can tell you to clean your plate, be quiet, and then call you my little treasure. I don't remember much more than that."

"German," he muttered, thoughtful. "They teach K-9 dogs using German commands. We had a unit give a demonstration at the last training conference."

"You think the guy is a cop?"

"I don't recognize him, but police dogs usually live with their handler."

"Do you remember any of the commands?"

"I took notes. On my phone. Which I no longer have."

Bowers considered the dog. "Can you make him listen to you?"

"Only if I take a quick course in German."

I remembered another term that Penny's grandmother had applied to her, usually while pinching her cheeks. Using my most syrupy-sweet voice, I said, "Schnuckel."

The dog's tail wagged.

"What did you say?"

"I have no idea, but I said it in the same way Penny's grandmother used to say it to her. I think the dog might have been responding to my tone, rather than the word."

Skinny Guy glanced back at us, so Bowers rested his chin in his hand so that his fingers blocked his mouth. "The dogs are trained to respond to the voices of their handlers. It's odd that he would listen to you."

"I'm in his head. Maybe that's confusing him."

He fidgeted in his chair. I knew his fondest wish was to sprint across the room and tackle Skinny Guy, and that he was holding his place through massive amounts of self-control. "We have an advantage, in that you can—in that we have a connection—in that we have the dog's attention, but I'm damned if I can think how to leverage it. I don't suppose you can convince him to leave?"

"How would that help? Skinny Guy still has a gun." I gasped. "If the dog disobeyed, would Skinny Guy shoot him?"

You know how when you have a strong feeling about something, you play out the scenario in your head? It's pointless, because it hasn't happened yet, and you wind up getting worked up about nothing. Well, the thought came to me of Skinny Guy aiming his weapon at the helpless animal, and suddenly a low, throaty growl filled the room.

Skinny Guy didn't get it at first. He swiveled his head, looking over the customers to see where the threat came from. When all he saw were motionless, frightened people, he looked down at the dog, puzzled.

"*Ruhe!*" It sounded like *woo-eh*.

Still staring at him, the shepherd continued to growl quietly in the back of his throat.

"*What did you just do?*"

I gaped at Bowers. He had just yelled at me, albeit quietly. "It was an accident, I swear."

He took me by the wrist and pulled me toward him. "Don't play with the doggie, Frankie. His handler has a gun, and if the dog attacks him, there could be bullets flying around this restaurant and people could get hurt." He squeezed. "People could die."

I held up three fingers in the time-honored signal of a scout and said, "I swear. I had no idea I was still connected."

He let go. "You mean you can't control it?"

It wasn't very ladylike, but I snorted. "Dream on. If I could control it, it would *never* happen."

He rubbed his knuckles against his chin, which made him resemble a serious, young boy thinking furiously how to best sneak a turtle into the house without freaking out his mother. "Can you just listen? I mean, as a spectator. Without letting any of your thoughts slip through to the dog?"

"Hey! Stop talking."

I stared down at the table, too scared to look up, but Bowers said in a cool, controlled voice, "You have to make allowances. You're scaring the hell out of my girlfriend, and I'm trying to keep her calm."

"Well, hold her hand, without talking."

Instead of giving Bowers my hand, I inched my arm back toward my purse to dig through it for a pen and paper so we could write notes, forgetting that I had brought an evening bag. As soon as my fingertips touched the soft, crocheted cloth, I remembered I had only brought my wallet and house keys.

"How long do you think this is going to take?" Bowers called out, taking advantage of the fact that he and the crook were now on speaking terms. "Our food is getting cold. I don't know what kind of money you make, but my job doesn't pay well enough to waste an expensive dinner like this."

A few of the customers stared at Bowers with wide-open eyes. You could practically hear them thinking: "*Stop irritating the armed man!*"

Skinny Guy cracked a grin. "I didn't tell anyone not to eat."

"But you took our utensils," the elderly lady blurted out.

"Use your fingers."

A few people decided they might as well eat, maybe to take their minds off the robber and his gun. The balding guy picked up his salmon between his index finger and thumb and took a delicate bite. The elderly lady had gumption. She used her straw to round up some green beans and got them down with dignity. Other patrons followed suit, some opting for rolls, and some picking up baked potatoes as if they were finger food. The newly affianced guy reached for a bread stick. His wife-to-be held up the butter dish for him with a smile. He wiped one of the pats over the bread, broke the finished product in half, and shared it with her.

Din-din.

When I got the message, I tried to keep my thoughts from sending out a response, which is not as easy as it sounds. I forced my mind into a blank, but I couldn't resist sharing the news with Bowers.

"He's hungry."

"Join the club," Bowers muttered, refusing to use his hands to eat his steak.

I repeated it, slower, and with more emphasis. "The dog is hungry."

He met my gaze and considered what I'd said. "Look at your steak," he ordered.

"My appetite is gone."

"Look at your delicious steak and remember how much you wanted it."

I glanced down at my plate. The melted blue cheese had solidified, trapping browned, tasty mushrooms in gooey heaven. Since the steak had rested for longer than usual, the juices were now nestled safely inside the filet. My mouth watered.

"Look," he hissed.

As Skinny Guy and his sidekick in crime headed our way, long strings of drool oozed out of the shepherd's mouth and soaked the bag. I hope the guy didn't have a lot of cash in there. He'd have a job drying it out. Dog spit is thick and slimy. If you don't believe me, just try washing out the water dish. Enterprising environmentalists should coat the outside of oil tankers with dog drool.

It was our turn. Skinny Guy loomed over me. He seemed a lot bigger up close. "Hand over the necklace," he said in a rough tenor.

My hand moved to my throat and covered the pearls. I'd never been attached to jewelry. I only wore earrings under protest, but this was a present from Bowers.

"Come on. Hurry it up."

My eyes watered, and my lips began to tremble. I gasped in a deep breath to control the tears. I would not cry in front of this creep.

"Frankie, honey," Bowers said, gently. "Give it to him. I'll get you another one."

And how much would that cost him? On his policeman's salary, he'd have to stop eating to afford another. Okay. Slight exaggeration, but I wanted *this* necklace, the one he had so lovingly placed around my neck. Not some replacement he bought because he felt he should.

"Listen to your boyfriend, Frankie."

My breath came fast, and my cheeks felt warm. I no longer wanted to cry. I was too angry.

I glared up at him, and a tear escaped. "Only my friends call me Frankie, and you're not my friend, scumbag." Scumbag? It just came out.

As I said this, I inched my plate toward the edge of the table with my elbow.

"Frankie." Bowers voice held a warning note.

I gazed down at my delicious blue-cheese-and-mushroom smothered steak and said good-bye as I knocked the plate to the floor, and as it fell, I said in a loud, clear voice, "Din-din!"

The dog dropped the bag and grabbed the steak. I misjudged how much time I would have, because the dog swallowed the filet in two gulps, so I directed him to Bowers' porterhouse, and he jumped up, placing his front paws on the table. Bowers was so startled that he jerked back and stood, his chair falling to the floor behind him.

I was taking an awful chance. What if the dog wasn't a police dog? What if someone trained him to eat cops for breakfast? It was too late to turn back.

Recreating the fear and sorrow I'd felt watching the newly-engaged woman give up her ring, I painted a quick picture of the customers in need of a big, strong, smart German shepherd to protect them from the bad guy. I tied the source of their fear to Skinny Guy, and the dog stared up at him and whined, confused.

With the gun trained on me, the robber squatted down and picked up the bag. "Looks like you and your boyfriend need a lesson in manners."

He gave an order, and the dog reluctantly abandoned the steak and obeyed. He faced off with Bowers, barking at him in a sharp, deep voice.

"One word from me and he attacks."

I expected Bowers to tighten up and freeze like a normal human being faced by an impressive set of sharp teeth. Even the dog's bark was making my shoulders twitch. Instead, he relaxed his muscles and smiled, careful not to move his limbs. When he spoke, it was in a conversational tone, though he had to raise the volume to be heard over the barking.

"It's a shame this animal can't understand what you're really doing. I don't think he would cooperate."

The shepherd, holding his position, trembled with anticipation.

"It's pretty low that you would use a trained police dog to commit a crime."

"That's enough!" The crook's voice shook, and I sensed panic.

"What are you?" Bowers continued, running a quick gaze over him without hiding his distaste. "An animal trainer? I hate to believe that a man who served as a cop would fall to your level."

A slow, evil grin spread across Skinny Guy's face, and I shouted, "No!" At the same time, he uttered a word.

As my world fell apart in slow motion, I mentally covered Bowers with the uniform of a police officer and said my first prayer in a long time.

My heart dropped into my stomach. It didn't work.

The dog soared through the air like Rin Tin Tin's stunt double. Bowers threw up his arms to protect himself. The ninety-pound propellant hit his target straight on, his paws over his victim's shoulders. Bowers stumbled back from the force of the attack. My scream tapered off as the dog proceeded to...lick Bowers' face.

I'm sure it was a reflex, but Bowers wrapped his arms around the dog to hold it up while it rained kisses on him. A few customers tittered.

It took Skinny Guy a moment to react to the spectacular failure of his attempt to intimidate Bowers. Then his face scrunched up with fury, and he raised the gun.

I don't remember thinking, but I must have reasoned it out. The guy was left-handed, so he held his gun in the arm closest to me. Pushing the gun away might have him shooting into the restaurant and shoving his arm up might make him shoot Bowers or the dog who were both directly in front of him. I lunged forward, wrapped myself around his arm and fell back in a dead weight. The gun went off, and people screamed.

Suddenly, a frenzy of fur and drool descended, and Skinny Guy joined in the screaming. The dog, jaws clamped over the criminal's wrist, jerked his head from side to side until Skinny Guy dropped the gun. I shoved the weapon under the table and tried to back away from the melee, but my heels got caught up in my dress.

"Freeze!"

The voice belonged to a female, and when I looked up, Detective Gutierrez stood over Skinny Guy, covering him with her own gun. I'd never been so happy to see her. In fact, I'd never been happy to see her before now.

Several uniformed policemen and women moved about the restaurant, secured the location, and made sure the other customers were alright.

Bowers knelt at my side, his voice a mixture of panic and fury. "Are you hurt?"

I untangled my heels from my hem. "Only my pride."

"My God. You little idiot."

I followed his gaze to the shattered drywall behind me.

He gathered me to him and pulled me to my feet, and by that time, Skinny Guy was safely cuffed. His canine companion looked around, relaxed, and wagged his tail. He seemed to be grinning up at us, expecting praise, so I walked on shaky limbs, using the table for support, and took Bower's remaining steak from his plate.

"Good boy!"

The dog moved forward and sat, and when I held out the porterhouse, he gently took it from me, set it on the floor, and went to work on his reward.

As a uniformed officer led the criminal away, Gutierrez holstered her gun and smirked at us.

"Enjoying your dinner?"

"How did you know?" I demanded.

She jerked her chin at Bowers. "He called us."

I swiveled my head. "When?"

"When I got rid of my gun. Which reminds me."

He went to the bathroom to retrieve his weapon.

I rubbed my temples. "I don't get it. We didn't know we were going to get robbed at that point."

Gutierrez shrugged it off. "Cops have instincts. He said something was going down, but he wasn't sure what yet. It was smart of him to hide his weapon. A crowded restaurant is not a good place for a shootout."

She held up the robber's bag. "It's kind of nice having so many witnesses and so much evidence for a change."

I caught sight of the engaged couple, comforting each other. "Then one less piece of evidence wouldn't hurt your case?"

I wouldn't say that Gutierrez always thought the worst of me, but...Okay, she always assumed the worst of me. She tightened her grip on the bag and frowned at me with suspicion. "I'm sorry if you're inconvenienced, but you'll have to wait along with the rest of the victims to get back whatever he took from you."

"What's up?" Bowers said, giving his shoulder holder one last adjustment.

"I was just telling your girlfriend that the evidence would have to remain intact. She'll have to wait to get her baubles back."

He raised one brow at me, and I glanced at the table of the engaged couple. Bowers nodded and motioned with his hand to Gutierrez.

"Can I talk to you for a minute? Privately?"

Gutierrez followed him, happy to exclude me. As he spoke and gestured, she lost the happy smile. She shook her head no, but her gaze softened as she looked at the young man and woman, holding hands as they waited their turn to be interviewed. She shook her head again and left him there.

Bowers returned to me, the hands on his hips pushing his jacket open. He shrugged. "No dice. It was a nice thought."

I heard a cry, but this voice held joy, not fear. Gutierrez, standing by the engaged couple, stooped down and picked something off the floor, which she handed to the young woman. The newly engaged fiancée slipped the ring back on her finger and clutched her hands together, daring anyone—two-legged or four-legged—to take it from her again.

Gutierrez looked over her shoulder at us, shook her head as if disgusted, and left the restaurant.

Bowers and I were the last guests interviewed. By then my appetite had returned, and I had to hold my stomach in to keep it from growling.

The shepherd, gnawing on the porterhouse bone, hadn't moved from Bowers' side, and my date absently stroked its head while he answered questions. He finally told his colleague that he would come down to the station to fill in any gaps after he dropped me off at home.

Most of our fellow diners had bolted for the exit as soon as the cops were through with them, but a few, including the elderly woman and what I learned was her grandson, had opted to remain for the complimentary dessert offered by the La Hacienda management.

"Are you ready to go?" Bowers said, removing his jacket from the back of his chair as he stood.

"What about him?"

The dog, as if sensing he was the subject of conversation, looked up and licked his nose before returning to his bone.

The officer interviewing us grinned. "His handler is coming for him."

"Skinny Guy wasn't his handler?"

The cop looked at me funny, and Bowers interpreted. "The suspect."

"Gosh no. He's——"

A woman in street clothes pushed through the front doors and called out the name of her favorite pastry, I assumed.

"Muffin?!"

The dog dropped his bone, shot between the tables, and leaped into her arms, knocking her flat. She laughed and rolled around with him on the floor before getting to her feet. Any woman who will roll around on a strange floor to make her dog happy gets points in my book.

She brought the dog to heel and strode back to us. As she shook hands with Bowers, she introduced herself as Officer Stacey Howard from the Phoenix police department.

"And this is Muffin. I've been frantic. He was stolen from his kennel three days ago by a dropout from the Academy."

Off Bower's expression on the name Muffin, she laughed.

"I couldn't pronounce his original German name, so I picked a new name that sounded similar. I guess I got it close enough because he responds to it."

I had been holding myself together with effort, but now that I knew the dog would be alright, the energy drained out of me. It had been a long and disappointing night. Bowers put his arm around my shoulder and led me outside.

We ate burgers from a drive-through on the way back to my house, and once we arrived, Bowers turned off the ignition and came inside with me.

"Are you sure you're going to be okay? I could come back after I'm through at the station."

Memories of a night when Bowers spent the night on my couch in a t-shirt and sweatpants because he had concerns for my safety came to mind, but our relationship had progressed to a point where a repeat performance might be too great a strain on my self-control.

"I'm fine. Just a little disappointed. It took all my willpower to let the dog eat my steak."

He clasped my shoulders and nodded, solemn. "That was very brave of you. I'll recommend you for the Citizen's Act of Bravery award." His grip tightened. "Though grabbing the guy's gun arm was not very bright. You could have been killed."

"I thought he was going to shoot you. Or the dog. Either would have been terrible."

He pulled his head back. "I don't rate any higher than the dog?"

"That's not what I meant."

He touched noses with me. "I was teasing you." Then he adjusted his head and kissed me. He lowered his hands to my waist, and when he lifted his head, he squeezed.

"I better get going. I've got to hit the station and then be back to work at five a.m."

"Bowers? I've been thinking."

He let me go. "Uh-oh."

"Maybe you should call June and schedule a date for us to visit. Not maybe. You should."

Instead of jumping up and down and applauding, he said, "You've had a shock tonight. Give it some thought."

"No. Really. When I thought that guy was going to hurt you, the idea of not having you in my life, well, it made me crazy. Crazy enough to make a grab at the gun. So, if it's important to you that I meet your sisters, then it's important to me."

His response was another kiss, this one gentle and lingering. Then he gave me a peck on the forehead and walked out my front door.

I watched him drive away until the car's tail lights were no longer visible. After closing the front door, I leaned back on it, dazed.

It occurred to me, with a bit of excitement and a lot of fear, that I loved Detective Martin Bowers.

The Harlow Brothers

Edward Harlow ghost writes the Aunt Civility etiquette series. His brother, Nicholas, is his secretary, assistant, and general dogsbody.

The combination of Edward's logic and romantic nature and Nicholas' common sense and need for action makes them a formidable duo when it comes to solving crimes.

Death of a Christmas Tradition

"I don't think I can stay in a home that's anti-Rudolph."

I was standing in the middle of my brother's living room, which was not a surprise since I lived with him. It was an agreeable room, with maple floors, matching leather recliners, walnut furniture, and a white couch so large and deep that anyone under my six-feet who sat on it would be left with feet dangling above the floor. The only blot in sight was Edward—the source of my anger—who was on his hands and knees in front of the fireplace. I had a perfect view of his rump and was itching to deliver a swift kick.

Edward stopped arranging a vase of white poinsettias in the hearth long enough to glare at me over his shoulder.

"I have nothing against Rudolph except he'll clash with my color scheme."

I flung my arms out to my sides. "Who in their right mind has a color scheme for Christmas? I can understand if you want to try a few new decorations, but why take it out on the tree? You're supposed to buy an evergreen, drop it in a bucket, and decorate it with whatever you have on hand. And another thing. You're supposed to cut down your own tree, or, if it's a fake, put it together yourself. Ordering a tree that's already decorated is un-American."

He ignored me.

"And how are we supposed to light the yule log with that vase of flowers in the way?"

"We live in San Diego. It's not as if we depend on the fireplace to keep us warm."

"But I *like* the crackle of a fire on Christmas Eve."

"So do I, but this year I'm trying something different. It's not good to get into a rut."

I folded my arms across my chest and said a dirty word. "Claudia."

His shoulders stiffened. "I don't want to talk about it."

"You're going to kick aside all our traditions because of one snotty remark by a woman. Traditions we've had since we were kids."

Edward shook his big head. "Nicholas, Nicholas, Nicholas. Forever a ten-year-old. And I suppose you expect Santa to drop down my chimney on Christmas Eve?"

When he said my name like that, it made me want to show him little brother was all grown up, but I had to resist the urge to grab him in a headlock because the doorbell rang. Since my job as his secretary—on call 24/7—included answering the door, I answered it.

A stocky man in his forties with a jagged scar above his eye stood on the front stoop next to a ten-foot-tall Douglas fir decked out in blue-and-green tartan bows, gold tinsel, and a string of rope lights. I couldn't tell what color the lights were because they weren't plugged in, but I suspected they might be *something different*—like fuchsia.

His blue work jacket was covered with splotches of dirt

and sap from a day of delivering balsams and firs to other people too arrogant and pig-headed to decorate their own trees.

"Sign here," he said, and he held out a clipboard. I did so, and he returned to his rusty, tan pickup truck without offering to help me get it inside.

I sized up the tree, which was on the thin side. Edward had given a lecture at a women's guild this afternoon, and I still had on my dress shirt, slacks and tie. After flipping the tie over my shoulder, I wrapped my arms around the middle of the fir and dragged it into the house, not caring if it scuffed the floors. When I got to the living room, I stood the tree straight and said, "Haggis."

"What's that?" He didn't turn around.

"It's a wee bonnie tree you have here. We can put candles in whisky bottles to keep up the theme. I know I could use a drink. And another thing. Rudolph's red nose will match the green plaid just fine. It's known as a comple-mentary color."

To show how little attention Edward paid me, he didn't jerk his head around until I said *plaid*. He shot to his feet. "That's not my tree." He grabbed hold of the giant Christmas decoration and said, "Catch the delivery man. Hurry!"

The guy was long gone. When I returned to the living room, I left Edward holding the tree upright and sat down on the couch. "It's your tree now. I signed for it, and the guy left."

Edward ran his gaze over the decorations and sneered. "Nonsense. I'm not keeping this abomination. My tree is coral and seafoam green."

I gaped. "For Pete's sake. Consider yourself lucky and keep that one."

"Get Kaiser's on the phone right now. And where's the stand? They were supposed to deliver a stand."

Since Kaiser Tree Farm was a family-operated business, Mrs. Kaiser answered the phone. After I explained the situation, she looked up Edward's sales record.

"It says right here that Mr. Harlow ordered the Misty Memories theme. I remember my surprise. He seemed like the Old Fashion type. I'm usually spot-on at matching customers to themes." She tittered. "Maybe I'm losing my touch. His was the only Misty Memories this year. You say that isn't what James delivered to you?"

"This tree is Scottish, and it's wearing a blue-and-green kilt."

She made a noise that was a cross between a shriek and a yell. "Oh, good heavens. That's Mr. MacNeil's tree. He'll be livid. I better get James over there right away to switch it out."

I told Edward the good news. He was still holding the tree, since he didn't want to leave sap marks or needle scratches on the wall. When he tried to hand it over, I ignored him and went to my bedroom to sulk. Christmas was one of my favorite holidays. My brother was going to ruin it.

When I was ten years old, we moved to San Diego from Illinois after my parents' separation, since Mom had family here. I was devastated. The ocean was okay, but you couldn't fish from a canoe on the ocean. You couldn't dip a tin cup in the ocean and enjoy an icy cold drink of fresh water. There were other oddities like palm trees, mountains that got in the way of your view, and women who didn't wear nylons. When our first Christmas rolled by without one stinking snowflake, I didn't come out of my room for a week.

Over the years, I'd grown to appreciate the relatively

mild San Diego weather, and as a driver, I had to admit I wouldn't want to risk spinning out on black ice just to enjoy building a snowman, but there was still a part of me that missed Christmas in the Midwest. I compensated with traditional holiday decorations and rituals, which included a stuffed Rudolph I'd had since I was seven. He was a little on the scruffy side and missing one eye, but every year, he took his rightful place next to the Christmas tree. I'd be damned if I'd shove him in a drawer just to keep Edward happy.

Our holiday traditions were one of the few things my brother and I agreed on until this year. His change of attitude came after his long-distance love referred to him as a stick-in-the-mud when he refused to fly to Illinois to attend a pumpkin painting festival. He said, quite correctly, that jack-o'-lanterns should be carved, not painted. How else would the candle shine through at night? Technically, I think the term she used was *inflexible* stick-in-the-mud.

Now he was performing penance and killing my Christmas spirit. He planned to send her pictures of his non-traditional tree and decorations to get back into her good graces. What a sap. Women don't have good graces. Before she was through with him, my brother would be hanging heart-shaped garland and baking lemon bars instead of iced sugar cookies. It had to stop.

To calm myself down, I turned on a CD that included Perry Como and Andy Williams crooning out carols, so by the time the doorbell rang again, I worked up a grin as I passed Edward, still holding the tree, on my way to answer the door. It was the same guy with the scar. His hands were stuffed into the pockets of his jacket and he wore a scowl that was missing the right note of apology.

"Where's the tree?"

His attitude irritated me. We weren't the ones who

screwed up. When he moved to enter the house, I blocked his path.

"Aren't you missing something?" I asked, keeping my tone polite. "This is supposed to be an exchange."

"Uh, yeah. I'll take your tree and return with the right one."

I shook my head. "I signed for that tree. It's not leaving until I have one to replace it. Not that I don't trust you, but my generous holiday spirit only extends to people I like."

"I need that tree," he said. He tried to shove his way in, which was silly. I was at least seven years younger and stood four inches taller than he did. My arm shot out and I gripped the door frame before he made it past.

Edward appeared behind me. "What's the problem?"

The guy took a step back. At six-feet-two, Edward has the muscled bulk of a lineman that not even a red sweater vest, plaid shirt and red knit tie can disguise. And there were two of us.

"James here—You are the James referred to by Mrs. Kaiser?" When he said yes, I continued. "James wants to take your tree without replacing it. I declined his offer."

"Naturally." He glared at James. "Where is *my* tree? I can't imagine Mr. MacNeil accepted it, since his own is obviously a tribute to his family lineage."

"It's probably back at the farm," James said.

Edward made a scooting motion with his hands. "Run along and get my tree and then I will be happy to surrender Mr. MacNeil's. And don't forget the stand this time."

James didn't like that option, but he had to accept it.

I suddenly realized that my brother's hands were empty. "What did you do with the tree?"

In the middle of the living room, Edward had plunked the evergreen into an ice bucket and shored it up with a couple of boxes of his latest release, written under the pseudonym of Aunt Civility. He put his hands on his hips and frowned at the Scottish nightmare.

"Tube lights. It's the latest thing, you know. I can't help thinking it will look like a giant slinky once they're lit."

He took the plug for the lights and attached it to our extension cord. Nothing. He fiddled with the connection and tried again. When they still didn't work, he unwrapped the string from around the tree. I disapproved.

"That's not your toy, you know."

"Mr. MacNeil will be disappointed when the lights don't work. He may be an old man, and the problem might present difficulties for him as well as an inconvenience."

"Maybe he wants to save on electricity. He's Scottish."

"A stereotype."

He finished unwrapping the lights, wound them up and tucked them away on the bookshelf. "Don't forget to give those to James when he comes back. And make sure he knows they don't work."

By ten o'clock that night, James still hadn't returned. Edward, with a huff of indignation, said people couldn't expect him to stay up all night for their convenience. He was having a fit. He rarely went to bed before eleven.

After locking up, I went to my own room to think about gifts. I got out paper and pen because I like things neat, and I wrote a column of the people I had to buy gifts for. Once I got past the tip for the paper boy and my barber, my list only had three names left.

Our mother was headed on a cruise to Hawaii the day after Christmas with her girlfriends, so I opted to stuff an envelope full of spending cash for her. Next came Dad. It was hard to come up with a gift for a man who wasn't interested in anything but old books. He collected first editions and sold the ones he could part with in a dusty, one-room store outside of Naperville, Illinois. I couldn't afford a first edition, and anyway, he probably wouldn't like anything I would choose. I'd wind up sending him a gift card just like I did every other year.

Edward was going to be a pain. He could afford anything he wanted. Ever since he retired his dreams of reporting on athletic games from the press box in favor of the lucrative job writing the Aunt Civility books for Classical Reads, he had stopped doting on sports. He didn't like electronics, and they didn't like him. Maybe I'd buy him his own stuffed Rudolph so he could remember back to when he was a man instead of a dog being led around on a leash by his lady love.

I looked up when a noise like splintering wood came from the living room. Edward probably hadn't put water in the ice bucket, and who knew how dried-out Kaiser's stock was? I tossed my pen on the desk, stood up and stretched. The Scotsman probably wouldn't want his Christmas tree delivered in pieces, so I went to see if I could minimize the damage.

The lights weren't on in the house, so when I opened my bedroom door, it must have given the intruder a heads up. I was about to the middle of the living room when he rushed me.

Taken by surprise, I went down on my back, but I swung a fist as I fell, and it connected. We both struggled to our feet, but when I heard a metallic click, I froze.

With help from the outdoor security lights that bled through the windows, my eyes adjusted to the dark. I could make out a shadow standing a few feet away in front of the door between the kitchen and living room that led to the backyard. The light also reflected off something shiny in the figure's hand.

I made regular trips to the firing range and knew the lethal power behind even the smallest gun, so when a man's voice told me to take a step back, nice and slow, I complied. Then he flashed a light in my face, and I squinted and held up a hand.

"We have ourselves a problem," he said. My spine stiffened at the way he said it—in a calm whisper that seemed to look forward to the solution.

"If you scoot back out the front door, I promise to count to ten before I come after you."

He chuckled, a sound that didn't make me want to laugh along. "I don't think that will work."

It's amazing how your senses tune in when there's danger. There wasn't a creak or a click, but I'm sure I heard a movement as the back door opened. Edward must have heard the commotion, gone out the sliding glass door in his bedroom, and come around from the outside.

Before I could warn him about the gun, there was a commotion. Someone swore, and the light swung away from my face.

I felt the burning pain in my side at the same time I heard the retort and saw the muzzle flash. Doubling over, I cried out and dropped to my knees.

"Nicholas!"

The struggle stopped. The raspy voice said, "Get over there by the other guy and sit still."

My brother was at my side in an instant. He knelt beside me and whispered, "Are you hurt?"

"My side is on fire," I said, panting a little from the pain.

A low growl started at the back of his throat. He would have gone after the guy if I hadn't grabbed his arm and held on. If he got shot, who would call the ambulance?

"You," the voice said. "The one I didn't shoot. Pick up

the tree and walk slowly to the front door. And stay in front of me or I'll plug you."

Edward complied.

I struggled to get to my feet to follow, because I couldn't imagine a scenario where the thief would let my brother go. Rolling to my left side and pushing off the floor with that arm got me to my hands and knees, but the room wasn't cooperating. It kept spinning. So, I crawled to the coffee table, got my left forearm onto it, and pushed myself to my feet.

Edward walked into the room just then, and when I spun my head at the sound, I wound up back on my rump, leaning against the couch. He took one look at me, and the skin on his face not covered by his Van Dyke beard turned an off shade of white. I worked up the courage to look down and fought back a wave of nausea when I saw the blood on my hands and shirt, though I'm sure it looked worse than it was because the shirt was white.

He hooked his arms under my armpits, hoisted me off the floor, and half-dragged me to the couch, with me protesting that I couldn't afford to have the white fabric replaced.

"Stop fussing," he snapped. Then, conceding I had a point, he spread the Christmas tree skirt over the cushion before he sat me down.

He peeled my shirt up and took a long look.

"How bad is it?" My voice was shaking, and I think I was, too.

"You're fine."

He once said the same thing to me in the same firm, reassuring voice back when I was ten and wiped out on my bike. Turned out I had broken my arm in two places. However, the blood had returned to his face, so I risked a peek. The bullet had only grazed the skin under my ribcage, leaving a burnt, bloody furrow. He went to the bathroom and came back with antiseptic and bandages.

"I don't think you'll need stitches. However, if you like, I can take you to the hospital."

"Forget it," I said, more confident now that I knew the injury wasn't life-threatening. "What did the truck look like?"

He raised his brows. "Who said it was a truck?"

"I did, because nobody comes after a ten-foot Christmas tree with a hatchback."

"It was parked down the street by the empty lot. There aren't any street lights there, so I couldn't tell."

"But it was a truck? Not a van?"

"A truck."

"James drove a tan truck."

He answered with a nod. "Not very subtle of him."

While he wiped up the blood with a face towel, Edward talked about his plans for Christmas dinner, his voice a soothing drone. My breathing slowed down, and my shoulders relaxed. He was being surprisingly gentle with me, which I appreciated until he poured on the antiseptic.

"Dammit!"

"Don't whine. You've been more seriously injured playing flag football."

Only when I played with him.

After he bandaged me up, he helped me to my bedroom despite my protests. He covered his big-brother concern by saying, "I don't want you fainting on my newly polished floors. You might drool."

After he helped me out of my bloody clothes and into pajamas, I lay back on the bed. He paused in the doorway.

"I'm sorry, Nicholas. If I had known the man had a gun, I wouldn't have jumped him."

"Forget it. I think he was planning to shoot me, anyway."

He immediately brightened. "Then I might have jostled his arm and saved your life."

"You hang onto that thought, Edward. But I still got shot."

"But it's not as bad as it might have been."

"Maybe."

He turned off the light. "Tomorrow morning, if you're up for it, I suggest we pay Kaiser Tree Farm a visit."

"Sounds like a plan," I mumbled, and then I was asleep.

———

I woke early the next morning because my side throbbed as if Edward had finally stabbed me with his fountain pen. Then I remembered last night's adventure and grabbed two aspirin from my medicine cabinet before heading to the kitchen for something to eat.

Edward stood over his recliner and folded a blanket into a neat square. When I asked what for, he pointed to the back door. The crack I heard last night was the sound of the wood splintering around the lock. Edward had slept in his recliner to guard his castle.

"Call someone to repair that, Nicholas. As soon as you're dressed, we can go." He gave me a quick glance. "If you're up to it."

I said I was, but first I had to answer the door. It was a delivery, and the driver kept grinning at me as I signed for the package. I assumed it was because I was still in my pajamas.

"Late night at the office party."

"Takes all kinds," he said before he left.

"Ah!" Edward took the box from me. "My Christmas cards."

While I got dressed, he took his prize to his office. He was still in there when I came out of my room, so I joined him. He sat at his desk and stared down at something with an expression just short of horror.

"What's wrong?"

The item on his desk was a greeting card. I reached for it, but he slapped his open palms down to cover the image.

I made a gimme motion. "If you don't show me now, I'll just sneak in here later."

Reluctantly, he handed over the card. The front image had a few things wrong with it. First, Santa was a woman, though a very sexy, well-rounded woman in a tiny, fur-lined, red outfit. She held a whip that I admit might have been for the reindeer. The fundamental problem was the elf, and I guessed he was an elf because he wore a pointed green cap that matched his thong, and he had pointy ears. He was a handsome guy who was squatting down with his sculpted rump sticking out as if, having been a bad boy, he eagerly awaited his punishment. They both wore bright smiles. The verse inside read: *Hope your holidays make you tingle with joy.*

I flipped the card over. "Alternative Greetings?"

"I thought it meant an alternative to traditional Christmas cards."

"It is that. You can't send these. Did you even look at them before you placed the order?"

"I ordered over the phone and asked them to send me their best-seller." He slapped the desk. "Good gad! That means they have my name on file."

I sat on the edge of his desk and looked down at my pathetic sibling. "Have you considered you might be taking things too far? I've called you lots of names before, and

143

you haven't tried to change yourself to make me feel better."

"Claudia deserves someone who will meet her halfway. She doesn't like traditional celebrations? Then I must come up with new ones."

"Did she actually say that? Women are impulsive. She called you a stick-in-the-mud—"

"*Inflexible* stick-in-the-mud."

I based my lack of friendly feelings for Claudia on the way she led my brother around by the nose. While it was his life, I hated to stand by and watch him get hurt by a conceited, self-centered woman.

"She called you a name. Big deal. It's over and done."

"I assumed so, but she was cold the next few times we talked, and when I phoned her on Thanksgiving, five minutes into the conversation, she had to go. I haven't been able to reach her since."

This was serious. Thanksgiving was ten days ago. The formerly happy couple had been in the habit of talking every night. Their relationship might truly be over. Being a good brother, I wasn't about to let Edward see my relief.

"Maybe she really is busy. This is probably a hectic time at Inglenook Resort." Claudia and her brother Robert owned Inglenook.

He looked up at me with the sad but hopeful expression you usually find on puppies. "You think so?"

I stood. "Sure. Holiday travelers. Family visiting family. The place is probably booked solid. And for all you know, some of her staff are sick, and she's working double-time."

"It could be." He didn't sound as if he bought my explanation.

"You should take advantage of the break to finish your book."

Edward was working on a spring release that covered

everything from the proper way to hold an Easter egg hunt to how to conduct a co-ed Maypole dance without descending into debauchery.

"I've hit a wall."

"You've had writer's block before. Don't you have a ritual or something to get you moving again?"

"I usually discuss it with Claudia. She's been very helpful in the past."

I tossed the card on the desk in disgust. "But you must have done something before you met Claudia."

"Maybe I've run out of ideas."

Since those ideas were how Edward made money, and his money is how he paid me, a wave of panic shot through me. I pushed it aside because one of us needed a clear head.

"Look, Edward. You're stressed. You just need to get rid of some tension. For starters, why don't we go yell at the Kaisers? That will make you feel better."

Before we left, I arranged for temporary security by wedging a walking stick under the handle of the back door.

Kaiser Tree Farm didn't open until ten a.m., but we got there at nine-thirty. Farm was misleading. Things grow on farms. I don't know where they got their trees, but none of them sprang forth from the ground. A chain-link fence surrounded dirt lots on either side of a small, permanent structure painted red and decorated with ornaments and lights.

Edward knocked on the door. When nobody answered, he went in search of a back door.

I peered through one window and called him over.

"Give me your cell phone."

"Why?"

"So I can report the dead body on the floor to the police."

He shoved his face against the window. When he stopped gaping, he rubbed his trim Van Dyke with his fingertips and glanced up and down the street.

"No one knows we're here. We should let the Kaisers discover their own body."

"You would let Mrs. Kaiser walk in on that? For shame."

"Maybe the man isn't dead."

"He just got sleepy and decided to nap on the floor?"

Edward jiggled the window until it slid open. "One of us should check before we alarm everyone unnecessarily."

One of us meant me. In consideration of my injury, Edward had allowed me to wear sweatpants and a loose flannel shirt with tennis shoes today instead of the usual dress clothes he required me to don as his employee. He, however, had worn a navy-blue sports jacket, pale-blue dress shirt, tan slacks, and Oxfords.

Resigned, I said, "Give me a leg up."

There wasn't anything under the window on the inside, so I dropped to the floor head-first, caught myself with my hands, and let the rest of my body slide through. The contortions weren't helping my injury any.

I stood, dusted myself off, and looked around for the light switch. It was next to the door. Inside, there were a few chairs in front of a sales counter. Behind it were a desk with a computer and a file cabinet. Mrs. Kaiser kept things neat and clean, except for the mess on the floor.

Someone had buried a small hatchet in the man's back, and he had leaked blood all over his blue work jacket and the surrounding floor. I leaned over to get a better view of his face and confirmed my suspicions when I saw the scar above the man's eye. Jimmy hadn't returned with our tree because he was busy getting himself killed. With all the blood and the wide-open, staring eyes, I didn't bother to check for a pulse.

There was a phone on the desk, but I thought the police might not appreciate me adding my fingerprints to the instrument, so I leaned my head out the window and told Edward to make the call.

Twenty minutes later, Detective Jonah Sykes arrived on the scene with his crew. He was Edward's twin—standing six-feet-two with a trim goatee and a critical attitude, only Detective Sykes had skin the color of nutmeg and topaz eyes, which he aimed at us in an unfriendly glare.

He led us to a bench outside so the deputies could do their job inside.

"Kaiser's wasn't open, but you wanted a tree so badly you broke into the place."

"We had good cause," Edward said.

He nodded. "You saw a body on the floor while peering in their windows."

The way he said it made us sound like the neighborhood snoops, which was understandable. He didn't work for Edward, so he had no way of knowing what a pill my brother could be when he was obsessing over something— like a Misty Memories tree.

"I explained about the mix-up," Edward said. "When no one showed up last night, I wanted to get the error straightened out as soon as possible this morning. I'm a busy man."

Before the police arrived, we had agreed not to mention the attack at our house because Edward didn't want it to sound as if we came here courting trouble. More important, he didn't want his name in the paper. As Aunt Civility's official representative, he tried to keep a low profile when it came to things like guns and hatchets. He had a vested interest in the series, mainly because he *was* Aunt Civility, a fact known only to his publisher and me.

But then Sykes noticed the blood on my red plaid shirt.

He motioned to my middle. "Did you cut yourself coming through the window?"

I looked down. Blood had soaked through the right side of my shirt in the area under my ribs.

"I must have."

"You should get that looked at." He waived over the coroner, an older woman with gray hair who was exiting the building. She strolled over.

"What have we here?"

"I just need a Band-Aid."

She motioned with her hand, so I lifted my shirt to show her. When she whistled, Sykes raised a brow in my direction. There wasn't a good explanation for how I had bandaged a cut I had just discovered, so I kept my mouth shut.

The doctor peeled back Edward's handiwork and studied the wound. "This needs a couple of stitches. If you don't want anesthetic, I could just take care of it here."

Edward clapped a hand on my shoulder. "Nicholas can handle it, if you wouldn't mind."

Once the doc finished stitching me up, she retrieved a prescription book from her car and wrote me out one for painkillers.

"You were lucky, young man. A little to the left and the bullet would have pierced your lung."

We thanked her and rose to leave, but Sykes blocked our way.

"Sit back down." He stood over us, hands on his hips, and smiled. Really, it looked more as if he were in pain. "Bullet? I think you better start at the beginning, and this time, don't skip the good parts."

So we spilled. At least Edward spilled. With my head pounding and my stomach doing flips from the experience of getting stitches without a painkiller, I mostly grunted to acknowledge my brother's points. He glossed over the shooting, making it sound as if I had broken a fingernail, but by the time he finished, Sykes was breathing fire.

"And it didn't occur to you to report this to the police?"

"The man was gone, So was the tree. I don't imagine you have the resources to send a patrol unit in search of a Christmas tree."

Sykes stared.

I leaned my head close to my brother's ear. "You're missing the point, Edward. The police don't like people using guns on human targets. It makes them nervous."

The detective spread his hands. "Thank you! That's exactly the point." He narrowed his eyes. "Another minor point. Did you come here to get revenge on James Worthington?"

Edward didn't fake his surprise. "Why would we do that? While I want that tree, I wouldn't take a life over it."

Sykes' voice rose an octave above his usual baritone. "Because he *shot your brother*?"

"Which is secondary to the tree," I mumbled.

Edward glanced over his shoulder through the front window toward Mr. and Mrs. Kaiser, huddled in the corner with a female officer. Mrs. Kaiser sobbed into a handkerchief.

"I don't suppose this is a good time to ask them—"

"Don't even think about it," I said.

Sykes blew out a long sigh. "There wasn't anything unusual about the tree?"

He wisely addressed the question to me.

"Other than its general hideousness, no. It was about

ten feet tall, a little on the skinny side. It was a tree. We didn't frisk it."

There wasn't anything left to say, so Sykes let us go. He wouldn't have had he known Edward had peeked at the sales book while we were waiting for the police to arrive. We were headed for the home of Dougal MacNeil.

———

The house was a disappointment. It didn't look Scottish. Because of the bows on MacNeil's tree, I expected blue-and-white decorations to honor the Scottish flag and a Santa wearing a kilt. And regardless of what Edward said about stereotypes, I still expected a Scotsman to be stingy. Not Dougal MacNeil. He'd wrapped every tree, shrub, and bush in Christmas lights. A life-size crèche sat in the center of the lawn, complete with wise men, shepherds, livestock, and angels, while a blow-up Santa and his reindeer pranced through fake snow on the roof.

Edward rang the bell. The man who answered didn't live up to his name. Dougal means "dark man." I know that because I looked it up when I got home.

Mr. MacNeil, all five-feet-five of him, was a study in white. He had hair on the back of his hands, a thick, white mane on his head, and when he turned sideways, I could see tufts of white scruff pushing up under the collar of his green sweater. His cheeks were rosy red, and his blue eyes, set under a single scraggly eyebrow, sparkled.

"Merry Christmas!" he boomed in a voice too big for his size that still carried the remains of a brogue.

"Merry Christmas to you, Mr. MacNeil," Edward said. "I've come about your tree."

MacNeil frowned. "Did you now. Do I know you?"

"You ordered your tree from Kaiser Tree Farm. Is that correct?"

He smiled fondly and chuckled. "Every year. Mrs. Kaiser is a dear, sweet woman. I knew her back when she was Fiona Duncan." Then he seemed to consider the oddity of a strange man knocking on his door to ask about his Christmas tree. He took a long look at both Edward and me. "Why do you want to know?"

Edward hesitated. He expected the man to clutch his jacket by the lapels and shake him, crying, "*My tree? You know what's become of my tree? Tell me, man, before the sugar cookies grow stale!*"

But he didn't.

"I received your tree by mistake."

MacNeil's eyebrow shot up. "Impossible."

"I'm sure it wasn't Mrs. Kaiser's fault," Edward demurred. "Who knows how these things happen?"

"I mean it's impossible, because my tree is standing in the den right this moment." He opened the door wide. "See for yourself."

He led us through a house properly decorated for the holiday: snowmen grinning down from shelves, silver bells hanging from the mantle, and a ceramic Santa sliding across a decorative table, his team led by Rudolph.

We came to the den, and there it was. A tree identical to the one James had delivered yesterday, except this one stood proudly in the room's corner surrounded by piles of presents.

"I don't understand," Edward muttered.

The Scotsman narrowed his eyes. "Neither do I. Is this a scam?" Then he caught sight of the blood on my shirt and said, "Who are you? What's going on? Ethel! Call the police!"

Mrs. Santa's clone peered into the room. She even had

little round spectacles perched on her nose over twinkling gray eyes. "Donny? What's the problem?"

Edward made a slight bow in her direction. "I assure you, Madam, that I don't mean to cause you or your husband distress." He motioned to the MacNeil's tree. "I have an identical specimen in my living room. My own Misty Memories is missing."

"Impossible!" MacNeil sputtered. "They make my order to my specifications. That's my family's tartan on that tree."

She moved into the room and stood next to her husband.

"Misty Memories," she repeated, thoughtful. "Isn't that seascape colors? Coral and seafoam green? It reminded me of where we grew up, by the North Sea."

Her husband shuddered. "The shoreline off Aberdeen has great, hulking rocks and gloomy, dark water like any respectable coast." To move the conversation away from the dangers of a Misty Memories Christmas next year, MacNeil escorted us to the door. Then, regretting his lack of hospitality, he offered an encouraging word.

"It'll turn up. Don't you worry. Trees don't just walk away, except maybe the fairy trees. Possibly."

———

Edward suggested we return to Kaiser Tree Farm, but I objected.

"The woman has had a shock," I said with a strong snort of disgust.

"If we find my tree, we may find her employee's killer. That might give her some comfort."

"We don't even know if she liked James," I grumbled, though I knew he had a point.

By the time we arrived at Kaiser's, the police and other emergency personnel had gone and taken the body with them. With a little rearranging, they had allowed the Kaisers to continue to operate, since most of their business took place outdoors. When we walked into the shack, I noted the police tape blocking off the half of the room where James had spent his last moments.

Mrs. Kaiser, a white-haired grandmother type, and a gray, grizzled man who I had assumed was Mr. Kaiser sat in chairs behind the counter. She rose when we entered, and then her welcoming smile froze in place.

"Mr. Harlow."

"Madam." He nodded, first at her and then at the man. Mrs. Kaiser introduced him as her eldest brother, Tom Duncan, and said he was helping her through the tragedy. He must have been there solely for moral support because he had one leg stretched out in front of him and his arms crossed over the top of a cane.

"I hate to bother you at a time like this, but my tree is still missing."

"Misty Memories, right?"

Tom Duncan snorted.

"With James not around to ask, I don't know where to look for your tree." Her eyes watered at the mention of her late employee, but she looked like she would hold it together, so I asked a question.

"Was James with you long?"

"This was his first season."

"So, he was a stranger?"

"Hardly that. His mother is my sister. She asked us to find him a job." She shook her head. "My poor sister. I don't know how I'm going to tell her. She's on a plane to Scotland to visit family, so I haven't been able to get hold of her yet."

"She'll probably celebrate," Tom said. "That boy's been nothing but trouble from day one."

"Shush. He's still flesh and blood. Or was."

"You say he was troublesome?" Edward said. "Because I've had nothing but trouble since I ordered my tree."

He explained about the attack and theft. She made an appreciative audience, gasping and shrieking where appropriate. Her brother sat still and listened. When it got to the part where I got shot, he gave me a skeptical look. It seemed to say that if I'd been properly shot, I wouldn't be here wasting my breath over a lost tree.

"Sounds like something James might do," he admitted when Edward had finished. "Still, the lad wasn't bright enough to come up with these ideas on his own. He hung out with a foolish crowd and went along with whatever nonsense they planned. I blame them."

"Do you know who those people are?" Edward asked. "Because I would like to speak with them."

"Me too," I added.

Mrs. Kaiser leaned across the counter and took my hand in hers. "I'm sorry James shot you, but I'm sure it was an accident."

Tom rubbed at a spot on the floor with his cane. "The boy's aim was lousy. Probably meant to shoot the tree."

I was about to protest, but Edward cut me off and assured them on my behalf and without my say-so that the injury was a trifle. Nothing for them to worry about.

"Then you no longer have the tree in your possession?" She put her hand on her cheek. "Oh, dear. I can't offer you a refund without the tree. Do you still have any part of the tree? Some token piece you can return?"

"I don't want a refund. I want my tree."

"Well, the police are working on that. They're very good. I'm sure you'll get your tree back."

"I'd like it up before New Year's Eve," Edward growled, losing some of his manners. "I'll pay for another."

She looked over her shoulder at her brother. "Do we still have any of the Misty Memories materials?"

He reached out with his cane, dragged over a large box and peered inside. "Looks like we do. Not a popular choice this year."

She turned back to Edward, wearing a professional smile, and asked, "Cash or credit?"

My brother wanted to wait until his purchase was ready, but I needed to pick up my pain prescription if I was going to keep up this pace. Mrs. Kaiser assured him that Tom would personally deliver the tree.

———

The first thing I did when we got home was pop two pain killers and change out of my shirt, which I put in the laundry room sink to soak in cold water. The second thing I did was talk Edward out of calling Claudia. I found him in his office, reaching for the phone.

"What are you doing?"

"Without Mrs. Abernathy around to take messages, I don't know if Claudia phoned while we were out," he said.

Mrs. Abernathy was our housekeeper and cook. She was off for a holiday to enjoy her grandkids.

"Claudia can try back later." I glanced at the clock. "It's the middle of the day. She'll be dealing with late arrivals, people checking out, and she may have to grab a cart and do housekeeping duties."

He dialed anyway. "It wouldn't hurt to check in."

I made a noise of disgust and snatched the phone from

him. "For Pete's sake, don't be so needy. Give it some time."

Then I went to my room to take a nap, which is something I never do. Edward only woke me up three times. The first was to ask where I had put the printer toner. The second was to ask if I wanted some lunch. I didn't. If he was hinting that I should make his, he was out of luck.

The third time he woke me up was to ask if I wanted to meet with Detective Sykes in my bedroom or in the living room. I opted for the living room.

By the time I joined them on the couch, Edward had brewed coffee and set out a plate of butter scones, the last of the baked goods left behind by Mrs. Abernathy before she took off on her vacation. Sykes stuck to coffee, so I loaded two scones on my plate and gave them the attention they deserved.

"Detective Sykes wanted to view the scene of the crime. I've already described what happened, though there's not much to see."

Edward had scrubbed away the blood from the floor before it set. I'm sure if Sykes had brought a forensics team with him, he could have found some in the cracks between the floorboards, but he wasn't that interested.

"Did you see the gun?"

"No, but I heard it when he cocked the hammer. And it was shiny."

Sykes passed a hand over his mouth. "Cocked the hammer? Shiny? That would be an older revolver. Do you still have the bullet?"

Edward went to his bedroom and returned with a small box, which he handed over. Sykes opened it, took out a flattened piece of metal and held it between his pointer finger and thumb.

"A twenty-two short would be my guess."

I leaned forward for a closer look and then glared at Edward. "Were you keeping it as a souvenir?"

"I thought it might be wise to hold on to it."

"It was." Sykes closed the box and stuffed it into his pocket. "I'm keeping it as evidence."

While he was there, Sykes thought he'd ask us about our relationship with the Kaiser's and James Worthington.

"Have you ordered a tree from Kaiser's before?"

"This is my first experience with them. We won't be doing business again."

"You'd never seen James Worthington before you argued about the tree?"

Edward gets flustered when he faces unpleasantness. He spouts the truth and incriminates himself. There didn't seem to be any danger with this situation, but I got my answer on record first.

"Correction. We didn't argue. We expressed customer dissatisfaction. And I had already met him when he delivered the tree an hour earlier."

"What exactly did he say when he came the second time?"

I closed my eyes and replayed the scene. My memory is excellent, and I can repeat conversations verbatim, if they aren't too long. This time, it didn't seem necessary to put out the effort.

"He said he came for the tree. I told him it was an exchange, and he was empty-handed. He tried to push his way in, unsuccessfully. We sent him on his way."

"Didn't you find his persistence excessive?"

I considered the question. "Not then. I understood from Mrs. Kaiser that Mr. MacNeil, the owner of the tree that got delivered here by mistake, was prone to fits." I gave my brother a steady look to let him know what I thought of men who throw fits.

"What were his exact words?"

I raised one brow. Sykes was taking this tree theft seriously. "He said *I need that tree.*"

"Need. An odd word choice."

I shrugged. "Maybe he meant he needed to fix his mistake or else he would lose his job."

"That's possible. Can you think of another reason?" He looked from Edward to me as if he seriously expected an answer.

"Why else would he break into our home but to retrieve it? Although, bringing a gun along was pretty excessive, now that you mention it."

"Are you certain the man who shot you was James Worthington?"

Edward roused himself. "No. We're not. The lights were off. Obviously, we didn't get a good look at the man's face."

"But you saw the truck," I argued. "James' truck."

"It could have been anybody's truck."

"You seemed pretty certain last night."

Sykes held up a hand to stop our bickering. "James has an alibi. He was with friends."

I raised my brows. "Friends can lie."

Edward barked out an unfriendly laugh. "So, he never planned to bring me my tree. Instead, he was drinking at some bar. Probably with ex-convicts who were teaching him the ropes."

"He was babysitting."

I didn't like that alibi. "That's no good. The attack occurred within a half hour after I locked the place up at ten o'clock. Depending on their age, the kids were probably in bed. How would they know if he left them alone for half an hour?"

"That's true, but the parents were home by ten. Then

they discussed the movie they had seen with James for at least twenty minutes before he went home."

I waved my hand. "Forget it. Put it on your list of unsolved crimes."

Sykes gave me his full attention. He wasn't just being polite. "Explain what you mean by that."

I shifted my position on the couch, uncomfortable with his intense gaze and unfriendly tone. "It's all too stupid. What was the gig, anyway? Steal trees and resell them to make some Christmas spending cash? Doesn't sound very lucrative. And did they only target Kaiser's pre-decorated beauties? Or were undecorated trees in danger, too?"

Edward was quicker than Sykes to recognize my sarcasm, probably because he's used to it.

"My tree wasn't cheap. Five hundred dollars."

I gaped. "You spent five hundred dollars to save yourself the effort of putting up a few ornaments? You could have bought five or six naked trees *and* their decorations for that much money. And all because you're too lazy to get on a ladder. Hell, you wouldn't need a ladder unless you got a twelve-footer."

Edward's jaw muscles flexed. "The point is, those trees are worth money. Someone would be glad to pay half Kaiser's asking price, and the thief would be two-hundred-and-fifty-dollars richer." He leaned toward the detective. "Have there been other tree thefts?"

Sykes stood and gave us a hard stare, one I couldn't interpret. All he would say before he left was, "We're looking into it."

—

We found Mrs. Daniel Stafford by phoning Mrs. Kaiser

and asking about James' friends. Three of them were married, but only one had kids.

Edward drove, so I looked out the window and appreciated the decorations on Tamarack Avenue as we approached the house. Four yards had blow-up Santas, three had blow-up snowmen, one house displayed a menorah in the front window, and one humbug didn't have any holiday decorations at all.

The Staffords had sided with the majority, though they lacked creativity. Their Santa was made from painted pressed plywood on a stand. When Edward rang the doorbell, a stampede of feet approached the door from the other side.

Mrs. Stafford was slim with long brown hair. She wore a white sweatshirt with Christmas trees embroidered on the front, and as she stood in the open doorway, she used her limbs to block the escape of three children under ten.

"May I help you?"

Edward cleared his throat. "Mrs. Stafford, there isn't a delicate way to put this, so I will just ask. Have you heard about James Worthington yet?"

When her face crumpled and tears escaped, the five-year-old boy charged out from under his mother's arm and kicked Edward's shin. With small fists jammed into his hips, he said, "You made my mom cry. Pologize."

Since his encounter with Claudia's young nephew and niece at Inglewood Resort last winter, my brother has developed a tolerance for children. He leaned down to eye level. I admired the kid for holding his ground.

"I'm sorry I made your mother cry."

The kid sneered and pointed to his mom. "Not me. To her."

"Oh." Edward stood up. "I—"

She waved him off. "Don't worry about it. It's just that it's still a shock."

As she reached for the first child, the two-year-old made his move and kicked Edward's other shin. I think he was just imitating his big brother because afterward he leaned his head back and gave my brother a snot-covered grin.

With the help of a tall girl around nine, Mrs. Stafford herded the boys back inside, but she remained in the doorway. "What about James?"

I knew Edward, with his honesty hang-up, was about to tell this woman we suspected her late friend of breaking into our home, shooting me, and robbing us of a Christmas tree, so I got in ahead of him.

"Someone has suggested James might have been somewhere he shouldn't have been last night, and we don't think they're right, so we wanted to check with you about times. We knew he was going to babysit here."

"Are you friends of his?"

"More like acquaintances, but we'd like to clear his name on principle."

She nodded. "We came back here after the movie, and we brought a pizza with us. The kids were already in bed, and the three of us ate and discussed the movie. You know how James was about movies."

Since I didn't know James, I just nodded. "Do you have any idea what time he left?"

It had taken us about seventeen minutes to make the drive from our house. The attack occurred around ten-thirty, give or take ten minutes.

"I can get it pretty close." She rubbed the head of the smallest child, smiled down at him, and said in a cooing tone meant for the child's ears, "Tom-tom let me know he had to tinkle like a good boy." She switched back to her adult voice. "I checked the time because I wanted to know how long he had made it. We're trying to break a certain habit."

"Tom-tom wets the bed," the older boy said, giggling.

"Do not!"

"Boys! Be quiet. Billy, go to your room."

"Aww, mom!"

The older child retreated up the stairs, but when Mrs. Stafford turned back to us, I could see him sitting on the fourth step from the top.

"When I went to check on Tom-tom, it was twenty-seven minutes after ten. James was just leaving when I got back downstairs. Does that help?" she asked.

"It does, indeed," Edward said. After giving her our sincerest thanks, we headed back home.

"It wasn't him," I said as Edward pulled away from the curb.

"Obviously."

"She had to get Tom-tom out of bed, take care of business, and tuck him back in. Say she finished in ten minutes. If he drove fast, he might have made it to our place in fifteen minutes."

"If he didn't hit any lights."

"James wouldn't have made it in time to take the tree." I rubbed my chin. "So, it was just a random tree-stealer who saw your unlit tree through the window and couldn't resist."

"Now you're being deliberately obtuse."

"Can you come up with a better explanation? And another thing. Tom Duncan said that James hung around with bums. I don't have a lot of experience hanging around with corrupt influences, but did Mrs. Stafford strike you as a criminal type?"

"Movies and pizza," Edward said to let me know he'd been thinking the same thing.

That was the end of the conversation until we were back in the house. I made ham sandwiches and brought them to the kitchen table. As I handed Edward his plate, he said, "But why? Why make a duplicate of Dougal MacNeil's tree?"

"Maybe there's a rash of Scottish patriotism in the neighborhood. Maybe there are other MacNeils floating around and they saw his tree last year at the Christmas party and thought it was a fine idea. Maybe someone on the assembly-line made a duplicate by mistake. Maybe there were leftover bows and the Kaisers, being thrifty, didn't want to waste them."

"You have an idea there."

I halted, mid-bite. "Seriously?"

"Perhaps the tree was a mistake. A simple error."

"Then why go through so much effort to steal it back?"

"That's the part I don't understand." He took a large bite of sandwich and masticated, although I think it's cows that masticate, and Edward's more of a bull. When he swallowed, he said, "I think we must assume that whatever was going on ended with the theft of our tree. We'll never know the why. We should just forget about it and move on."

But it would not be that easy.

———

Edward almost refused to let Tom Duncan in with the tree that night. He had a point. There *was* some coral and seafoam-green mixed in the decorations along with purple, red, blue, and about a dozen other colors. Polka-dot bows with contrasting backgrounds covered the boughs. It looked like someone had set a ten-year-old girl loose with a box of markers and sparkle.

My brother pointed the finger of shame at Tom. "That is *not* my Misty Memories."

Tom took Edward's reaction in stride. "Once you move away from the traditional colors, you take your chances. Does it really matter?"

"Edward." I snapped my fingers to get my brother's attention. "You've got a tree, and it's definitely not traditional. Claudia will be thrilled."

He relented and held open the door, directing Tom toward the living room. I offered to help, but the old guy had his pride. He limped his way through the foyer, and when he got to the living room, he took in the scenery. Based on Edward's choice of tree, it must have surprised him to find dark wood and leather instead of satin and teak.

While he held the fir upright in the base he'd brought along, Edward turned the screws to secure his prize in place.

"Nice place you've got here." Tom nodded approval.

Since Edward has an ego just like any other human being, only larger, he gave the man a brief tour of the house, pointing out the changes he had made since buying the place six years ago. I didn't go along because I received the tour when I moved in last year. When they got back to the living room, Tom ran his hand along the side of the walnut bookcase.

"Sturdy," he said with approval. That launched a discussion of well-made furniture, built to last. Finally, with one last look around, he said he had to get moving, and he probably would have if his gaze hadn't landed on the string of lights tucked into the shelf on the bookcase.

"Is that from the original tree?"

Surprised, Edward retrieved the lights. "They don't work. I'll save you the trouble and throw them away."

Tom held out a hand. "I'll take those. They are the property of Kaiser Tree Farms."

Edward stopped moving forward and narrowed his gray eyes. "That would be the same Kaiser Tree Farms that never delivered the correct tree to me. The one I ordered from you over a month ago."

Tom walked over to the tree and reached inside the branches. "Hand 'em over or I'll take back the tree."

To normal people, a tree mix-up wouldn't have been a big deal, but Edward was processing much more than that. It was his first Christmas dating Claudia Inglenook, and not only was he apart from her, they weren't even talking. The same lady love had called him a stick-in-the-mud, and he was acting against every instinct to have a traditional Christmas to please her. A Christmas tree thief had shot his brother—I'm assuming that would have caused him some stress. He had a looming deadline for his next book, a case of writer's block, and he still didn't have the right tree. Duncan's impolite attitude was the last straw.

Edward folded the lights up, a small smile on his lips, and when he looked at Tom Duncan, he had a dangerous gleam in his eyes. "I will keep these as a souvenir. Consider them payment for the inconvenience I've suffered."

Tom grinned. "I really don't want to take the tree back, but I *will* take those lights."

For the second time in two days, I heard a metallic click. Having already experienced what follows, my knees went weak.

Tom Duncan pulled a revolver out from the branches of the tree and pointed it at my chest. There wasn't a chance he would miss this time.

Attempting a show of bravery, I heard myself say.

"Nuh-uh. You already shot me once. It's his turn." I jerked a thumb at Edward.

"Now son, just tell your brother to give me the lights and I'll be on my way."

"I would, but he never listens to me."

On the appearance of the gun, Edward must have tightened his grip on the tube lights, because one bulb squeezed out of the end and clattered on the floor without breaking.

"What the devil is that?"

Duncan fired the gun. I flinched, but the only casualty was a vase to my left that shattered on the impact.

"Next time, I won't miss. Now hand them over."

My throat tightened up, and I choked out my words. "Edward, give him the damn lights."

"Of course." Edward took a step forward and tossed the string to Tom.

To understand what happened next, remember I'd already been shot, and I hadn't enjoyed it. Tom Duncan wanted those lights, but once he got them, what guarantee did we have that he wouldn't kill us both? So, when Tom reached out to catch the lights, I made my move.

I hit him around the middle, but I wasn't at full-strength. He was surprisingly solid for an old man. He didn't go down, and being the guy that shot me, he knew where to land his punch. I doubled over, still hanging on as he struggled to right his gun. Which went off.

I heard a grunt and feared the worst, but I wasn't letting go. We struggled over possession of the revolver for what seemed like an hour but was probably two minutes. With my side on fire again and my head spinning, my hold on him weakened. I had enough energy for one last move.

When I jerked him forward, he instinctively leaned back, so I shifted my weight and used his momentum to push him into the tree. We all three—Tom Duncan, me, and the tree—went down.

As I struggled to get out from under the fir, a hand reached out. I grabbed hold and someone hauled me to my feet. Once I got upright, I saw the hand belonged to a burly deputy. Two more gripped Tom Duncan's arms. All were under the supervision of Detective Sykes.

I went directly to Edward, who was leaning against the bookcase for support. One of the advantages of sturdy furniture.

"You're bleeding," I said, nodding at this thigh. A tear in the fabric of his tan slacks exposed an ugly gash.

"So are you." I looked down at my shirt and sighed. The past few days had been hard on my wardrobe.

He winced and shifted his weight, so I leaned into him and said, "Come on."

Edward threw one arm over my shoulders. Since I knew he would refuse to bleed on his good furniture, I helped him limp to the kitchen and deposited him on a chair.

Sykes squatted down and peered at his leg. "Looks painful, but it just grazed you. You boys are on a lucky streak." He stood. "The bullet is embedded in your recliner. Do you want it back when we're through with it? That way you can have matching souvenirs."

He called for an ambulance, and when the paramedics arrived, Sykes insisted I go along to have my stitches checked. After Edward made the detective promise to lock up, we climbed aboard and the EMT told the driver he could go. The driver muttered back.

"The holiday season always brings out the nuts."

The next day, we were back in the living room, each of us on a recliner. Sykes had the couch to himself.

"Tell me what the devil happened," Edward demanded.

"James was working for the Kaisers."

"I know that. He delivered their trees for them."

"He was also helping them with their sideline. Moving stolen diamonds."

Edward's brows went up. "The diamonds were in the lights?"

"And James delivered them right to our door." I snorted. "Tom Duncan mentioned his nephew wasn't very bright."

Sykes laughed and shook his head. "James came into the store when there were customers around and asked which tree belonged to their *special client*. We got that from one witness who was insulted that James wasn't referring to her. Since Tom couldn't spell it out, he told his nephew the correct tree was the one-of-a-kind. What he meant was a duplicate of MacNeil's made-to-order tree. Since Tom didn't handle the day-to-day operations at Kaiser's, he didn't know that there was another one-of-a-kind-tree, the only Misty Memories ordered this year."

I nodded. "Mrs. Kaiser said this was James' first year with them, so he wouldn't have known about the Scottish tradition."

"Instead, he delivered *your* tree to their partner."

"It was nice of you to return it," Edward said.

Sykes grinned. "The gentleman we arrested wasn't interested in keeping it."

A quick glance at the coral and seafoam-green balsam that occupied the corner behind Edward's recliner made me lose the desire to be happy.

"How could you arrest someone for receiving stolen property when we still had the string of lights?"

"That's not what we charged him with. Let's just say the client took James' mistake personally."

"And you're not going to tell us who that client was?"

Sykes shook his head. "You'll find out with the rest of the public."

"I guess that makes me feel better, that the guy wasn't killed by his own uncle, though it doesn't help James."

When the detective smiled, it was almost friendly. His mother must be proud of his teeth. "You helped James Worthington, in a way. You helped clear his reputation. Mrs. Kaiser and her brother became spooked when James died. To deflect attention from what they were doing, they made out he was into some shady stuff with an imaginary gang. That he was to blame. I doubt he even knew what he was delivering."

"I told you his friends seemed nice," I said, but Edward had something else on his mind.

"I want to know how you got here so quickly last night." My brother made it sound as if the police had goofed up by arriving just in time.

"We already suspected Kaiser Tree Farm was involved in fencing diamonds. We had them under surveillance... and you."

"Me? Why?"

"Face it, Edward. You were having three kinds of fits. Sykes here couldn't believe it was over a tree. Lucky for us. I don't think I could have handled Tom Duncan much longer."

"I can't believe you thought I would buy stolen property," Edward mumbled.

Something was bothering me. Something that didn't add up. "How did your deputies know Edward and I weren't fighting with Tom Duncan over the diamonds? You already suspected us, but you only arrested Duncan."

Sykes suddenly had to leave, and I escorted him to the door. As I handed him his coat, I said, "Did you at least get a warrant?"

He looked back at me with innocence and feigned surprise. "For what?"

"For whatever device you used to eavesdrop on us."

He grinned. "Go ahead. Search the house. You won't find anything."

I nodded. "Thanks for locking up yesterday. That was very considerate." And it gave him and his men the time they needed to remove any spyware.

Out on the front stoop, he turned back and sent a nervous glance toward the living room. "I would keep your completely unfounded suspicions between us. I wouldn't want you to upset your brother."

"Trust me. It's not on the agenda."

As I locked the door behind Sykes, the phone rang, followed by a panicked bellow.

"Nicholas!"

I made it to the kitchen and grabbed the receiver on the third ring. A cool, husky female voice said, "I could call back later when you're not busy."

"Save that tone for Edward. And for your information, he couldn't get up to answer the phone because of the bullet wound in his leg."

"Bullet wound?" Claudia whispered. Then she roused herself and demanded to speak with him.

"He might be asleep. I'll see."

I walked to the living room where Edward was leaning forward, his hand reaching for the phone. I held it out of reach. "What's that? Claudia who? I'll tell her you're waiting for a call from Nancy."

I had pity on him because I thought he would pull a muscle flailing around like that. I handed him the phone.

"Claudia? Ignore what he said…Claudia?"

I grinned. "It's on mute. And before you unmute it, I suggest you pull yourself together."

Since this was a strictly private phone call, I went to my room and quietly lifted the extension.

"It's not bad. I'm sure Nicholas exaggerated."

"But someone shot you. How on earth did that happen?"

"It's a long, boring story." Edward cleared his throat. "More important, I've given what you said a lot of thought."

A pause. "What did I say?"

"Oh, I don't remember exactly, but it was something about me being an inflexible stick-in-the-mud."

"Did I say that? I must have been angry. I'm sorry."

I had to jerk my head away from the receiver to cover my laugh.

"—and you're right, so this year, I ordered a coral and seafoam-green tree. I'll send you photos. There was an unfortunate accident with the Christmas card order, but you'll find what I send will be completely untraditional."

Silence.

"Did you say a coral and seafoam-green tree?" She made a noise that sounded like *ack.* "You're having fun with me. A man of your excellent taste and sense would never get something so—so hideous."

"But I thought you wanted—"

"Edward, I love you just the way you are."

Silence. Then my brother, his voice strangled with emotion, said, "Did you just say that you love me?"

It was time to hang up. I'd figure out how to jump this latest hurdle after the holiday season. I puttered about my room until my brother called for me again. He was using his pleasant voice, which meant he wanted something. I returned to the living room and found a new Edward. He was practically glowing, but in a manly way.

"There's a pitcher of spiced cider in the refrigerator. And could you move that vase out of the fireplace and replace it with the yule log in the closet? I feel like a fire tonight. Oh. You will need to put a rush order on new Christmas cards. Something with a snow-covered scene, I think. And could you bring me my laptop? I have to get moving if I'm going to meet my deadline."

This was more like it. Before he let me get to it, he had one last instruction.

"And Nicholas?" He pointed at the tree and then jerked his thumb toward the backyard.

"With pleasure."

But first, I went to my bedroom. When I returned, I set my Rodolph on the coffee table and patted it on the head. Then I opened the back door, picked up the Kaiser pre-decorated coral and seafoam-green tree, and heaved it into the yard.

Once I completed the other tasks, I returned from the kitchen and handed him his glass of cider. He held up his mug and said, "To tradition."

I toasted him back and sat down. "Did you finally stand up to Claudia?"

"Well, a woman has to want a man for who he is." He said it as if any man with common sense would see this obvious truth, but his face flushed and he tugged at his collar. "It's warm in here. Must be the fire."

"I haven't lit the log yet. So, why the delay between phone calls?"

He smirked. "A pipe froze and burst on the second floor. They had to move the guests around, dry everything out, have a plumber in." He waved a hand. "Just as I suspected. She was busy. And you know how hectic the Christmas season is for tourist venues."

"Uh-huh."

He flushed again and stared down at his laptop screen. "That was an exciting few days, but it's time to get back to routine."

"Edward?"

"What?" he snapped.

"Balsam or fir? We're still missing a tree."

"Let's go with a spruce this year. It, er, wouldn't do to get into a rut."

"Edward?"

He sighed. "Yes, Nicholas."

"Merry Christmas."

The Wilder Women

Roxanne Wilder finds herself back in Illinois in the arms of her family—scatterbrained mother, Deana, and cranky sister, Vanessa.

Whenever her mother launches into crime solving mode, it's all Roxanne can do to keep up. Steering her mother away from dangerous and embarrassing situations is a lost cause. And if she ever needs cheering up…well…Vanessa is not the one to do it.

Rubies for Christmas

"I hate Midwestern winters," Roxanne Wilder said as she jammed her shoulder against the solid metal door and shoved.

Deanna Wilder, plump and festive in a forest-green velour sweat suit, the jacket smothered in a spray of rhinestones, struggled to unwrap a peppermint nougat.

"Just yesterday you were telling your father how you missed the seasons; how the Los Angeles weather blends into *one, long, boring* year. You even said you might return to Wilton for Easter."

"I lied." Roxanne rammed her shoulder into the door again. "You *could* stop eating the table decorations and give me a hand, Mother."

Successful at last in freeing her nougat, Deanna Wilder popped the candy into her mouth. "It would be a wasted effort. You will not get it open." In between chews, she cheerfully added, "There must be three feet of snow on the other side of that door."

The Wilton Elementary School Old Hall was an underground structure added on in the late thirties as a

gathering place for school assemblies, community func-
tions, and scout meetings. In the fifties, its underground
feature provided the illusion of shelter for those students
and staff who hoped to survive an atomic blast through the
handy practice of Duck and Cover. Its cavernous belly
could have held the entire school and half the neighborhood.

Today, people ignored the hall in favor of a modern
gym, but community organizations still made use of the
large space and conveniently attached kitchen. Last weekend, the Barmy Beaders and Crazy Crocheters held their
annual Holiday Craft Extravaganza, and tomorrow the
Wilton Women's Guild planned to host a Christmas party
for the retirees of Slumbering Hills.

The building's exit doors were located up a small set of
stairs at ground level and led out to the school parking lot.
Roxanne pressed her face against the windowpane hoping
to spy a school employee making a last-minute departure
for the weekend, but nothing outside moved except the
assault of snow illuminated by parking lot security lights. It
pained Roxanne that she could see her car parked a mere
twenty yards away, and it seemed cruel that her escape
route should be blocked by something as pretty as crystal-
lized raindrops. She blew a huff of warm air onto the icy
glass and traced out HELP in the resulting fog before
following her mother back downstairs.

The wooden steps creaked and popped under their
weight. Roxanne recalled the days when her own second
grade class had stampeded down these very steps for school
assemblies. So long ago. The expectant faces waiting for
her at the bottom of the stairs didn't share Roxanne's fond
memories. Most hadn't seen grade school in well over half
a century.

The Christmas Decorating Committee was made up of

a small group of women who had optimistically agreed to brave the weather to prepare the space for tomorrow's luncheon. They couldn't imagine disappointing seniors eager for an afternoon's respite from boiled chicken and tapioca.

Though twelve ladies had originally committed to help, only seven had shown up. The truants included a mother whose child had come down with a sudden and convenient illness the woman refused to name, a widow whose car wouldn't start but who promised to go at the engine like a pit stop mechanic and come as soon as she'd fixed the problem, and Wanda Lake, the current President of the Women's Guild. Wanda hadn't bothered to make an excuse other than to say she was dog-tired after picking up supplies from the grocery store. Roxanne suspected that, as an amateur volunteer, the professionals had hoodwinked her into coming and then abandoned ship.

In the three hours it had taken those present to fill the room with card tables, folding chairs, and holiday cheer, the snowfall outside had accumulated to a level high enough to jam the exit doors. And now she had to break the news.

"What's the verdict?" Annie Verona, the wife of Judge Gerald "Rummy" Rumbottom, chuckled at her own joke.

"Aren't you a clever cuss?" Ida Nichols, Annie's chief nemesis, pursed her wrinkled lips to show she'd meant the opposite.

Roxanne raised her voice and interrupted before the exchange could evolve into a geriatric catfight. "We won't be able to leave for a little while longer. Just until we get someone to clear away the pile of snow by the doors."

"Oh, foot fungus!" Ida, the more fashionable of Roxanne's aunts, had already draped her black cape around her shoulders in anticipation of a hasty goodbye.

She whipped it off and threw it over the back of a nearby chair. "What in the flipping angels are we supposed to do now? I've got a date."

Gina Halfax, the youngest member of their group, put her hands on her hips and took deep breaths. She'd looked a little queer since Roxanne had first pointed out the high level of snow packed against the windows lining the upper walls of the room.

"I'm starting to feel...there's a tightness in my..."

Gina recited a Hail Mary, interspersing the prayer with, "We're trapped!" She shook her head, mumbling, "No, no, no!", and burst into a sprint for the fire doors that led directly into the elementary school.

Roxanne had already checked those. The students had fled long ago, followed by relieved teachers desperate to escape for the weekend. Max, the custodian, had locked the connecting doors before he left with a promise to return and finish his closing procedure around nine o'clock. That way, the ladies would have plenty of time to work their magic.

It was only seven o'clock now. That didn't stop Gina from hoping Max might still be wandering the halls, scraping gum off chairs and spitballs from the walls. She pounded on the solid barrier to freedom and screamed, "Help us! Let us out! I can't breathe!"

"I'm sure that's extremely useful, Gina," Deanna said over the shouting, "but maybe my cell phone is a better option." She rummaged through a handcrafted tote the size of an overnight bag and pulled out a large, outdated phone. She jabbed at several buttons large enough to thrill Mr. Magoo, but without producing results.

Roxanne took it from her and pressed the ON button. Nothing happened.

"When's the last time you charged it?" she asked.

Deanna snickered at her daughter's ignorance. "It's rechargeable. It gains power while I use it, like a car battery."

Roxanne handed back the phone. "That's not how it works, Mother. It's dead."

"I wondered why no one was calling me," Deanna muttered. "I'm usually very popular."

"I must get home soon." This quiet statement, delivered as an apology, came from Valerie Elliot. A petite woman who had the personality of gray wallpaper, Valerie was a paragon of volunteerism who readily—almost feverishly, Roxanne thought—worked to support the various groups within the community. Her husband, Bob, had lost his job a few months ago, but still she showed up wherever needed, tireless and uncomplaining.

"Bob starts a new job tonight as a watchman at the mall. I've got our only car. We had to sell the station wagon after…." She let the sentence trail off.

"Does this mean we're going to have a slumber party?"

Roxanne sighed. Mabel Popp, Ida's fraternal twin, hovered just outside of reality most days. Roxanne reeled her back in.

"No one is spending the night here," she answered.

"Don't panic." Annie flipped open a slim, bling-encrusted phone and pressed a single button. "Gerald gave me this little trinket for my birthday. It's guaranteed to work under the most trying circumstances. Goodness knows we wouldn't want Bob to miss his first day of work in—how long did you say it was, Valerie?"

The small woman flushed.

Gina's outburst had descended into quiet whimpers. Roxanne felt it was safe to approach her.

"Are you alright?"

Embarrassed, the young woman averted her eyes.

"Sorry. The idea of being trapped in here with—" She looked over her shoulder at the older ladies, and, realizing half of them were related to Roxanne, she adjusted her comment. "Being trapped made me feel claustrophobic. I just—couldn't breathe."

"I feel that way every time I come back to Wilton and stay with my mother." Roxanne led Gina to a chair and forced her to sit. A wooden built-in bench lined sides of the room. A long metal pole with a hook on one end rested on the far end. Roxanne stepped up onto the bench and slipped the hook into the latch of one of the upper windows. With a few turns and pulls, she cracked it open. A pile of snow dumped into the room.

"There!" Roxanne jumped down and dusted snow off her sweater. "Fresh air. And we can kill some time admiring our hard work."

They'd done a spectacular job with the decorations, from the holly wreath centerpieces and snowman place markers to the cheerful ornaments on the Christmas tree. The latter included Mabel's handmade cotton ball angels, Ida's old-fashioned paper ornaments, Deanna's bubble-lights, Gina's gingerbread men, an eclectic assortment from Valerie, and Annie's red, blown-glass Santa Clauses.

And there were lights. One of the red bulbs seemed to wink at Roxanne. Again. It was just that one red light near the base of the tree, and it was driving Roxanne nuts. About to check if the bulb needed tightening, she paused to listen as Annie's call went through.

"Gerald, darling. We seem to have a problem." And then Annie explained how tiresome the evening had been and now, wouldn't you know it, she'd wouldn't get home in time to make them their evening hot toddies.

"Yes...Yes." Annie giggled and turned her back on the

group. "*She's* here alright, and in her usual form. Don't worry your handsome head. I'm ignoring her, as usual."

Roxanne wondered if *she* referred to her Aunt Ida, who had dated Judge Rumbottom before Annie had the pleasure of becoming his wife. Of course, *she* could always mean Deanna, who was a pain-in-the-butt on principle. It was a toss-up.

After wrapping up the call with a sugary sign-off and ignoring Ida's gagging noises, Annie told the women it might be an hour before Gerald-darling could rescue them.

"We might as well wait for the janitor to get back," Ida said.

"He's a custodian," Valerie murmured. "And his name is Max."

"Same difference." Ida leered at Annie. "I guess Rummy must be working on something important to leave his wife stranded for an hour."

Annie's stiff upper lip twitched. "He's having drinks with a *very* important man." She neglected to name this community paragon, only adding that everyone knew you should wait an hour after consuming alcohol before taking the wheel of a car. As she slipped her phone back into its matching case, she let out a shriek, held up her right hand, and stared.

"My ring! I must have left it by the kitchen sink." She scurried through the swinging double doors.

"If I have to hear about that ring one more time," Ida snapped, "I'm going to strangle an elf."

When Annie had walked in at four-thirty that afternoon—fashionably late—the first thing she did was shove her bony hand under everybody's nose so they could *ooh* and *aah* over a gigantic ring made of ruby chips in a gold setting that resembled a Victorian crown. The ring wasn't just big. It was enormous, the kind of thing that might cripple a less ambitious woman.

"Looks like something the dog coughed up," had been Ida's response, but that hadn't stopped Annie from joyfully complaining the entire evening. She couldn't *possibly* hang tinsel; surely, it would snag in her setting. Unfolding tables and chairs might scratch the stone. She had condescended to hang her one-of-a-kind ruby-red Christmas Santa's—handmade by some toiling child in a third-world country, Roxanne suspected—and she'd only done that bit so she could comment how her ring glowed amidst the other reds.

When pressed to do more, Annie had taken a few swipes at the kitchen counter with a damp cloth, though she had removed her ring to protect it from the alleged hazards of water.

"She's a born leader," Deanna said with a smirk. "She avoided doing any work, but she'll be first in line to grab the credit."

"She's good at delegating," Roxanne said, trying to remain neutral. Before her mother could think of a pithy response, a loud wail pierced the air.

———

Followed by the rest of the volunteers, Roxanne burst into the kitchen to find Annie standing next to the stainless-steel sink, lifting soap bottles and scrubbers in a frenzied search.

"It's gone! I left it right here." She looked at Roxanne. "I took it off to clean the coffee pot," she said, pointing to the large forty-cup urn resting on the counter, ready to caffeinate large parties in one fell swoop.

"Don't panic," Roxanne said. "Did you check the drain? It might have fallen in."

Annie held up her perfectly manicured fingers. "Maybe you could do it for me," she murmured.

"That's right," Deanna muttered under her breath. "Delegate."

Roxanne squeezed her eyes shut, reached through the rubber splash guard, and felt around. "I've got something." Annie leaned forward, eager, but stepped back when Roxanne pulled out a large wad of hair and a peach pit.

As Roxanne scraped the crud off her fingers into a plastic wastebasket, she addressed the group. "We need to do a quick search of the kitchen."

There wasn't a lot of clutter hanging about, but the members did their duty, peering alongside the ancient refrigerator and opening up cupboard doors as if the gem had taken flight and settled next to the white, ceramic coffee cups.

Deanna pulled her daughter aside. "Do you really think that ring is…*lost?*" She arched one brow to make her point.

"You can't mean that one of us *stole* it," Roxanne hissed.

Deanna gave her daughter a pitying stare and then patted her arm. "We'll proceed under the assumption it's lost. I'll arrange a search party."

Before Deanna could do so, Annie raised her hand and wiggled her fingers. "If I could have your attention, please. I think the best approach would be to arrange a search party."

"That was my idea!"

Roxanne shushed her mother. "Even your whisper carries like a foghorn. I'm sure everyone heard you suggest it first. And does it really matter?"

Annie wiggled her manicure at Roxanne's aunts. "Ida and Mabel, you check out the table decorations. My little bauble might have come off while we were setting up the candles. A ruby would blend in with the holly."

"I don't remember *you* helping," Ida said.

"I was around," Annie said with a vague wave in the air. "Gina, be a dear and check under the tree. As we speak, my ring could be tangled up in the skirt. Valerie, you keep looking in here. I might have searched the drawers for a dish rag or something."

"And what will *you* do?" Ida said. "Supervise?"

Unable to resist a chance to put in her own two cents, Deanna said, "I think the table decorations are our best shot. Annie might have felt the need to sit down to rest after all her efforts." She turned her back on Annie's glare. "Roxanne, why don't you try the door again? We're going to be here a while, so I'll put on some coffee."

Valerie said, "I'll get it." She hurried to the urn and pulled a gigantic can of grounds down from the shelf above.

Deanna nodded with approval. "Valerie is a real trooper. No wonder she's Grand Marshall for the Christmas parade."

The honor of sitting atop Santa's sled and pelting small children with candy usually went to the most aggressive party. Politicians, business owners, and social activists bribed, cajoled, and harassed with unrelenting campaigns until the morning when *The Wilton Chronicle* announced the lucky name on the front page, including a picture of the winner posed with this year's neediest, usually orphaned children or puppies.

This year, the naïve event coordinator, a woman new to the job, had decided the representative of Christmas should be a person known for their *year-round* charitable work in the community. Once committee members got the message that gifts from potential candidates were off limits, they warmed up to the idea of a fair competition. Valarie had won by a large margin, much to the chagrin of Ida and Annie. Both women had high hopes of using the honor to beef up their community service resumes before the election for President of the Altar and Rosary Society at the Mother of Good Faith parish. Public opinion was the only reason either woman had shown up tonight.

Roxanne knew how much Deanna liked to create her own excitement, so she grabbed her mother's elbow and led her to a corner. "And what kind of trouble do you plan to cause while the rest of us are busy searching?"

Deanna straightened her shoulders. "I'll keep an eye open for suspicious activity. And, since Annie's the victim —and it's possible she really is a crime victim and not just a senile pain-in-the-butt who mislaid her ring—she should sit down so she doesn't go into shock. I don't suppose there's a shot of whisky around here."

"In a school hall?" Roxanne asked. "I doubt it. Anyway, searching the room is pointless. Annie didn't help anywhere but in the kitchen."

Annie, who had been listening, walked up. "But I did that all by myself."

"Then I suppose the ring just sprouted legs and walked away," Ida said.

"Well," Annie admitted, "I suppose a few of *you* might have popped in while I had my back turned." She narrowed her eyes at Ida. "I remember seeing you in here."

"I was looking for the Scotch tape."

Annie whirled around. "And you!" She pointed an accusing finger at Valerie.

Valerie cringed. "But I—"

"I'm sure we were *all* in the kitchen at one point or another," Roxanne pointed out.

"There's only one thing to do," Deanna said, her face holding that intent expression that Roxanne had learned to fear. "We need to search everyone."

Mabel cheered. "We're playing strip poker?"

Deanna approached Gina first. "No offense, dear, but you're the newest member and we really don't know you."

Gina stepped back. "I have rights. You can't touch me."

"Are you refusing?"

"You better believe it."

Deanna snapped in the way one might summon a waiter. "Grab her, Roxanne. We need to be extra vigilant with this one and make sure we don't miss any crevices."

"Mother!"

"Everyone warned me not to hook up with the decorating committee," Gina said to herself with a touch of wonder at her own stupidity. "*They're all a bunch of crazy old women. Why would you want to hang out with them? There isn't one under fifty.*"

"Really?" Roxanne snapped. "You think I'm fifty?"

Gina blinked. "I assumed because your mother has to be at least—" Her gaze darted over to Deanna, and the rest of the statement trailed off. "Never mind."

"A wise move, *young* lady." Deanna patted her hair. "I don't look a day over fifty myself, though my daughter doesn't wear her years as well."

Roxanne's mind was already on other things. "You have to admit it *is* strange the ring hasn't turned up yet. It has to be somewhere."

Ida waggled a finger. "It's not in my underwear, so don't bother searching."

"Isn't anyone going to search me?" Mabel asked, disappointed. "I wonder what we would have found?"

Deanna punched her open palm. "We have to think of

a motive." She eyed each committee member. "Which one of you has the criminal tendencies and finesse to pull off a theft?"

"Take it easy, Miss Marple."

Roxanne dragged her mother into the hall, the suspects close behind.

———

Valerie followed with a tray of coffee service. "Who could want to hurt Annie?" she asked as she handed out the cups. "No offense, Annie, but you *are* difficult to like. To do something about it, though, takes a scary mindset."

"I don't know about that." Ida scrutinized Valerie's outdated clothes and hair that hadn't seen a professional stylist in years. "It could be someone who needs the money."

Valerie flushed. "I would never insult Bob or God by resorting to crime." Then she put on an innocent face and said, "How's the election coming?"

"Ha!" Roxanne barked out, surprised at Valerie's pluck.

Annie Verona was the outgoing president of the Altar and Rosary Society and eager to renew her position. Ida was her only competition, and that competition was fierce.

Perhaps it was Valerie's mention of the elections, but Annie took hold of herself and became the Woman in Charge.

"If the ring turns up, I'll be happy to forgive whoever *accidentally* stole it. The holidays can bring out the worst in us, with all the stress and high expectations. Yes, I will forgive and forget," she said, her head held high and a noble expression on her face that suggested the gentry were about to thrill the peasants with a free goose for the holidays. "After all," she murmured, "it *is* Christmas."

Roxanne didn't buy that a normal person would suddenly develop the urge to steal. Maybe in extreme circumstances, like a father desperate to feed his children. But as far as she knew, none of these women were sucking on old cough drops for dinner.

She studied each one in turn. Ida's slim figure and arrogant face revealed a woman focused on herself. She was the type who wondered why the starving poor didn't just rouse themselves from their weakened state and make an extra effort. Although she was the vindictive sort, and she didn't like Annie one bit, it probably wouldn't occur to her to do something as active as steal. She was confident in her own ability to get what she wanted, *fair-and-square.*

Gina just looked miserable. The only thing Roxanne knew about her was that she had arrived a chirpy blond, happy to help and intent on doing something nice for old folks. Prolonged exposure to Deanna, Ida, and Annie had caused her to readjust her concept of goodwill. While the others chatted, Gina sent frequent surreptitious glances toward the exit. It was possible she had committed the crime and wanted to make certain of her escape route, but Roxanne thought it more likely the young woman needed the reassurance that there was light at the end of the hallway; that she preferred a hazardous and solitary drive home to the current company.

Valerie perched on the edge of her chair ready to respond to any call for Wilton's number one volunteer. Roxanne had known the woman to whip up dozens of bake sale cookies from an original recipe, crochet a few lace doilies for the church bazaar, and then spend the evening doling out punch at the high school sock hop. On the same day.

The source of her nervous energy could be guilt, but it was difficult to tell in a woman who seemed to regret breathing as long as someone less fortunate might need the air. Roxanne thought the woman carried humility to an annoying conclusion, which didn't suggest a person who would steal what belonged to another.

"You know," Deanna said, as if reading her daughter's mind. "There is another possibility."

The women turned as one toward the back of the room. Mabel, dressed in Goodwill castoffs—her fashion choice rather than a necessity—had one foot leveraged on the lowest branch of the Christmas tree in an attempt to scale it. The tree tilted. Valerie cried out and rushed over to help, but Annie beat her there.

There was a light, tinkling noise. Annie crouched on the floor and picked up ruby-red shards of a Santa ornament.

"Look what you've done!"

Mabel, assisted by Valerie, dropped off her perch. "But Gabriel was flying cockeyed."

"Gabriel?"

Mabel pointed to the lopsided angel fastened to the top of the tree. "He has to announce the birth of Jesus to the shepherds. He's biding his time up there until he's ready to strike."

"Makes him sound like a serial killer," Roxanne said.

Annie stared at the jolly remains in her hands.

"Maybe we should take Mabel up on her offer and frisk her," Deanna said, her voice heavy with implications.

"But she usually sticks to calendars," Roxanne said. Mabel had a habit of lifting other people's calendars from their homes and living vicariously through their engagements. Though her habit caused some confusion —like the time she insisted she needed a ride to breast augmentation surgery. The appointment belonged to Cousin Clara. While embarrassing, it seemed harmless enough.

Valerie disappeared into the kitchen and returned with the wastebasket. She held it out to Annie, who clutched the broken Santa to her chest as if it were her firstborn child.

"Maybe I can save it." She turned her back and bowed her head, presumably to perform emergency surgery.

Deanna leaned her head toward Roxanne's. "Doesn't she remind you of that Glum person in Tolkien's book, defending the Precious?"

"Gollum," Roxanne automatically corrected her Mother. "And yes. She does."

Annie must have realized the strange bent of her behavior, because she at last consented to dump the remains of Santa into their final resting place, right next to the coffee grounds.

"Gerald gave me those ornaments the first year we were married. They have sentimental value."

"Nonsense," Deanna said. "You can find them at ACE Hardware."

"Can you really?" Roxanne asked.

"At least the tree looks better," Deanna mused. "There was too much *red*."

"Some people couldn't color coordinate to save their lives," Annie snapped, but then her face fell. "I'm sorry. That was uncalled for." With a martyred sigh, she turned away. "This has been a terrible day. I just wish whoever is playing this little joke on me would put an end to it. I promise I won't be angry."

As Annie wandered away, despondent, she slipped a balled-up hand into the pocket of her wool slacks. Roxanne wondered what she held in that tight fist. Why would the woman want to keep a broken bit of cheap ornament? *You only think it was cheap because of what Mother said.*

Roxanne caught herself. She had begun to see the situation through a filter of suspicion influenced by her mother's ability to see the nefarious in the perfectly ordinary. The ornaments probably *did* hold sentimental value for Annie, just as she'd said. Of course, the rest of the set remained intact, so why so much bother over one broken ornament?

"Okay, everybody." Roxanne stood up and made a call to action, more to stop her train of thought than because they could do anything more to find the ring. "We've checked the kitchen, under the tree, and the tables. Have we checked the floor? The corners of the room are in shadow. Maybe it was on the floor and someone accidentally kicked it."

While the others fanned out and walked around the edges of the room, Roxanne took another shot at the tree. Empty boxes, dressed up as presents, rested in attractive piles on a candy cane-striped skirt. She tapped each gift with her toe to make certain they were empty.

"That's not very nice."

Roxanne gave a start when Deanna spoke. She pulled a bell from the Christmas tree and hung it on her mother's sweater.

"That's so I can hear you coming."

Deanna looked down. "I didn't think of the presents. They would make a good temporary hiding place." She squinted her eyes and rocked on her heels, like a television detective considering the points of a case. "There are only seven of us, and no one has left the building. The ring isn't in the drain, and it didn't get tangled up with the other decorations, since Annie didn't help put them up. I wonder where the little stinker is." She brushed through the needles of the tree as she said this. "If we're looking at motives, we have two good suspects. Ida can't stand Annie, and Valerie is in financial difficulties."

"Suppose Valerie took it," Roxanne said. "Where would she hock it? The Wilton gossip machine reaches beyond our humble borders. She'd practically have to go all the way to Chicago. Her schedule is packed with volunteer work this time of year, so the other volunteers would note her absence. And if Ida did it, she would want to tell the entire world how she'd put one over on Annie, but even she would realize people would take a dim view of someone who steals. It would ruin her chances of winning the election to president of the Altar and Rosary Society."

Deanna scanned the room until she settled her gaze on one person. "I think it's a shame the school hasn't invested in security cameras."

Roxanne scoffed. "Why? So, the thief could obligingly pose for a headshot before stealing the gem?"

"No-o-o. So I could figure out what your Aunt Mabel just stuffed down the front of her shirt."

"I don't believe this. Has she been hiding the ring this entire time?" Roxanne's initial storm across the room petered out as she approached her elderly aunt and realized the awkwardness of asking a relative to reveal what she hid between her bosoms.

The old dear looked pleased with herself.

"Aunt Mabel, I—that is—*Mother* noticed you were tucking something into your shirt, and she—we— wondered if we could have a look?"

Aunt Mabel readily complied, pulling out a wadded-up tissue. "Most people tuck them up their sleeves," she said, jiggling her arm to show how loose the ends of her sweater were. She handed over the prize. Roxanne had no option but to reluctantly accept. "I've got cough drops in here too, if you need one."

A sudden pounding on the door made them all jump. Gina cried out with joy. Annie rushed up the stairs and translated for the group as a muffled voice told them to sit tight for the next ten minutes.

———

The doors eventually burst open. The loud clump of boots preceded the entrance of Gerald-darling in a long, black wool coat and trilby hat. The snowplow driver—Dick, according to the embroidered name tag on his overalls— followed close behind.

"I cleared out the parking lot, so you ladies can leave," Dick said. "I'd go straight home. It's dangerous out there."

Gerald's hawkish eyes and bulbous nose gave him the appearance of a stern clown, but he seemed genuinely delighted to see Annie. He clasped her shoulders and moved to plant a kiss on her lips. She demurely turned her face and accepted a modest peck on the cheek.

"Have you ladies been having a good time?"

Deanna whispered to her daughter. "It'd take champagne and Liberace before that woman would condescend to have a good time."

"Liberace is dead," Roxanne pointed out.

"She'd still consider him a step up from the current company."

Annie arched one brow and let her gaze wander over the decorating posse, who held their collective breath. Would she tell the judge about her missing ring?

"I'll tell you all about it, later," Annie finally said, indicating there was *much to discuss.*

Something flickered in Judge Rumbottom's eyes, and

Roxanne didn't think it was anticipation. She wondered how much complaining Annie did in the privacy of their living room.

"I'll just wait for you in my car, so I can follow you home. Give me your keys and I'll warm up your car."

The judge exchanged a few words with the other ladies as he waited for his wife to retrieve her keys—mostly grunts and *Really? How nice.* Then he gladly escaped to the estrogen-free parking lot, followed by Dick.

Ida flung her cape around her shoulders, while Annie retrieved the mink wrap she had positioned carefully over the back of a chair, far from the rest of the woolen and fleece riffraff. She swung a formerly happy fox around her shoulders and watched as the rest of the ladies grabbed coats and scarves from a pile tossed onto a folding chair.

Gina held up a worn, red wool jacket. "Whose is this?"

"Mine."

Gina held out the jacket toward Valerie. With the movement, something solid clunked onto the floor. All eyes fixed on the ruby ring as it rolled to a stop at Gina's feet.

"My ring! Where did it come from?" Annie demanded.

Gina's eyes darted frantically from Valerie's horrified expression to the ring at her feet. She crammed the jacket into the latter's arms and said, "I didn't see a thing."

Annie swooped down to pick her prized gem off the floor. Rather than thank her lucky stars she had recovered her ring, she moved in for the kill.

"It dropped right at your feet, Gina. Seems to me like you're trying to cover up. Do you have experience at slipping trinkets into your pocket, *Gina*? We don't really know you, *Gina*, if that's even your actual name!"

"I think she looks like a Trudy," Mabel said.

"You're making a mistake," Gina said, rallying her last remaining nerve. "You probably dropped the stupid thing yourself, and it just fell out of the pile when I moved the jackets."

Annie would not let it go. She slipped the ring onto her finger and then shook her hand. "That story will not fly. See how well it fits? This ring isn't going to just slip off my finger. And I hung my fur over a chair. I didn't go near your jackets. I bet you thought you'd get away with it. You nearly did. That's probably why you panicked when you found we were snowed in. Because you lost your chance to escape before I noticed my gem was missing."

"Hey-there-ho-there," Roxanne said. "What happened to the Christmas Spirit?"

"Looks like he had other obligations and couldn't stick around," Ida said.

Annie circled her prey. "Do you have a rap sheet? Stealing from helpless old, er, middle-aged women? I wonder what the police will have to say."

Gina folded. She pointed her finger at Valerie and said, "She did it." Then she turned and headed for the exit, venting as she went. "No wonder you can't get anyone to help out. You're all crazy."

"Hey. I'm just visiting," Roxanne said.

"Can we keep your name on the list of volunteers?" Deanna called after her. Gina picked up her pace.

With Gina's exit, an embarrassed silence fell over the group. Valerie, pale and trembling, was the first to break it.

"I didn't take your ring." Her voice retained a quiet dignity.

Annie pursed her lips in prim disapproval, and Roxanne marveled at how closely she resembled the faces carved into dried apples.

"There's no point in going to the police, but I *will* have a word with the City Council. I don't think Wilton's representative in the parade should be a common thief, do you?" And with a dramatic flip of the fox's tail, she stormed up the steps.

"This is going to kill Bob." Valerie's face crumpled. Mabel dug deep into her cleavage and offered a fresh tissue.

Ida gave her glum summary. "People never fail to disappoint me. I've come to expect it."

"I'm just glad it wasn't me," Mabel said happily as she followed Ida out the door.

"Even if it's true, no one will believe Annie," Deanna said. "In fact, it will probably become a Wilton tradition— hide Annie Verona's ring. College students will remember you fondly as the woman who gave them something fun to do on Christmas break."

"Will you please stop it!" Valerie closed her eyes and took a deep breath. "*I didn't do it.* I know you're just trying to make me feel better... It's too humiliating."

Deanna put her arm around the woman's shoulder and walked her up the steps, her hearty words of comfort carrying through the Old Hall. "You're still young. You must learn to take these things in stride. First, you defend yourself so loudly people would rather agree to your innocence than listen to one more tirade. Then, like anyone who had *really* experienced an injury, you take the offensive and go after your target. Let's start plotting revenge against Annie. That phase always makes me feel better."

"Why don't I stay behind and shut everything off?" Roxanne said to the empty room.

She checked to make sure someone had unplugged the coffee pot and left cleaning the urn until morning. Finally, she flipped off the kitchen lights. Roxanne didn't believe for an instant Valerie had stolen the ring, and though she'd only known Gina by sight before tonight, she couldn't swallow a scenario where the young woman would steal the ring and then carelessly drop it.

Roxanne unplugged the string of tree lights, and with a last look to make certain all but the main lights were off, she headed for the door. Halfway to her destination, she skid to a stop.

The winking light, the one that had irritated her all night, had been red. She ran back to the tree and plugged the lights in. The string wrapped around the tree only had white lights on it. On impulse, she pulled down one of the Santa ornaments, and with grim satisfaction, she found the seam. Santa's head unscrewed. His hollow belly was the perfect size to hide a ring.

Outside, she stepped in front of Annie's warmed up BMW, just as it was maneuvering around a pile of snow left by the plow. Roxanne held up the Santa ornament in two pieces. Annie put the car in park and rolled down her window.

"ACE Hardware?" Roxanne asked.

Annie glowered. "Target."

"After you made a big deal about removing your ring and leaving it by the kitchen sink, you slipped it into one of your Santas. Or had you already hidden the ring before then when you were hanging your ornaments? It's not as if anyone checked. We only have your word that you had the ring on when you went into the kitchen.

When Mabel started messing with the angel, it gave you the perfect opportunity to rush over to the tree, break poor Santa open, and retrieve your *stolen* property. Then you hid it in Valerie's pocket, where it fell out when Gina handled the coat."

"You can't prove a thing."

"No. But the ornaments were yours. Who else would know they unscrewed? And you hung them yourself."

"Someone else must have handled the ornaments."

"Nope. You made a huge deal about how you had to hang them yourself. You overplayed your part."

Annie closed her eyes and leaned back against the headrest. "It was a fit of madness." Her eyes snapped open. "I'm going through the change, you know. And I have PMS. And post-MS. And postpartum depression."

"You gave birth to your son forty-five years ago."

"A delayed reaction. Whatever you call it, I've got hormones raging all over the place. I wasn't responsible for my actions." She put her fingers to her forehead. "Oh, no! I feel another wave coming on. Stop me before I do something else I can't be held accountable for."

"Nice try."

Annie's left eye twitched. "What are you going to do about it?"

"Let me think. You were going to malign a woman's character, and all for a shot at Grand Marshall of the Christmas parade. That stinks."

"I wouldn't have let her go to jail. I *said* I'd forgive the culprit."

"But she would have a reputation as a thief. There would always be doubt, because people will always believe you can't have smoke without a fire."

"I'm not going to grovel," Annie said, her arrogance popping up for an encore performance. "Do with me what you will. I can take it."

It would serve Annie right to have her cruel trick explained to the authorities, but Roxanne didn't know if the woman had actually committed a crime. Besides, people could learn their lesson in other ways. No need to embarrass Judge Rumbottom.

"I have the perfect way for you to make up for your, er,

loss of control," Roxanne said. "And I think it will guarantee there aren't any other mishaps. In fact, I sense a cure coming on."

Annie narrowed her eyes. "What does it involve?"

They opened wide as she listened to her punishment.

Deanna had the car running when Roxanne slipped into the driver seat.

"Annie hid the ring herself."

Roxanne gave an irritated huff. "Now how did you figure that out?"

"Because Annie is vindictive, and Valerie had something she wanted. I bet she was trying to frame that poor woman. Are you going to tell me how she did it?"

Deanna nodded as if it were all obvious after Roxanne explained. "Of course." She rubbed her hands together. "How much time will they give her for framing an innocent person? And should we force Rummy to sentence his own wife? I want to be there!"

"Your Christmas spirit is dumbfounding."

"Crime is crime. If you think about it, Santa's just a strange man breaking into people's houses through the chimley."

"Chimney," Roxanne corrected.

"Whatever. You're not going to let Annie get away scot-free, are you?"

Roxanne grinned. "Not a chance."

"Her punishment should be public. I'd force her to make her apology at the City Council meeting."

"Oh, her penance will be public. Remember those huge foam fingers the church council bought for everyone to wear when the Cardinal came to visit?"

"The ones that say *You're number one*? They're hideous."

"Annie will have one on each hand. To make up for

embarrassing Valerie, Annie's going to stand front and center at the Christmas parade. She's just become Valerie's biggest fan."

Evan Miller

Unsociable crime reporter Evan Miller fled Los Angeles when he ticked off powerful people in the LAPD. Now he's living in Settlers' Ridge in an old house his aunt willed to him and fending off the friendly (and nosy) overtures of his elderly neighbors.

Life in this small, rural town does offers some rewards, including Evan's elusive childhood crush, Sheila Baker.

Murder at Friendly Farm

Two months prior to this cold December afternoon, Evan Miller had been shot twice while trying to protect his young cousin, Joseph, from a murderer determined not to leave behind witnesses. He felt *that* episode had earned the top spot in the worst days of his life. However, the man standing in his living room—the one with the curly black hair and bulbous nose—had just threatened to make Evan's harrowing surgery and painful recovery seem like a fond memory.

"Normally, I'd say you should go house-to-house and invite people yourself. Make it personal. But since you're not good with *personal*," the man gave Evan a pointed look, "you would be better off mailing the invitations. In fact, I think that's best, because, no offense, you're not a good conversationalist. It takes a certain salesmanship to get people to come to your home. And you should *definitely* have the guests RSVP to Joseph."

While Evan had slowly warmed to his elderly neighbors in the months since moving back to Settlers Ridge, and he wouldn't pretend he wasn't home if one of them rang the doorbell, the reclusive crime reporter wasn't yet ready to embrace a full-scale invasion. Impersonal talks with sources about gang shootings, drugs, prostitution, and murder had no effect on Evan. Personal conversations with his elderly neighbors about petty rivalries, health complaints, casually overheard secrets and—Heaven forbid —their sex lives…the mere thought of it made his knees weak.

Evan tried, unsuccessfully, to keep the panic from his voice. "But I don't *want* to give a Christmas party."

Jefferson "Crooked" Crookshanks, Evan's childhood friend and the person who had suggested the party, waved him off as if his opinion didn't matter. "Joseph and I will handle the details. Right, kiddo?"

When Crooked put an arm around Joseph's shoulder, Evan realized for the first time how much his eighteen-year-old cousin resembled his best friend. Whereas Evan stood six-feet tall with chestnut-brown hair and gray eyes, Joseph Dempster, a freshman at Sleepy Valley College, had dark eyes, curly black hair, and had stopped growing at five-foot-ten. Anyone would think the two of them were related, and that gave Evan an unreasonable twinge of familial jealousy. Unreasonable because, until recently, Evan was the last person to care about family.

"Well?" Crooked asked.

Joseph's blank expression showed a complete lack of interest which Evan knew meant the teenager was *extremely* interested and the battle was lost. Still, he wasn't going down without a fight.

"If the idea appeals to you so much, why don't you throw your own Christmas party?"

"It would be a pleasure, but you're the one who's under an obligation to your neighbors."

"*Obligation?* How so?"

Crooked raised his thick eyebrows. "I seem to remember them coming to your rescue several times during the Robinson murder case."

"Three times," Joseph offered. "At *least* three times."

Evan gave a derisive snort. "They were being nosy."

Crooked responded with a brief nod. "Good thing for you or you'd be dead."

Evan reluctantly admitted that his friend had a point, and Crooked pushed his advantage. "I don't see what the big deal is. You had them all over while you were recovering."

"Not by choice. The first day I could tackle the stairs, they were waiting for me in the living room. It was an ambush."

"You survived. Rumor has it you even laughed."

Joseph raised his hand. "I'm a witness."

"That was the pain medication." Evan sighed in defeat and put his hands on his hips. "What would I be expected to do?"

Crooked made a long face at Joseph. "Your uncle's never thrown a party before. Isn't that sad?"

"I'm not his uncle."

Evan had little hope of getting rid of the honorific bestowed upon him when he met Joseph a few months ago, given to him because of the large age gap between him and his cousin. He supposed he should be grateful no one had mistaken him for Joseph's father.

The teenager gaped. "Seriously? Never? Oh, man. It's really simple, Uncle Evan. There should be music and dancing and lots of booze. There's this one drink—"

Evan narrowed his eyes. "I assume you're not speaking from experience, since you're underage." He bit the inside of his check. Too often lately he sounded exactly like a parent. In his discomfort, he crossed his arms over his chest. "I suppose I could put on a CD and set out some chips or something."

"Chips or something." Crooked slapped Evan on the back. "Joseph and I will take care of everything. You'll pay for it, of course." He rubbed his hands together like a fiendish elf and glanced around the living room. "You'll need to decorate."

"Decorate?"

"And I think that corner next to your desk is the perfect place for your tree."

"Tree?" Evan winced. "I don't suppose there's a chance you mean a small ornament I could set on the coffee table."

"Seven feet should be about right, don't you think?"

Joseph high-fived Crooked's outstretched hand. "Friendly's Farm is open."

If Evan was going to be stuck with a tree, at least he could make the purchasing process as painless as possible. "There's a lot just around the corner on Main Street. We won't have to cut those down."

Joseph made a face. "Do you have any idea how old those trees are? They're dried out and shed needles and make a mess. And they catch fire easily."

"Oh, come on. It's not as if I plan to decorate the thing with candles."

"No, but the bulbs get hot. Besides." The teen hesitated. "Me and Grandma always got our tree at Friendly Farm." He shrugged. "It's tradition."

Crooked clapped him on the shoulder. "Then Friendly's it is."

"Right now?" Evan motioned toward his desk. "I've got a story to write. Since the two of you seem to be doing some sort of holiday mind-meld, why don't you and Crooked go pick something out?"

The teen's grin faltered. "We can wait for you. Anyway, if we go at night, the corn maze will be creepy." When Evan hesitated, Joseph cocked his head. "Come on, Uncle Evan. It will be fun." Then he straightened his shoulders, lowered his chin and said in a blustering voice, "You haven't had your minimum daily requirement of fun in a while, Mister. I prescribe a night at Friendly Farm."

Crooked snickered. "That was good. You sounded exactly like Doc Bellevue."

Evan was secretly pleased that Joseph wanted him to tag along, but he kept his expression solemn. "On one condition. Your cell phone stays here. I don't plan on doing all the work while you text friends and play mobile games."

Joseph wrinkled his nose. "I guess that's okay. Deal. But only if you leave yours here, too. *I* don't want the night to get cut short because you get a call that someone's lost their cat."

Evan had to agree with his cousin's dismissive attitude toward his job as *The Signal*'s crime reporter. Unlike Evan's former haunt, Los Angeles, Settlers Ridge had a Mayberry-like atmosphere that left him reporting on minor thefts and traffic accidents. He ignored the dig and agreed to the terms.

"I don't suppose you have a tree stand," Crooked said, but Joseph assured him there was one in the garage out by the alley.

"And a saw, too." Joseph grinned. "And maybe an ax." He slipped a glance at Evan. "All work and no play makes Jack a dull boy."

While Crooked laughed, Evan said, "Who?"

Joseph shook his head slowly. "Haven't you ever seen *The Shining*?"

"Great movie." Crooked patted the teen's shoulder, and

the two of them headed out the back door toward the garage, braving the cold without putting on jackets.

Evan felt another twinge of jealousy.

Crooked had always been able to talk to anyone, whereas Evan, after years of tiptoeing around a father ready to explode at the slightest provocation, had avoided personal ties with people. He moved to Los Angeles right after college. His social life had consisted of monthly phone calls to his Aunt Flora.

When she died and left him the house in Settlers Ridge along with an income, it had come with the responsibility of a cousin he'd never met—her grandson, Joseph. Their relationship had suffered a rocky start, with the teenager struggling to meet life without the one person he had loved and Evan struggling to start over in a position that required him to consider someone else's needs.

He gathered his notes and slid them into a manila folder. As he continued to straighten the papers on his desk, he felt guilty about his lack of enthusiasm. To Evan, Christmas had always meant spending the evening alone with a bottle of scotch and the police scanner, but now there was Joseph to consider.

It was disconcerting how much his reality had changed in such a short time. He'd been snatched from his comfortable existence as a loner who watched life from the outside and dragged into a messy, noisy world occupied by a teenager and retiree neighbors who demanded his participation. Like a Christmas party. He might still fall short of other people's expectations, but he was amazed at how well he'd adjusted to the changes.

He grinned, thinking of Flora's reaction if she could see him now. With a sparkle in her eyes she would have told him it was about time he settled down. He missed Flora, but it had to be much worse for Joseph, who had been raised by her after his parents had died in an automobile accident. It suddenly hit him that this would be Joseph's first Christmas without his grandmother.

Evan was the kid's only living relative. Like it or not, he needed to make an effort.

———

Friendly Farm had been at the northwest edge of Settlers Ridge since Evan had been a boy. Flora used to take him there over thirty years ago on those weekends he escaped from his abusive father. Back then, the Friendly family sold produce out of an old barn. The matron of the family used to give him candy she called "moth balls" because they looked like their namesake. Sugary goodness layered over a nut center.

The first sign that Friendly Farm had changed over the years was the kid standing in front of the entrance with a glow stick, motioning Evan to park among the rows of cars already lining a gravel lot.

"You used to be able to pull right up to the barn," he muttered.

"Back when I was young," Joseph called out from the backseat in a creaky voice, "I used to walk through twenty feet of snow to get to school."

Crooked chuckled.

Evan pulled into a spot at the end of a row and turned off the car. "You could both walk home."

"You're old and feeble. Who would help you unload the tree?" Joseph said as he exited the car.

Evan grimaced at Crooked. "He thinks we, in our early forties, are old and feeble."

Crooked opened his door. "He didn't mention me."

As Evan joined him, he said, "At least he couldn't find the saw. Or the ax. Maybe they'll cut it down for us."

Crooked shook his head sadly. "You're missing the point of this exercise."

"To annoy me as much as possible?"

Crooked sighed. "It's a good thing I know you so well. Otherwise, I might think you're an ass."

They walked along with dozens of families, most of them with children, until they got to the farm proper. A line formed next to a sign that read *Free Ride on Santa's Sled.* A team of two Morgan horses, patiently waiting, puffed steam from their nostrils into the frigid air, a reminder to Evan that he should have worn a hat. The teenage boy in the driver's seat, perched on top of a bale of hay, stared at the screen of a cell phone, killing time while his partner helped passengers to their seats. Santa's *sled*, an open wagon filled with bales of hay, looked suspiciously like a hayride except for the strings of colored lights hanging from the sides.

To the left of the barn, rows of evergreens resigned to their fate stretched out on a snow-covered field lit by spotlights hung from poles. They all looked the same to Evan. Hopefully, Joseph would agree to take the first tree they came to.

A couple passed by sipping steaming drinks. A young boy, concentrating on his candy cane lollipop, bumped into Evan. After the boy's mother handed him half her supply of napkins, he rubbed at the sticky spot left on his jeans, muttering, "This place is a zoo."

Crooked grinned. "And you haven't even been inside yet."

The three of them joined the people streaming into the barn through a side door. Inside, Evan paused to take in the changes. He sniffed the air. Instead of the nostalgic aroma of dirt, dust and old hay, the barn smelled of baking spices mixed with the scent of people—aftershave, damp shoes, and sweat. The dirt floor had been covered over with concrete. Instead of a muffled quiet broken by an occasional barking dog or bleating goat, the barn was filled with the chatter of adults and the high-pitched squeals of children. The fresh produce, now mostly gourds, pumpkins, and Indian corn, had been moved to one wall, while knick-knacks, including woven baskets and canned preserves, filled displays in the center of the room. Evan picked up a mug and studied the Friendly Farm logo—crossed sheaves of wheat over a barn.

"Another quaint childhood memory shot to hell. This place is like a theme park."

"I thought you said it was like a zoo. More important than your personal impressions, they still have cider donuts," Crooked said.

Evan set the mug down. "Seriously?"

Half a dozen picnic tables with attached benches were arranged in front of a counter decorated with tinsel and lights. Evan bypassed a popcorn stand and led the way to a large, wooden menu on the wall. Eggnog, hot and cold cider and coffee were on offer as well as heartier fare: chili, bratwurst, and bowls of apple slices drenched in caramel. He purchased three cider donuts and handed one each to Joseph and Crooked.

The first bite, crunching through a layer of sugar, cinnamon, and a spice Evan couldn't name, made the trip worth it. The tables were full, so they wandered the room, detouring past a queue of parents and children waiting to have their picture taken with Santa. The jolly man sat on a giant red-velvet chair set on a wooden platform in front of a winter-themed backdrop. There was a small tree in the stage's corner surrounded by piles of stuffing that passed for snow. At Santa's side sat a large black bag filled with presents.

Two young girls with mousy-brown hair held hands and approached him together.

"Who's first?"

They stared back at him.

"Come on. I won't bite." He added an extra ho-ho-ho.

"Katelin, why don't you go first and show Shelby how it's done?" said a man with round glasses and brown hair who watched from in front of the stage. The slim blond woman next to him shifted the colorful backpack hanging over one shoulder and nodded encouragement. The older girl got on Santa's lap. A few people chuckled when the younger girl reached up with her hands and the jolly man struggled to lift her onto his other knee.

Joseph, bored by Santa Claus, asked, "What's the plan?"

Evan pulled a tape measure out of his jacket pocket and pointed it at Crooked. "You haphazardly threw out seven feet for the size of the tree, but did you consider circumference? I did."

"Oh, boy," Joseph muttered, which immediately set Evan on edge. He was, after all, trying to get into the spirit of things.

"We only have so much space. We can't have the tree taking over the living room."

"Why don't you try being spontaneous for once?" Joseph said, with a mixture of pleading and exasperation. "Not everything needs to be deliberated and planned. Geez. Haven't you ever just grabbed what you wanted without thinking about it?"

"I've never had that luxury." Evan put the measuring tape away. This was a waste of time.

"Grandma and I used to just pick one we liked."

Crooked put a hand on each man's shoulder. "You, Joseph, are responsible for finding a tree worthy of the Miller-Dempster household, and then your uncle can measure to his heart's delight."

"I'm not his uncle."

By then, the two sisters were through reciting their Christmas wish-lists for Santa. When their mother handed off the backpack to their father and stepped onto the platform to help the girls down, Evan noticed she was a beauty. Blond hair framed a face with a pert nose, full lips, and wide-set eyes. Her winter jacket cinched at the waist to emphasize an hourglass figure.

"What do you say, girls?" she said.

They turned back to Santa. "Thank you."

"Such good manners." Santa smirked at the woman. "I hope you've been a good girl."

She flashed him a smile. "I certainly tried my best."

He reached into his bag and handed her a present, too.

"What do you say, Mom?" the six-year-old said.

The woman curtsied. "Thank you, Santa Claus."

A few people clapped, and the next child in line climbed onto the platform with the help of a short, stout woman dressed as an elf.

Crooked gave a low whistle. "How'd you like to find her under your Christmas Tree?"

"I don't think Cindy would approve," Evan said, referring to Crooked's wife.

"I didn't say *my* tree. I said *your* tree."

Once Santa's lap was free again, a woman in her late seventies who looked like everyone's favorite grandma joined him. Even with her softly wrinkled face and hair that was now grey instead of brown, Evan recognized her as the original Ma Friendly. She waved her hands to get everyone's attention. "Santa needs to take his nap."

A few people groaned. The couple at the front of the line scowled. The man behind them checked his watch. Ma Friendly was quick to read the crowd's mood.

"He'll be back from his break in ten minutes. In the meantime, I hear there's a fresh batch of warm cider donuts. Everyone can have one on the house."

The news cheered the crowd considerably, and they moved toward the food counter except for a few families who refused to lose their places in line.

"I'll be right back." Joseph took off without further explanation. Crooked glanced toward the newly formed line in front of the food counter.

"I could use another donut, and I love free."

"Go for it."

Other people might have found it awkward to stand alone in a room filled with chatting and laughing couples, families, and groups of friends, but Evan preferred it. He was comfortable eating alone in restaurants, too. He stood, hands in his jean pockets, without feeling the need to employ the tactics of the self-conscious attempting to look busy, which most recently meant playing with a cell phone. Instead, he watched.

A short, brunette woman, her mittened hands wrapped around the arm of a tall blond man, led her partner toward the exit. She looked up at him with an expression of such adoration that Evan guessed they must be on a first date, or at least a date early in the relationship.

The parents of the two girls had set the backpack down on a table and were looking properly impressed over each child's gift from Santa. The youngest, Shelby, obviously loved her present, because she was jumping up and down. Or maybe she had to tinkle. When it came to kids, Evan had no idea how to interpret their body language. He was wrong on both counts. The woman reached into the pack, pulled out a plastic bag and two stainless-steel sippy cups, one large and one small, and settled both girls onto the picnic table bench with their snack.

A movement from behind the stage caught Evan's eye. Santa was in conversation with an olive-skinned man who looked as if he had crashed the wrong party. He wore an expensive cashmere coat, a trilby hat, and a scarf around his neck that Evan guessed was silk. They bent their heads close together as if in conference. Maybe the man was telling Santa what to get him for Christmas.

Next, his gaze landed on Joseph, who chatted with a pretty girl with long, honey-blond hair pulled back by a thick, colorful headband. She slouched, probably an intentional move to look confidently casual, but her face was animated as she said something to his cousin. Joseph was a good-looking kid. Evan was surprised more girls didn't drop by the house, not that he wasn't grateful for their absence. He had a sudden, horrible thought. By Evan's standards, Joseph had led a sheltered life. Please, God, let Flora have filled him in on everything he needed to know about relationships and intimacy. Evan wasn't ready to have that kind of talk.

Joseph caught Evan looking, and he excused himself and joined his cousin just as Crooked returned.

Evan eyed his friend's donut. "Where's mine?"

Crooked froze in the act of taking his first bite. "You didn't say you wanted one." He lowered the donut, gave it a mournful look, and held it out. "You can have it."

Evan smirked. "I don't want it, but you should have asked."

Crooked shook his head and took a large bite. "Ass."

"No one asked if I wanted another donut," Joseph said.

Crooked swallowed. "You're too late."

Keeping his voice casual, Evan broached the subject of the pretty girl. The territory of teenagers was still unfamiliar ground, but he had learned that questions were usually taken as criticisms. "Who was that you were talking to? I ask because I didn't recognize her."

"Just a girl from calculus."

Evan left it at that rather than run through the questions on his mind, such as *are you dating, is it serious,* and the one that made his stomach turn, *are you having sex?*

Crooked wasn't as subtle. "Young women. They're more trouble than they're worth."

"How would you know?" Evan asked. "You only dated Cindy. Speaking of your wife, I'm surprised you didn't bring Cindy and the twins with you."

Crooked took another bite of his donut and spoke with his mouth full. "Are you kidding? We practically live here. I'm taking a night off." He stopped chewing. "Speaking of trouble."

He was looking at Santa and the man in the cashmere coat.

Evan's brow wrinkled. "Trouble? I admit he's a little overdressed for the festivities."

Crooked shook his head, disappointed. "You're going to be the local crime reporter, but you don't even know who Lucky Lozano is?"

"Lozano. It sounds familiar."

"Word is that his family—and if you don't know what I mean by *family,* you're not fit to report on a catfight at the mall. The rumor is he was too crazy for them, so they shipped him to the suburbs."

Santa smacked the back of one hand on the upturned palm of the other to make a point, while Lozano stood perfectly still, like a reptile waiting to strike.

The reporter shook off his imaginings and smirked. "Are you saying he's mafia?"

Crooked turned his back on Lozano and Santa. "Keep your voice down. Yes. That's exactly what I mean."

"Do you have any proof? Did the body count in Settlers Ridge rise after Mr. Lozano moved here?"

"*Everybody* knows," Crooked insisted.

"I'll be sure to watch my step." Evan glanced around the room. "Where do we pay for the tree?"

His gaze landed on an auburn-haired woman in jeans and a thick, green, crocheted sweater under her parka, and his heart skipped a beat. About to raise his hand in greeting, he checked the motion as a blond man about four inches taller than Evan, his chest and arm muscles pushing against his black-and-white flannel shirt and quilted vest, and his thigh muscles straining against his jeans, handed Sheila Baker a Styrofoam cup. Knowing Sheila, it was hot apple cider. When the man smiled down at her, he showed a set of straight, white teeth. He looked like an advertisement for healthy, outdoor living.

When Sheila bent her head to blow on her drink, she glanced Evan's way. Their eyes met. She parted her lips as if to say something, but then she ducked her head and turned back to her date, flashing him an ultra-bright smile, as if Santa had delivered her the best Christmas present ever. The man grinned back, delighted.

Crooked joined Evan, who was still gazing at his childhood crush. Current crush, really. "You practically accused her of murdering Andrew Robinson." He chewed and swallowed the last of his donut. "It may take a while for her to get over that. In case you're wondering, that's Mark Weathers with her. He's a relation of the Friendly's. Quite a catch."

Joseph chose that moment to step in front of Evan to

get his attention. "We're going to hit the corn maze first, right?"

Evan tore his gaze away from Sheila. "For the love of Mike, it's winter," he snapped, and then, remembering his promise to make an effort, he adjusted his tone and added, "It's probably closed."

Joseph grinned and shook his head. "Open until the week before Christmas, and it's lit at night." When Evan didn't jump up and down with joy, Joseph issued a challenge. "What's the matter, old man? Afraid I'll beat you to the middle?"

Evan leaned back his head and looked down his nose. "A maze takes concentration, a good memory, and a slow, careful approach. Skills you haven't yet developed, young pup."

"You're on. I'll get the tickets."

Once he left, Crooked grinned. "Very clever. You got him to pay for the maze."

"I manage his trust fund. He can afford it."

In no time, Joseph was dragging them outdoors to a path lined with colored lights. The maze of dead corn stalks loomed large ahead and gave off a subtle, eerie glow that came from the lights placed throughout the interior.

"First one to the center wins. What's the prize?"

"Aren't we just here to enjoy the experience?" Evan said with faked innocence.

"Forget that. Whoever loses has to be the other person's slave for a week."

Evan's brows shot up.

Joseph backed down. "Okay. Two days, but that's my final offer."

"How do I know you haven't memorized the layout?"

At his cousin's sputtering, Evan held up his hands. "All right. We're on the honor system."

Joseph agreed, but as he took off, he was smirking. Evan and Crooked followed at a leisurely stroll. The path of trodden down snow inside the maze was about six feet across, so they were able to walk side-by-side. About ten steps in, they had to choose to go right or left.

"Which way?" Evan asked.

"I'm a neutral party. It would be cheating if I told."

Evan went left.

"Good choice. The natural inclination of most people is to go right. I think that's because most of them are right-handed."

They turned a corner and ran into a dead end.

"I thought you said left was a good choice."

"Statistically speaking, it was the unique choice. And I said good, not smart."

As they retraced their steps, Evan asked after Crooked's wife, Cindy.

"The separation did us a world of good. It's like we're on a second honeymoon."

"You never left home."

"It was a mental separation while I found myself."

"And where were you?"

Crooked grimaced. "I went back to accounting."

"What about your clients? I imagine they all moved on when you took your sabbatical."

"Most of them didn't even notice I was gone. They like me. I'm good at my job. It's not personally fulfilling, but it does pay the bills."

"I'm glad to hear it, because you're going to chip in for the party." When Crooked protested, he added, "It *was* your idea."

"It's a good idea."

"Good as in unique? Or good smart?"

Two turnings later, they reached another split. Evan

went left again, explaining, "I'll be right one of these times."

This wasn't one of those times. As soon as he saw the dead end, he spun on his heels and retraced his steps back to the split and went straight. About every fifty feet, electric lanterns illuminated the ground, reflecting off the snow and giving off just enough light to see the path, so when they noticed a large shadow in the middle of the stretch ahead in front of a wooden bench, they weren't able to tell what it was until they got a few yards closer.

Evan paused when he made out a red shirt, black pants and shoes, and gray hair, and on jogging closer, his stomach tightened. "Oh, no." He knelt and, gently pulling on one shoulder, turned the man over.

"Frederick? Frederick. It's Evan."

Evan's elderly neighbor moaned and squinted his eyes to focus. It was pitiful to see him sprawled out on the ground in an undignified position, his red cable-knit sweater pulled up to reveal a softly wrinkled belly and wiry gray curls of chest hair—like seeing your grandmother in her underwear. Something that, once seen, could leave scars. Frederick's thick, gray hair, always neatly combed with pride, had been mussed by his fall. Evan resisted the urge to brush it back into place.

"Evan? What are you doing here?"

"Take it easy. Did you fall?"

Frederick touched a spot on the back of his head and winced. "Someone hit me."

"Help me get him up."

Crooked took one side, and they slowly raised the old man to his feet and helped him to the bench. When he shivered, Evan took off his jacket and wrapped it around Frederick's shoulders.

"How long were you on the ground?" He took his

neighbor's hands in his and rubbed them. "You're freezing."

"Not long." Frederick pointed at something on the ground.

Crooked picked up a black knit hat and handed it to him. Frederick put it on. "Much better."

Evan crouched in front of him.

"You said someone hit you. Are you certain you didn't slip and then hit your head when you fell?"

Frederick narrowed one eye. "I haven't got dementia. I can tell the difference between a whack on the head and a senior spill. The latter at least has the ring of respectability."

Evan laughed with relief. There couldn't be too much damage, because the old man's sense of humor was intact.

"Besides," Frederick continued, "I wasn't totally out. Just dazed."

After glancing around at the empty stretch of maze, Evan frowned. Something wasn't right. The seniors he knew traveled in packs.

"What are you doing out here on your own?"

Frederick grinned. "Seeking solitude like an elephant who knows his time has come? No, no. I'm not alone. I told the others to go ahead, because I had hay in my shoe. Have you been on the sleigh ride? No? Not worth the price. Anyway, I was leaning over to put my shoe back on when I heard something move. Next thing I know, I'm seeing stars."

"Did you get a look at the person?"

"How could I? I was looking down at my shoe."

"Guess who I found?"

Evan's head jerked up. Joseph stared down at him, his hands stuffed into his jacket pockets. Behind him hovered the core group of Evan's neighbors. The ghoulish Timid

Tildy stood close to Gus, both of them wearing hooded parkas. It should have been a surprise to see any woman standing within ten feet of Evan's cantankerous next-door neighbor, but it wasn't. Not since Evan had discovered they were secretly dating. According to Gus, they didn't want the other *old farts* to know.

Dot, true to form, had donned a stylish leather jacket with a fur-lined hood and wore an amused expression. Evan suspected the source of her amusement was every other person on the planet, including him.

"If we had known you had an interest in trees," she said, "we would have invited you to join us."

The others shared uncomfortable glances, but Even was too busy being dazzled to notice. He blinked several times at the sight of a Christmas sweater with colored, winking lights worn by a slender, old man with a sweet expression. As Samuel was Frederick's partner, Evan addressed him.

"Don't get excited, but it seems Frederick was attacked."

"Attacked!" Samuel yelled, ignoring Evan's advice and swooping onto the bench next to Frederick. The first thing he did was pull off the black hat and brush Frederick's hair back into place. The second was to lick his thumb and rub a spot of dirt from his partner's forehead.

"We found him on the ground," Evan explained, because the look Samuel gave him demanded an explanation. "He'd been hit on the head."

Tildy, a retired nurse, slipped behind Frederick and ran her fingers over his scalp.

"Are you sure you didn't have a stroke?" That optimistic question came from Gus. "You're old enough. How many fingers am I holding up?"

"Four," Frederick snapped as he held up one particular

finger in Gus's direction. "And you're six months older than me. Sorry about the vulgarity, ladies."

"How do you know my age?" Gus demanded.

Frederick smirked. "I looked at your driver's license at the last Neighborhood Watch meeting at Tildy's house. You shouldn't leave your wallet lying around."

"Children," Dot said with a tolerant smile. "Aren't we missing the point? Who would want to attack Frederick?"

Evan stood. "Did you pass anyone headed the other way as you were coming back here with Joseph?"

"Lots of people," Dot said. "But not anyone who looked like, well, nervous. Or running. No one on his own."

"Except Joseph," Gus offered.

The teen gaped.

"Don't be ridiculous, Gus." Dot smiled at Joseph. "We know you wouldn't hurt Frederick."

"I didn't mean I thought he'd done it, but he was the only person on his own, and he moved past us in a hurry."

"That's true." Tildy turned on her cell phone's flashlight application and shone it in Frederick's eyes.

Evan glared at Gus. "It was still a damn stupid thing to say."

When the old man winced, Evan regretted his sharp words. It was hard to remember the wrinkled, old curmudgeon had feelings.

Tildy patted Frederick on the shoulder. "You don't appear to be confused."

"No more than usual," Gus called out with a cackle, refusing to be quieted by Evan's admonishment.

"Your pupils look fine." Tildy turned off her flashlight application and tucked the phone into her pocket. "You say you weren't ever unconscious. I think you'll be all right, but don't take any long naps." The former nurse tittered, and Evan assumed it was because old people depended on their naps.

He thought the situation called for someone to take charge. "Why don't you all help Frederick back to the barn and Crooked and I will check out the maze." To his surprise, they listened.

"I'm coming with you guys." Joseph mumbled. "If Frederick stumbles, I wouldn't want to be accused of tripping him."

As they moved ahead, Evan asked his cousin who he had seen since entering the maze.

"I saw someone sitting on the bench, but I didn't stop to look and see who it was. That must have been Frederick. Then I turned the corner, and on the next stretch, I had to scoot by a group of slowpokes. They turned out to be our neighbors. I passed a few other people, but I only remember a dad with his kids, a tall guy with his short girlfriend, and—" Joseph cleared his throat.

"And what?"

"And I saw Miss Baker with some guy."

"That would be Mark Weathers," Crooked cheerfully offered.

"Is that it?"

"That's all I noticed. There were others, but I was focused on getting to the middle of the maze."

Evan turned left at the next fork and glanced into a dead end. Empty.

"Do you really think the guy who attacked Frederick is hanging around?" Joseph plucked a dead leaf from a stalk and twirled it in his fingers. "I know I wouldn't."

"I'm with Joseph." Crooked rubbed his hands together to warm them. "Anyone who sticks around in this weather is going to freeze to death."

The next dead end came up sooner than the last, but this one was occupied.

"Stay here," Evan instructed. He crossed to the man and crouched at his side, tapped his face, and shook his arm. Unlike Frederick, Santa Claus didn't wake up.

Evan pulled down the man's black, leather glove and felt for a pulse. He looked up into the faces of his companions. He could tell from the way Crooked set his jaw that his friend understood the situation, but his worry was for his cousin. Joseph had been with him last October when he had discovered the body of Andrew Robinson in his swimming pool, and the teen had almost passed out. Now he was hyperventilating.

"Is he—oh, man. Not again."

"Crooked, take Joseph with you and call for an ambulance."

Joseph sucked in air and exhaled. "I'm fine. You stay here, and I'll go."

As his cousin hurried away, Evan checked the dead man for signs of injury.

"Give me a hand."

With Crooked's help, he turned Santa over. A large area on the back of his costume was matted with a darker red that stained the snow underneath him.

"It looks as if he's been stabbed, don't you think? I'm sure we would have heard a shot."

Crooked swallowed hard. "I have no clue. I just see blood. Lots and lots of blood."

Children's voices sounded from within the maze. They were headed this way.

"Turn him back over," Crooked said. "Hurry!"

They got Santa back to his original position just as the man with round glasses came around the corner with his wife and two daughters.

"What's happened?" she asked, frowning down at them.

At the same time, her husband said, "Can we help?"

"I'm afraid this man is—"

Crooked elbowed Evan in the ribs.

"Is Santa sick?" Shelby, the youngest daughter, asked. Her mother adjusted her backpack to one side, hoisted the toddler up and held her tightly against her shoulder, but the girl craned her neck to see.

"Yes." Crooked nodded solemnly. "Yes, he is. He fell off his sleigh, but with a little Christmas magic, he'll be right as rain."

The older child twisted her fingers together. "Maybe you could tap his shoulder and he might wake up. This one time, in Miss Danvers' class, this one boy—his name's Johnny—fell asleep with his head on the desk." She put one fist against her cheek and closed her eyes. "Like this. And Miss Danvers tapped him on the shoulder, and he woke up." She jumped in the air and looked around, wide-eyed and confused. "Like that."

After giving his friend a wary glance, Evan said, "My cousin is calling for an ambulance—"

"The *elf* ambulance," Crooked interjected. "It's pulled by reindeer."

"If you could tell management to shut down the maze while we wait for the, um, elves, that would help."

"Of course," the man said. As the couple left, pushing Katelin ahead of them, Shelby, peering over her mother's shoulder, kept her eyes fixed on Santa. She let out a whine.

"I wanna see the elves!"

Once they turned the corner, Crooked shook his head

and made tsking noises. "You've got to protect children from ugliness like this. Can you imagine how traumatized they would have been if you'd told those girls Santa is dead?"

Evan stood and stomped his feet to get the blood flowing, scanning the surrounding area as he did. "Well, he is, and there's no sign of a weapon. I wonder if he was killed here." He studied the ground, but the snow had been packed down by many footprints and was now as hard as ice.

He shoved his hands into his jean pockets to warm them up. "You stay with the body. I'm going to check out the rest of the maze."

Two turnings later, Evan came across an occupied bench. A man held a woman in his arms and was kissing her. When Evan coughed to get their attention, he saw it was Sheila Baker and Mark Weathers. Sheila turned her head and, after gasping in surprise, ran her hand over her hair.

"Are you spying on us?" she demanded.

Mark looked from Sheila to Evan, uncertain what the situation called for. Feeling a need to respond, he asked his date if she *knew this guy*.

Evan ignored him. "How long have you been here?"

Mustering up her censorious, schoolteacher voice, Sheila said, "None of your business."

His face flushed, and when he averted his eyes, he saw a short cigar on the ground. He bent down and picked it up.

"You should head back to the barn and wait for the police. There has been a—an accident."

She stood, all irritation gone from her expression. "That's terrible. Not a child I hope."

"Not a child. Santa Claus."

Mark shot to his feet. "Uncle Ned?"

He moved to pass, but Evan blocked his way. "Don't touch anything. The police will want everything left the way it is now."

"Police? Don't touch—are you saying he's *dead?*"

"That's exactly what I'm saying, and the circumstances are suspicious."

Mark turned to Sheila and took her hand. "I've got to see to Aunt Helen. This will hit her hard. It's not going to be pleasant."

She smiled. "I'll be fine. Go."

To Evan he said, "Do my aunt and uncle know?"

"They may. Someone called for an ambulance, so probably. I've already given instructions to keep people from entering the maze, but there may be visitors farther in who should be told."

Mark looked toward a spot Evan assumed represented the center of the maze with an expression of frustration on his face. "I really should—"

"Evan and I will check for people. You go to your aunt."

Before he left, Mark leaned in for a quick kiss on the lips, and Sheila turned her head so he caught her cheek instead.

"And remember not to touch anything," Evan called out after his departing back. Then he stared at Sheila. He hadn't seen her in weeks. She had taken to attending a later Mass at Mother of Good Counsel parish just to avoid him. Or maybe he was being paranoid.

"You certainly know how to ruin a good time."

Okay. Not paranoid.

"It wasn't my intention to break up your make-out session, though you could have chosen a less public spot."

"Make-out session?" Her voice rose. "And what did you

mean by *suspicious circumstances?* Or were you just being dramatic to stick it to Mark?"

"Is that what you think?" Evan kept his tone even and impersonal. "That I'm so besotted with you I would stalk you through a corn maze and then make something up just to get you alone?" He dropped the cigar next to the bench, took her arm, and led her away. "Forget it. We need to shoo people out of here."

"You still haven't explained what you meant."

"The man was murdered. And Frederick was attacked."

"Oh, no. Is he okay?" She stopped walking. "Should we be out here alone?"

"Thanks for your confidence."

"Is the killer armed? It's not like you can stop a bullet with your bare hands."

Realizing what she had said, Sheila bit her lip.

"I'm well aware of my limitations at stopping bullets. However, Frederick was dressed in black jeans and a red sweater, and he was bent over at the time removing hay from his shoe. I think he was mistaken for Ned in his Santa suit." He ran a gaze over her fitted blue jeans and the sweater that skimmed her curves. "I don't think there's any chance that you could be mistaken for a guy."

They were at the next fork, and Evan looked both ways. "Do you have any idea where we're going?"

She pulled her arm away. "I thought you were the expert on everything."

"We didn't have a lot of corn mazes in Los Angeles. Or maybe we did. I never had the time or inclination to check it out." He glanced around. "I'm starting to feel claustrophobic."

"Don't worry, Evan. I won't let you get lost."

As they walked on in silence, Evan scanned the ground

and gaps in the stalks in case the killer had ditched the weapon. When he stopped to poke the toe of his tennis shoe at a small pile of snow, Sheila tried to break the tension with a joke.

"You're great company. I might as well not be here."

He glanced at her, then gave the ground an extra kick. "I assumed your thoughts were with your beloved."

"My beloved. Huh. I like that."

To hide his frown, he walked a few steps ahead and led them into another dead end occupied by a small group of teenagers. When he explained the situation, the teens responded with excited chatter, but none of them made a move to leave.

"Suit yourself," Evan said, "but you may not want to give the police any ideas."

Sheila was serious about knowing the maze. They went down several more dead ends, but it was a deliberate action on her part to round up stragglers, who they instructed to continue through the maze and return to the barn.

Soon they reached the center, which was an open circle of space about sixty feet in circumference with several benches surrounded by evergreen bushes shaped into animal figures: a wolf patrolling the perimeter, a bear looming over one bench, a deer poised to spring over the outer corn stalks.

"I thought there would be people hanging around in here," Evan said.

Sheila looked at her watch. "They've probably come and gone. It's eight-thirty."

He took another glance around. "Then we won't be interrupted." He stepped closer and looked down at her, fighting back a nervous grin. "You've been avoiding me."

She forced out a laugh. "I've been—as if I'd change

my routine because of—you think a lot of yourself, don't you."

"I think a lot of *you*. I think a lot *about* you. I thought you felt the same."

She pushed her hair behind her ear, but it fell forward again. "I'm not responsible for what goes on inside that head of yours."

He reached out to brush her hair back again but let his hand drop. "Was it all in my head?"

He held his breath while she considered the question.

"No. And you're right. I have been avoiding you, because it—it got so complicated. And you actually thought I was capable of—of murder." She shook her head.

"I'm sorry. I didn't know who to trust." He would like to have added that, with the additional stress of someone from Los Angeles trying to kill him, he hadn't been himself, but it wouldn't have been true. He'd spent his life expecting the worst from people and with good reason. It was a hard habit to break.

"Let's be reasonable. I hadn't seen you in many years. I didn't really know you anymore. Not that we were bosom buddies before."

He gave into the impulse and brushed her hair back behind her ear.

She gave an exaggerated shiver. "We should get back and see if—if everyone is okay."

So, she didn't want to talk about it. Evan swept out a hand. "Lead the way."

Since Sheila was familiar with the route, it only took another ten minutes to clear the rest of the maze and return to the barn. A deputy was stationed at the side door, but he didn't say anything and let them pass.

As soon as they were inside, Joseph jogged up, his face

flushed with excitement. "I told Mrs. Friendly to call for an ambulance. A few minutes later, the cops came and told us all to stay here. I saw Detective Simms go into the maze. Mrs. Friendly is crying, so her husband took her into the kitchen, and one woman that works here is making her some tea. Oh. Crooked came back a few minutes ago, and he doesn't look so good."

Mark Weathers stepped out of the kitchen, and when he spotted Sheila, he waved her over. Evan looked away and followed Joseph to Crooked, who was seated on a picnic table bench with his head between his knees. Evan's neighbors were at the same table and noticeably giving Crooked space by talking around him.

"Was it rough?"

The chatter stopped, and Crooked looked up, his face pale. "I was fine while I was by myself, even though it gave me the creeps to be out there with a dead body. Then the deputies and the paramedics got there and started talking, and it hit home that this *corpse*, as someone called it, had been alive a short time before. That someone had actually killed the man."

"I bet it was nothing compared to what we saw in 'Nam," Gus said. "Right Tildy?"

Evan pressed his lips together. "It isn't a contest."

Joseph snorted a laugh. "A deputy practically carried him back."

"Joseph." It was a reprimand, and the young man stopped laughing.

"Sorry."

Crooked rubbed at the dirt on the knees of his jeans. "I got light-headed. It's embarrassing."

"The first time I saw a dead body, I almost passed out." Joseph spoke as if he were an experienced man of the world. Evan hid a smirk until he added, "And Uncle Evan said he threw up his first time. At least neither of *us* did that."

Gus snickered. "Pansy." He slid a glance at Frederick and Samuel, seated next to him. "No offense."

Frederick raised his brows. "Why would we be offended? I'm not a pansy." He turned to Samuel. "Are you?"

"Not guilty." He waved a finger at Gus. "You weren't the only one in the war, you know. The rest of us just don't talk about it."

Gus hid his surprise by arguing. "Not a war. A conflict."

Frederick grinned. "Gotcha. What we call *Vietnam* was the Second Indochina War."

"Frederick," Evan snapped his fingers to get the old man's attention. "Are you certain you didn't see anything? The shoe of your attacker as you fell?" Frederick kept shaking his head no. "Did you get a feeling? Maybe smell a cologne or perfume? Anything might help."

Frederick hesitated. "There was something, but you'll laugh."

"I promise not to." He glanced at Frederick's fellow seniors. "Well? Do you all promise?"

"I'll only promise if it's not funny."

No one seemed to expect more from Gus, but the rest agreed, and Dot said impatiently, "Don't keep us hanging."

"I remember, it was right after I was hit and as I was falling," Frederick began, for once not pleased that all the attention was focused on him. "I got the impression of—of hot, buttered popcorn."

Evan's gaze moved to the bored teenage boy standing behind the popcorn machine. "Popcorn?"

"You know. Like you get at the movie theater."

"They don't use butter," Gus said. "Butter-flavored soybean oil. You shouldn't eat that stuff."

Frederick slapped his palm on the table. "I said I got the *impression* of popcorn. Not that I *ate* it. Haven't touched the stuff since I had an attack of diverticulitis ten years ago."

Gus wouldn't let it go. "How would you get the impression of something that you don't eat? Doesn't make sense. You'd have to have eaten it recently to remember what it smells like and tastes like, wouldn't you?"

"Leave Frederick alone," the normally mild-mannered Samuel snapped. "He's been through a lot tonight and he doesn't need you torturing him."

Evan put his fingers to his throbbing temple. "Why *are* you still here?"

Samuel shot a look of kindly exasperation at his partner. "Detective Simms offered to let him go home, but he refused."

"You bet I did. I don't like my gossip second hand."

Evan decided that was reasonable, since the rest of the neighborhood, those who weren't here, would, from habit, turn to Frederick for the gory details. The man had his reputation to uphold. Surprised at the path his thoughts had taken, the reporter wondered if living in a neighborhood of retirees had softened his brain.

Just then, Simms walked into the building. "If I could have your attention. There has been an accident in the maze. The deputies will take a statement from each of you. Please be patient." His eyes met Evan's, and he crossed the room. "Except you three. I'll talk to you myself."

After declining an eagerly offered invitation to join Evan's neighbors at their table, Detective Sergeant Walter Simms led the three men away and sighed as he settled his rear onto the picnic table bench in a corner of the room that gave them a semblance of privacy.

"I was on my way home. I'd still like to get there tonight, or at least before daybreak, so let's get this over with. Which one of you found the body?"

They exchanged glances, and Evan spoke up. "I suppose we all three did, though Joseph left right away to get help while Crooked and I checked to see if there was anything we could do."

Simms turned his thick neck to look at Joseph, who was still standing. "Did you see anyone on your way back to the barn to get help?"

"I don't really remember. Sorry."

"You all went through the maze together?"

"Heck, no." Joseph grinned, showing dimples. "I had already made it to the center and came back to see what was taking them so long."

Simms took the teenager through the people he had passed on his way into the maze as well as those he had seen in the center of the maze, which included a few classmates.

"So, you know the maze pretty well?"

Joseph had the grace to blush after making eye contact with Evan. "I've done it a few times, so yeah. I guess."

"Since you were the first one through the maze, did you see Mr. Roper? Alive, that is?"

"Mr. Roper is Helen Friendly's brother," Crooked explained. "Santa Claus."

"Sheesh. I know I wasn't paying attention to people's faces, but I think I would have noticed Santa Claus."

"How well did any of you know Ned Roper?"

Evan shrugged. "Never met him."

Joseph added, "I know he played Santa Claus and that he's Ma Friendly's brother."

Crooked, having spent his forty-two years in Settlers Ridge, had more detail. It helped that the Friendly's were his clients. "Ned Roper and his sister Helen own the place. Technically, I suppose, it should be called Roper's farm, but when they took it over from their parents back in the seventies, Ned and Helen liked the idea of using Helen's married name, and Josh Friendly didn't mind. Helen's daughter, Linda, works in the kitchen and hopes to inherit her portion of the business one fine day, but her other daughter, Shirley, moved when she married and isn't interested in the farm. Ned didn't have any children. I keep telling Helen she should gift some of her shares to her daughters, or at least Linda, to avoid estate taxes and take advantage of the cost basis of the stock, but, well, she's kind of a control freak."

Simms nodded. "Thanks for the accounting lesson, but I'm more interested in personal details. Did they get along?"

Crooked tightened his lips in reproach. "You can't expect me to bash my clients. It's not good for business. The control freak comment is common knowledge."

The detective glowered at Crooked, sending a clear message that he didn't appreciate the accountant's reticence, but never one to waste time, Simms dropped it and moved on. "The order of events we have so far is that Santa went on his break. His next move was to speak to Mr. Lozano, and right after that, he walked out of here. That was a few minutes after you three did. And since your nephew—"

"Cousin."

Crooked leaned toward Evan and spoke out of the side

of his mouth. "You're embarrassing yourself. You should give it up and accept that you're old enough to be his uncle." He winked at Joseph. "Unless you want him to call you Dad."

Joseph laughed a bit too hard, and Evan glared at his friend.

"Since *Joseph* went ahead of you," Simms continued, "but you all three entered the maze at the same time, Santa Claus should have passed you two, since he was found farther ahead of you in the maze."

"Not necessarily," Evan said. "We took a wrong turn right away and weren't on the main path for a few minutes."

Joseph whooped. "You got lost on the first turn? Hilarious."

"Yeah. Hilarious."

"So, while you were busy getting lost, Ned Roper got ahead of you." Simms rested his elbows on the table. "This maze is an investigative nightmare. With people taking wrong turns and going into dead ends, it's impossible to prove who was in the damn thing let alone where they were at specific times. And if he arranged to meet someone in there on his break—"

Evan felt a tingle of interest. "What makes you think so?"

Simms countered with another question. "What did you do when you found the deceased?"

"I felt for a pulse to make sure he was dead, and then Crooked helped me turn him over, since I couldn't see any signs of injury on him."

Crooked swallowed. "And then we saw the blood. So much blood. I—I got some on my finger, and it was still warm. Oh. That might be important. I wiped it in the dirt, so if you find any there, it was me."

Joseph leaned heavily on the table and sat down. Evan kept an eye on him as he said, "We heard someone coming and we put him back the way he was."

"Who was it you heard?"

"A family," Crooked said. "With children."

"Point them out to me."

Crooked nodded at the family of four, who were seated at a table. The enterprising mother had produced games from the backpack to amuse the kids.

"That's the same family I saw," Joseph said, "but only the dad was with the kids."

"What did they do when they entered the dead end?"

"Once they saw what was happening," Crooked said, his tone admonishing, "they didn't hang around, naturally."

"Did you remove anything from the body?"

The tingle of interest grew, but Evan kept it from showing in his expression. "Is something missing?"

"Not unless you removed it."

"You were expecting to find something on him that wasn't there. What? If I know what it is, I can help you find it."

"Or you can write about it for your paper. Nice try, Miller."

Evan shrugged it off as if he'd lost interest. "By the way, I found a cigar next to a bench, just a bit farther on from where we found the body. I picked it up without thinking, but I dropped it back where I found it. Not lit but chewed on."

Simms shook his head. "You two are a crime scene investigator's worst nightmare. Ned liked his cigars, so it could have been his." Simms rubbed his chin. "Was a cigar the only thing you found?"

"Are you asking if I saw the murder weapon?"

"No. I'm asking if that's the only thing you found."

Evan had a quick flash of Mark Weathers kissing Sheila. "The only thing of interest." Simms waited. "The cigar was the only thing I found."

After Simms told them to hang around in case he thought of anything else, Crooked stood. "I need to call Cindy."

Taking advantage of the break, Joseph told Evan he wanted to check on Felicity.

"Felicity?"

"The girl from calculus."

Left alone, Evan strolled around the room, pausing by clusters of people to hear what they had to say about the night's big event. Since the sheriff's people hadn't used the word *murder*, most complained about the inconvenience of spending the evening at the beck and call of the deputies. A few people had theories, such as a middle-aged man and his wife.

"I bet he was soused and died in a fall."

She looked at him in disbelief. "Ma Friendly wouldn't hire a drunk Santa."

"He wouldn't have been drunk when they hired him. I know I'd need a stiff one to deal with all those kids."

"Maybe he had a heart attack."

He gave her a superior smile. "They said he had an *accident*. A heart attack isn't an accident."

"You're crazy. Why would they need the sheriff's department for an accident?"

The man shrugged this off. "They probably need to take statements for the insurance company."

Evan smiled at the thought of Simms and the deputies performing their duties on behalf of the insurance company. He grew serious as he approached the Christmas stage. A young deputy stood on the platform to keep curiosity seekers from climbing up. The bag of presents still sat next to the chair, a reminder of gifts that wouldn't get delivered by this particular Santa.

"Please keep your distance from the stage, sir."

Evan gave the deputy a brief nod and continued around the stage. As he reached the area behind the back-drop, he came face-to-face with Settlers Ridge's lone mafia representative, flanked by Evan's neighbors. Lucky Lozano's face was lined with deep furrows, and the hair escaping from under his trilby was more gray than black, but his eyebrows were as thick and dark as Crooked's and he held himself as straight as a younger man. When he saw Evan, he waved the smoke from his cigarette away.

"They won't let him step outside to smoke," Gus explained.

Evan accepted the offer of a cigarette and a light.

"There you are." Crooked walked up and tucked his phone into his pocket. "I told Cindy not to wait up for—" The site of Lozano left him speechless.

Evan blew out a stream of smoke. "You have your cell-phone on you?"

Crooked kept his gaze on Lozano and spoke in a low voice with hints of reverence. "Naturally. I wasn't part of your deal with Joseph."

"Then why didn't you phone for the ambulance from the maze?"

Crooked finally transferred his gaze to Evan. "I wasn't thinking straight. Are you smoking? You shouldn't smoke in a barn. Not that there's any hay around. And the floors *are* cement. Still, it's not the done thing."

Lucky winked at Dot. "Reminds me of when we used to sneak a fag behind the garage when we were ten." His voice was low-pitched and smooth, like molasses.

Crooked held up his hands and stepped back. "I wasn't criticizing."

"You were such a handsome boy." Dot let her gaze travel over Lozano in a leisurely manner not open to misinterpretation. "Still are."

Frederick and Samuel snickered, and Gus rolled his eyes.

"You grew up around here? I heard that—" Evan paused abruptly, unsure how to continue without insulting the man and afraid to do so from the expression of alarm on Crooked's face. "Someone told me your family was from—" Crooked hadn't mentioned where *the family* resided. "From somewhere else."

"Yeah. Skokie."

Evan's eyebrows rose. Skokie, Illinois was a largely Jewish community. Lucky shook his head as if Evan was a bad boy.

"You never heard of Italian Jews?"

"Yes, but I thought—" He had been about to say that mafia were mostly Catholic, but that was based on his viewings of *The Godfather*. "Anyway, you were all friends with Ned?"

Lucky took a drag and exhaled through his nose. "Most of us went to the same grammar school. Ned was an okay guy."

Evan cocked his head. "I thought you were from Skokie. How did you manage to go to school in Settlers Ridge? I think your family would have been outside the district."

Lozano squinted at him. "You ask a lot of questions. You a cop?"

"A reporter," Samuel said, as if presenting Lozano with a gift. "And a very talented one. He has a column—" He touched his bottom lip with his fingers. "Or do you still?

Well, you did, and a lot of people read it. That's all that matters."

"I think his column went south with the rest of his career when he moved here," Gus said with malicious delight.

Lozano squished up his face as if he'd suddenly been exposed to an unpleasant stench. "A reporter is worse than a cop. My family has suffered a lot of embarrassment at the hands of reporters."

"I know," Evan said with full agreement. "We ask a lot of questions, like the one I just asked that you didn't answer. It's not a secret, is it?"

"I grew up in Settlers Ridge, but the extended family is from Skokie."

Crooked kept a smile on his face and, without moving his lips, whispered, "The *family*."

"This is cozy."

Evan turned at the sound of Simms' voice. When he dropped his cigarette butt and ground it out on the floor, he heard Gus say, "Goody-two-shoes."

Lucky took a final drag before tossing the remainder of his cigarette on the floor.

"I'd like a few words with all of you, including you, Mr. Lozano."

Lozano bowed his head slightly. "Of course."

Frederick looked pale, so Simms, whether motivated by compassion or a desire to remove the neighbors from the conversation, said, "Why don't you all grab a table, and I'll be right with you."

The group of seniors took the hint, and Crooked went with them, but the reporter preferred to wait until Simms specifically asked him to leave. He didn't.

"You and Ned Roper were pretty close."

Lozano gestured at Evan. "I was just telling this gentleman we were classmates when we were kids."

"I'm more interested in your current relationship."

Lozano, a thin smile on his lips, waited for Simms to go on.

"You and Ned used to be pretty tight."

"We're still friends, if that's what you're asking."

"And friends sometimes do friends favors. Sometimes those favors aren't so smart, but for a friend? Why not?"

All signs of friendliness left Lozano, but still he didn't speak.

"Did you know that Ned had a loft apartment upstairs?"

Lozano's glance darted toward the ceiling to where walls had been added to the formerly open hay loft. "Sure. I knew he lived here."

Simms smiled. "What do you think we'll find if we search his place?"

Lozano looked over his shoulder toward the kitchen where Ma Friendly was most likely drinking tea—or something stronger—to get over the shock. He stuck his hands in his trouser pockets and shrugged his shoulders to straighten the line of his coat. For the first time, he looked nervous.

"This has to stay strictly confidential."

"I'll decide what stays confidential." Simms turned his head toward Evan. "As far as *you're* concerned, it's off the record."

Lozano pressed his lips into a thin line, and it looked as if he wasn't going to talk, but then the big man's eyes crinkled up and he let out a long sigh. "If Ned weren't dead already, it would kill him if his sister found out."

Simms nodded, satisfied. "He should have thought of that before he got involved. Now, give me the details."

"He lost a substantial amount of money last week on the big fight. He didn't have ready cash. Most of it's tied up in this farm. He came to me for a short-term loan. His sister doesn't like it when he gambles. It's not as if he has a problem, it's not a compulsion with him, but Helen doesn't like gambling and there's no reasoning with her. He tries to do his betting on the quiet. He didn't expect to be killed and have it all come out."

Simms narrowed his eyes. "And?"

"And what? That's it. It was a personal loan between friends, but he insisted on an IOU 'cause he's that kind of guy. You might find it in his apartment, and I didn't want you asking Helen about it. Let the man lie in peace with his dignity."

This wasn't what Simms was expecting. His face reddened, and he got mean. "How much interest were you charging your *friend*? You know, you need a lending license to operate in this state."

Lozano took a step back as if afraid of what he might do if he didn't put some distance between him and the detective. "You got it all wrong. I make good money at my business. I don't need a sideline."

"What is your business?" Evan interjected.

"Construction." Lozano shook his head. "You guys have been listening to rumors. My family made a little money on bootlegging way back when, just like a lot of folks did. They're all legitimate now. Hell, my nephew's a doctor."

"Fine, fine. So, you lent Ned money, and he was in your debt." Simms rubbed his mouth, considering an idea. Then he nodded, confirming something in his own mind. "Now it makes sense. Is that how you got him to do it?"

Lozano frowned, and Evan didn't think he was faking

his confusion. "Do what? He needed money. I lent him money. End of story."

"What were the two of you arguing about?" Evan asked.

The formerly alleged member of the local mafia fixed his gaze on the reporter. "Who says we were arguing?"

"All right. Discussing. I saw you right about where we're standing now. Ned was making emphatic gestures. It looked like an intense discussion."

Lozano bared his teeth in a smile. "Ned was dramatic that way. Like my own Momma and most of my Italian relatives."

Evan raised his brows. "I think Friendly is a German surname."

"The Italians don't corner the market on hand gestures."

"Now I'm *really* curious," the detective said. Evan thought Simms looked more eager than curious. Eager in the way a lion might be about a gazelle that stumbled during the escape. "What were you talking about?"

Lozano smiled back. "Ned was just venting. He found it demeaning to put on a Santa suit and cater to the kiddies. I mean, the guy was half-owner of this place. You would think they would have hired someone else, but Helen had other ideas about where the money should go. It was a sore topic."

This news served to distract Simms. "Who gets his half, now that he's dead?"

"What do I look like? The family lawyer?"

A deputy passed along the wall behind Lozano. Evan's gaze followed him until the man stopped to talk to another deputy, this one a woman. He furrowed his brow and turned to scan the room. "Four. Five. Six."

Simms stopped in the middle of berating Lozano for

his bad attitude and narrowed his eyes at the reporter. "You practicing your sums?"

Evan turned back to him. "You know, Simms, I was wondering about something."

"What's that?"

"Joseph said you got here in a matter of minutes."

"You've got a problem with efficiency? We usually get criticized for taking too long."

"It's almost as if you were already here, or at least nearby."

Simms glared at Lozano. "Don't go anywhere." He pointed at Evan. "You, come with me."

———

Simms led Evan outside and headed for the maze.

"You know, Miller, if you want to stay on my good side, you'll keep your cleverness to yourself instead of blurting things out in front of suspects."

"You think Lozano killed his friend?"

"Right now, I don't know who killed Ned Roper, so I'm keeping my options open."

"Then I'm right. You were already here."

"You're talking nonsense." Simms gave Evan a blank stare, but then he gave up the ruse. "We got word something might happen in the area tonight, so we were in the neighborhood."

"It must have been a pretty big something. I counted six deputies in the barn alone."

They came to a fork, and Evan stopped Simms by taking hold of his arm. "Right. Turning left is a dead end."

The detective turned right and steamed ahead. "Ma Friendly says Ned showed up for work a little late, and he seemed keyed up. Touchy. She asked him if anything was wrong, and he told her no, but she said she recognized his mood. He was feeling guilty about something. That fit in with an idea I had. Now I find out he was all worked up because his sister might find out about a gambling debt."

"That's what Lozano said, but if you think about it, Simms, it doesn't make sense. It's not as if Ned lost the money this morning. If that's why he was feeling guilty, wouldn't she have noticed before today?"

"Of course, she might have mistook nervousness for guilt." The detective liked that idea and expounded on it. "A lot of people look guilty when they're talking to law enforcement, but they're just nervous. You certainly were the first time I interviewed you over that Robinson business."

Evan preferred not to remember that day. He had lost his cool when it looked like Simms was threatening Joseph, and he had come close to punching the detective.

"You think he was nervous about tonight? Why? Because he might run into Lozano and didn't have the money to pay him back? Or was he worried about something else? Well, he couldn't have been too worried. Ned lived in the loft. He could have stayed in the safety of the barn, yet he went for a stroll in the maze."

Simms stopped at the entrance of the dead-end where Ned Roper had spent the last minutes of his life. The body was gone, and portable spotlights lit the area where the forensic team worked. "Yes, he did."

Both men considered the implications.

"Did you find a weapon?"

Simms grunted. "But from the size of the wound we're pretty sure what we're looking for. One of the knives is missing from the kitchen. It's part of a set."

They started walking again.

"Stealing a knife from under the noses of the kitchen

staff was a bold move." Evan hesitated, unsure of his motive in making the next suggestion. "Mark Weathers would have had access to the kitchen, I assume. Have you questioned him?"

Simms ignored him and continued to walk, studying the ground and poking through stalks.

"You found the cigar I told you about?"

"We did."

"Then what are you looking for?"

Simms didn't answer him but continued down the maze. As they turned the next corner, they came upon a deputy who was shoving the base of stalks aside with his baton. Snow showered off the dead leaves.

"Anything?"

"Not yet."

"Keep looking."

Following Evan's memory of his walk with Sheila, the reporter led the detective to the center of the maze and sat down on the nearest bench.

"I'm not moving until you tell me what you're looking for."

"Suit yourself."

Evan grinned. "Are you sure you'll find your way out all by your lonesome?"

The detective chuckled. "Don't tell me you've never heard of the Right-Hand Rule." At the flash of uncertainty in the reporter's eyes, Simms explained. "If you put your hand on the right-hand wall and keep it there as you walk through the maze, you'll find your way out. It's not guaranteed, but I don't have to rely on that method." He smirked. "Swanson!"

Five seconds later, a brunette female deputy appeared at the exit across the open area. "Yes sir?"

Simms kept both his gaze and his smirk pointed at Evan. "Find anything?"

"No, sir."

"Keep at it."

"Yes, sir."

Evan shrugged. "It was worth a shot."

As Simms took the spot on the bench next to Evan, he gave the reporter a long look. "What do you know about the Bantam Burglaries?"

"Just what I've read in the papers. Becker assigned the story to Jim Sutton while I was recovering."

"Right. Like I said. What do you know?"

Evan smiled to acknowledge the compliment. "Named for the first house they burglarized on Bantam Street; the criminals seem to have inside information on every house they hit. Nothing but jewelry taken. Usually a small take, something that is probably covered under the homeowner's policy. A thousand bucks worth here, three thousand there. The owners are always out, even if it's for a short period, which means the criminals are either very lucky or they are in the know. The victims aren't usually out doing something routine, so it's not as if they've been studied. Pets are always okay. Not drugged. Word on the street is the police should be looking for a magician."

"That's about right." Simms leaned forward and rested his elbows on his knees with his hands clasped in front of him. "This last burglary, they hit pay dirt. The guy had just given his wife a white gold, opal, and diamond bracelet and matching earrings for their anniversary two days prior. Worth fifteen grand, which makes the bits and pieces they got from other burglaries look like paste. We got the word out quick, and we're watching the pawn shops and known fences."

"So, they're stuck with their haul."

"We think the thieves have a private buyer, but the difficulty will be in getting the merchandise to that buyer. They'll probably use an unknown middleman, not an actual fence. Maybe a member of the public who we wouldn't suspect. We got word from a source the exchange was going to happen here tonight."

"So, you're looking for the jewelry?"

"On the off chance we're right. It's always possible you three discovered the body sooner than the killer had hoped. Knowing there would be police around asking about everyone who was here tonight, the killer might have ditched the jewelry with the intention of coming back for it."

"If Ned was the go-between, why kill him?"

"Maybe Ned met the buyer out here, made the exchange, and then the buyer didn't like the idea Ned could finger him if he got caught. Or maybe the buyer decided to keep the money and the bracelet. What could the thieves do? Take him to court?"

Simms stood, put his hands on his lower back, and stretched. "Let's go. I meant what I said. I'd like to get home before dawn."

Crooked merely looked up on Evan's return and continued his conversation with Mark Weathers and Sheila Baker. Joseph, however, jumped up from the bench and charged over.

"Where *were* you." The implication being that Evan should have invited him along.

"I thought you were busy with Felicity."

"She left. Apparently, the police aren't interested in *her.*"

Joseph said this as an accusation, as if the only reason any of them had been inconvenienced was because of Uncle Evan's presence at the scene of the crime.

The deputies had moved through their interviews in good time. The crowd was noticeably thinner.

"It shouldn't be long now, I expect." Evan sat down. When he caught Mark's eye, he said, "How well did you know your uncle?"

"No, you don't," Sheila said. "Mark, he's a reporter, and he wants to grill you. Take it from me. You don't want to go there. He may come across as a friendly, even charming guy—"

Evan grinned. "Charming?

She narrowed her eyes. "But that's the bait. Then his evil twin shows up and he accuses you of murdering someone. Then he'll put it all in *The Signal.*"

He lost the smile. "For Pete's sake, you're exaggerating. Did you ever see your name in the paper? If so, it wasn't in any article I wrote, because I never mentioned you. As for baiting you, I never said anything I didn't mean, but I think you expected me to shut my brain off just because you're a beautiful woman."

Mark interrupted. "You're a reporter? Oh, man. You have to make sure you explain that this—this—"

Evan raised one eyebrow.

"That this unfortunate event has nothing to do with Friendly Farm."

"Not close, then," Evan said in reference to his original question.

"That's not fair." Sheila gave him one of her haughtiest looks. "Of course Mark's worried about the family business. All of them are worried. This could ruin them."

Mark held up his hands as if physically repelling the idea. "I wouldn't say it's as bad as that, but it would be hard on Aunt Helen and Uncle Josh. Definitely not fair. It's not as if they killed Uncle Ned. All they want to do is make a nice place for families to come and have an old-fashioned good time." He suddenly grinned, showing dimples. "A Friendly time." He winked at Sheila, and she obliged him with a weak laugh.

When he leaned in to kiss her, Evan turned his head away and scowled at his surroundings. The room had the look of the morning after a party. Discarded wrapping paper abandoned on tables and overflowing out of the large trash cans in the corner and by the exit. Popcorn spilled on the floor. Crumbs, drink cup rings, and blobs of chili left behind on the picnic tables by people too hurried or too frazzled to clean up after themselves, both conditions of wound-up parents and over-stimulated children. And Santa's chair, forlorn in its emptiness, watched over by a deputy.

Simms thought Ned's death might be related to stolen jewelry. That Ned might have been convinced to pass on the jewelry to his contact in the maze. Evan's frown faded and his expression became a blank as the problem pulled him in. Why go through the bother of meeting someone in a maze where he might be seen or overheard? Not when there was a simpler way to pass on stolen goods.

He got up from the table and walked to the platform. The deputy took a step forward.

"Can I look in Santa's bag?"

"No, sir."

"Can you dump the contents out on the floor so I can see them?"

The deputy's brow wrinkled. "I—"

"What are you up to, Miller?"

The deputy repeated Evan's request. Simms stared at the bag, chewing on his bottom lip while he considered what would motivate the reporter to ask to see the contents. When he hit on it, his eyes widened.

"Dump it."

The packages varied in size, and at Simms' say-so, the deputy grabbed the largest one and began to unwrap. Lucky Lozano, leaning against the back wall, stood straight, his eyes fixed on Evan. Simms and the deputies he summoned ripped the wrapping off every box and then shook the contents onto the platform to the amazement and envy of every child remaining in the barn. Within five minutes, wrapping paper had been stuffed back into Santa's bag along with the empty boxes, and Evan, Simms, and the deputies stared at an assortment of yo-yos, bouncing balls, jacks, nail art, and card games.

Evan shrugged, hiding his disappointment. "It was worth a shot."

The deputies couldn't hide their grins, and one blond female blurted out a giggle. She immediately sucked in a breath. "Sorry, sir. It just reminded me of Christmas morning when I was growing up. Seven brothers and sisters. We made quite a mess."

Simms tried at first to be pragmatic. "Either it's already been passed on, or it wasn't there to begin with." Then disappointment took hold of him. "I'm sure as hell not going to snatch back the presents from the kids." This brought guffaws and snickers from the deputies. "What are you all gaping at? Get back to work."

The detective turned on Evan, the obvious target of blame for his embarrassment. "In the future, keep your bright ideas to yourself."

"I will."

And since Evan had another theory about the gifts, and Simms had just ordered him to keep it to himself, he didn't feel any guilt about testing his theory without the detective's permission.

Funny how inaccurate first impressions often were, such as Evan's impression of the couple with the two girls.

Up close, Bill Seavers seemed the better-looking of the two. His round glasses covered intense, blue eyes, he had a good jawline, and his brown hair curled at the collar, giving him a youthful appearance. Carla Seavers, the beautiful blond who had caught Santa's fancy, owed much of her looks to the artful application of makeup. Smoky shadow opened up eyes that were actually on the small side and a bit too close together, liner provided her with an upper lip, and blush gave the appearance of cheek-bones in an otherwise round face made slimmer by the hair that brushed her cheeks. The marvelous figure was all hers.

"This evening took a turn for the worse," Evan said amiably as he stopped by their table. Little Shelby dozed on her father's lap, while Katelin hunched over the picnic table and drew on the back side of the wrapping paper from her gift.

Bill Seavers laughed. "You're not kidding. Next year, I'm getting a fake tree."

"Ah, but then you'll miss the cider donuts."

Bill grinned. "You have a point."

"Do the police know anything yet?" Carla put a hand on her eldest daughter's shoulder as if willing her not to listen.

Evan darted a glance at Simms. "I'm sure they'll tell us what they want us to know."

"I just thought, well, it seems like you and the detective are friendly."

"Not especially," Evan said, amused at the thought. Tolerated, yes. Friends? He didn't think Simms would agree with that word choice.

Shelby stirred and looked up at him with big, blue eyes. "Santa's dead."

Bill leaned his face close to hers. "No way, kiddo." He

pointed at Evan. "You heard the man. Santa fell out of his sled. He might have a bruise on his butt."

She giggled. "You said *butt!*" She looked up at Evan, begging him to get the joke.

"I saw someone's butt at our house, but Daddy made him put on his clothes." This came from Katelin and was delivered in an off-hand, bored tone.

Evan may not have known much about kids, but he recognized the sound of a witness who had a strong desire to talk. He leaned over the girl's shoulder to peer at her work of art.

"What are you drawing?"

She rolled her eyes up at him, displeased. "An angel. Duh."

She was using a set of mini markers she had received from Santa.

"Was it the angel you saw at your house?" Evan foolishly thought he could lead a six-year-old to reveal information using the same tactics he'd employed on adult witnesses.

"Angels aren't naked. They wear sheets, like ghosts. My friend, Anna, saw a ghost, or it was really her grandma, only her grandma was dead. But she wasn't scared, because her grandma used to make her cookies with raisins in them, the cookies that were Anna's favorite, but her mother said there's no such thing as ghosts and she must have been dreaming, but Anna wasn't asleep, so she couldn't have been dreaming, 'cause you have to be asleep to dream." She took a breath. "Have you ever dreamed?"

Evan, dazed by the unending flow of information, was slow to respond, and Shelby took advantage of the pause.

"From Santa!" She held up a set of stickers. When she motioned him over—at least that's what he thought she was doing when she reached out in his direction and wiggled her fingers—Evan bent down and allowed her to place an elf on his jacket.

"Thank you."

"Not that one." Shelby removed the elf and replaced it with a snowman. The process took so long that Evan offered to help, which brought on loud admonishments. Once the transfer had taken place, Bill covered the girl's ears and leaned her head against his chest.

"About what Katelin said," he whispered. "My brother-in-law invited his girlfriend over when he was babysitting. I'm afraid my daughter wasn't asleep as he thought."

"He made a mistake," Carla said, rolling her eyes. "It wasn't deliberate."

"He should have known better," Bill said, his voice hard. "He's been banished from the house."

Evan had no wish to be in the middle of a family squabble, so he grinned at Carla Seavers and asked the question that had brought him to this table. "And what did Santa give you?"

She looked at him, thoughtful, and then dug into her purse and handed him a small, square box. He removed the lid.

"Fluorescent slime." He frowned. "Kids like that?"

"Love it," Bill said. "I have to confiscate it all the time in my classroom."

"You're a teacher?"

Bill nodded toward Sheila Baker. "We're at the same school. In fact, Carla used to be a teacher before the children came along."

Evan's gaze stayed on Sheila, who was temporarily free of her farm-fresh boyfriend. He reasoned that he had spent enough time with the Seavers. He'd only stopped by to get a look at Carla Seavers' gift on the off-chance that Santa had passed her stolen jewels. He had struck out twice tonight. His instincts must be dulling in the fresh, Midwestern air.

He made his excuses and crossed to where Sheila sat alone, her forehead resting on one hand, and slid onto the bench next to her.

"How are you holding up? Full disclosure. I'm baiting you so I can tell *The Signal's* readers."

She turned her head without lifting it. "I'm tired, if you really want to know."

"Waiting is the hard part. Where's your boyfriend?"

She wiped her bangs out of her eyes. "Give it a rest."

"How long have you two lovebirds been seeing each other?" She didn't seem to hear him. "Sheila."

When she looked up, her forehead wrinkled, and her eyes reflected worry.

"What's wrong? I just asked you a question that deserved a caustic response, and yet here I am with all my skin." He pulled up his jacket sleeve and held his wrist out for inspection. "Not even a blister. So, tell me. What's on your mind?"

She folded her fingers together, twisting them. "Evan, I know I've been a little sharp with you, with good reason, but even so...can I trust you?"

The question took him by surprise. Sheila Baker could trust him with her life, but he couldn't say so without sounding like a melodramatic idiot.

"You tell me."

They held eye contact until she looked away. "There's something worrying me. It's just nerves, I'm sure."

"Tell me. I promise to do my best to help you no matter what it is."

"I'm worried about Mark."

He immediately wished he hadn't made the promise. "What about him?"

"We were in the maze, well, you know that, because you saw us." Her cheeks flushed. "Before that, Mark sat me down and said he'd be right back. He left—"

"Which direction?"

"Oh. Back the way we came from. Toward the start of the maze. Anyway, a few minutes later, he popped out of the stalks behind me. You know, he wanted to give me a fright."

"Rather infantile, don't you think?"

The flush in her cheeks deepened. "Unlike you, Mark has a playful side. It's not all doom and gloom."

It took great effort not to react. Sheila didn't know about his past. His abusive father. How he had cut himself off and retreated from personal relationships. How hard he was working to change that, not only for Joseph's sake, but because months of constant interruptions and annoying chatter from his nosy old neighbors had forced him to acknowledge how lonely and empty his life had been before his return to Settlers Ridge.

"Not everyone has your self-confidence, Evan. Some people cover their shyness, or maybe not shyness, but insecurity by doing silly things."

Self-confident? She was probably using that as a euphemism for arrogant. He was disappointed. He thought she understood him better than that. Fortunately, he had had long practice at keeping his emotions from showing, and his voice was even when he said:

"Have you told Simms?"

"No! And I don't want you to, either. He wouldn't understand." She turned on the bench to face him. "I want you to figure out what happened. To—to keep Mark out of trouble."

"And if he's *in* trouble?"

"If he did this, which I'm sure he didn't, he'll have to

pay for it. But he didn't do it, Evan, and I don't want his reputation to suffer because of a stupid joke."

At least she agreed it was stupid.

"I'll do what I can."

She smiled at him, and he knew he'd do anything to keep her smiling at him. Even lie to Simms.

"Thank you, Evan."

"No problem."

—

It was more difficult to keep his promise than he imagined, all because Mark Weathers had a big mouth. Five minutes after he'd made his promise to Sheila, Simms was telling him Mark's embarrassing secret, and the information had come directly from the handsome farmhand himself.

"It seems Mr. Weathers disappeared for a while. Long enough to kill his uncle."

"Did he say what he was doing?"

"He gave me some lame story about wanting to scare Miss Baker. Of course, that also leaves Miss Baker alone for the same period."

"Maybe he's telling the truth."

Simms squinted at Evan. "What do you know?"

"Know? Nothing."

"Okay. What do you suspect?"

"Still nothing."

"Look, Miller. You would be all over this guy if your nose wasn't pointing you in a different direction. Spill."

Evan wished he could make up something on the spot, but for a detective as good as Simms, it would be foolish to present an idea without testing all the angles to make sure the story would hold water. He shook his head.

"Fine. Keep it to yourself, but don't expect any favors from me."

Simms stalked off, leaving Evan to consider his next move. Lucky Lozano seemed like a good place to start, but when he found the Italian Jew, he was holding his jacket open while Samuel ran his fingers over the lining with an admiring gaze. Probably silk. Frederick would have to save up his pennies for Christmas.

Evan thought he should warn Sheila that Simms already knew about the joke. Maybe she'd let him off the hook. However, Mark was seated next to her at the picnic table, Joseph and Crooked sat across from them, and the neighbors filled in the rest of the seats and gazed on the Friendly Farm employee with open admiration. Though tempted, he knew Sheila would never forgive him if he embarrassed her boyfriend in front of witnesses.

"I didn't actually see the body." Mark seemed to be apologizing to Tildy.

"I did," Crooked said. "I don't think I'll forget it any time soon."

Sheila looked up at his approach and raised her eyebrows to inquire, and to avoid the desire to make Mark Weathers look like an ass, Evan altered his course, walked over to the popcorn vendor and asked if he was still open for business.

"Yeah. I guess so. It's kind of stale."

Evan smiled. "I love stale popcorn."

As the young man pulled out a bag and filled it, Evan glanced over his shoulder into the main space. "You have a great view of everything that happens in this place. Did you notice if anyone followed Ned outside when he left?"

"The cops already asked. I stepped out for some fresh air as soon as he went on break. Sorry."

Evan took his popcorn and handed over two bucks.

"Keep it. I mean, it's stale, right?"

As Evan put the bills back into his wallet, he said, "Did you go through the maze tonight? Maybe on your break?"

The kid pulled out his cell phone and punched in the security code. "Heck, no. I walked around the back of the barn. You know. To get away from the crowds."

"Did you see anyone else go into the maze?"

Without lifting his gaze from the screen, he said, "Can't see it from back there."

Evan held up his popcorn. "Thanks for the freebie."

"No problem." The young man glanced up from his phone and without any signs of irony added, "Have a nice night."

Evan handed the bag to a surprised couple seated at a nearby table and headed to the front counter where the tall, blond man and his girlfriend—the couple Joseph had seen in the maze—chatted with their heads close together. The Friendly family had set out free coffee for their inconvenienced guests and the hard-working deputies. Though he didn't particularly want coffee, he poured out a cup from the large urn and, turning around, intentionally bumped the girl's arm. His coffee sloshed onto the floor and she jumped back.

"I'm so sorry about that."

She brushed at her coat. "No worries. It didn't get me."

"I'm relieved." He looked up at the man. Early twenties. Not as muscular, but with the same good teeth and healthy aura. "You look familiar."

The man smirked, showing dimples. "We all look alike, or so I've been told." He held out his hand. "Ted Friendly, and this is my wife, Dana."

"I've met your—I've met Mark."

"My cousin."

Evan looked over his shoulder at the popcorn display. The young, blond attendant was leaning against the wall, still mesmerized by his electronic screen. "Is he a relation?"

"My younger brother, Tim. We're Ma Friendly's grandsons."

"How does Mark fit in?"

"My mom's older sister is his mom."

"Does she work here, too?"

He grinned. "You would think so, wouldn't you? My mom works here, but Aunt Shirley moved to Ohio with Uncle Joe when they got married."

"And Aunt Shirley would be Mark's mom? How did he wind up here?"

"When Uncle Joe died, Aunt Shirley was worried about him not having a male influence in his life, so she sent Mark to live here for a while. You know. With Grandpa and Uncle Ned around. That was a long time ago. I don't even remember it, but my mom has talked about it."

"I don't get it. You said *a while*. I assume that means he went back."

"Sure. Aunt Shirley sent for Mark when she remarried. She and her husband have an accounting business. Mark worked for them until he came for my wedding and decided to stay."

Glancing across the room, Evan studied the subject of their conversation with a critical eye. Imagining the big man in a dress shirt and tie didn't make him look any more like an office rat than he did in flannel and jeans. In looks, he was born to work outdoors surrounded by livestock and farm fields.

He discovered that Ted was watching him, amused. Evan's discontent must have shown in his expression. "He doesn't look like an accountant."

Ted grinned. "All the Friendly men inherited Great-grandpa Matthew's looks."

"So, you don't know Mark that well?"

Ted wrinkled his nose. "He's a cousin. I've seen him at the annual family reunions, but if you mean do I know what his favorite color is, I don't. I mean, he's at least ten years older than me, so it's not like we hung out. Still, when he expressed an interest in staying, Grandma was happy to have him."

"Will he be handling the books?" Evan wondered if he should warn Crooked.

"Not a chance. He said he wants to get his hands dirty, and we'll be happy to oblige. Once the Christmas season is over, he'll help me cut down the maze."

"Speaking of the maze, my cousin saw you out there. We had a bet on who would make it to the center first. He was definitely set to win." He'd have to discuss that with Joseph, later. "I imagine working here you know it pretty well." He gave an embarrassed grin. "I got lost on the first turning."

"Ted designed the maze." His wife rubbed his back.

"Did you?" Evan looked suitably impressed, thinking that would mean Ted would know every inch of the route through.

Ted tried to look modest but couldn't keep the pleased smile off his face. "Well, yes I did. I tried to make it tricky, but not too difficult. Otherwise, people would get frustrated and give up. It's supposed to be fun." He looked down at Dana. "Though I might have made it too easy."

She grinned, cocky. "Three minutes and twenty-five seconds tonight. A record."

"Dana's a little competitive."

"Am not!"

"Please." He nudged her. "I got a text I had to respond to, and she refused to wait for me."

She nudged him back. "Slow-poke."

Opening his eyes wide, Evan said, "You must have been out the other end before the tragedy occurred. That was lucky."

Dana scrunched her brows together. "I hadn't thought of that." She exchanged a worried look with her husband.

"Well, I'm sorry for your loss."

Ted pulled his wife close, and she put an arm around his waist. "I'm sorry Ned's dead, especially with the way—with what happened."

Dana lowered her gaze, and she pressed her lips together. Evan, wondering what she might be trying hard not to say, continued to watch her.

"Yes," he said. "Not a good way to die."

They stood there in an uncomfortable silence, and when she finally looked up to find him staring at her, she gave a guilty start. "It's just—"

"Now, Dana," her husband warned.

"Come on, Ted. I know you loved him, but maybe it's all for the best," Dana said.

The man darted a slightly alarmed glance at his wife and back at Evan. "She doesn't mean that."

"It *is* an odd thing to say," Evan agreed.

Ted roused himself to provide Dana's defense. "It's just Uncle Ned hadn't been happy lately. This farm was his life. He and Grandma inherited it from their parents. It was more than just a business. It meant family to him. A small, family farm." Ted shook his head ruefully. "He couldn't see the place wouldn't pay for itself if it stayed a—a produce stand. I mean, that's quaint, but customers are more sophisticated these days. They expect more."

"You tried explaining it to him so many times, didn't you honey?"

"I did, but Ned thought people could like the farm the way it was or lump it." He spread his hands, and the impression he gave was he was trying to convince Evan of the unreasonableness of his uncle's position. "As you might guess, he wasn't crazy about, well, the changes."

"You mean changes like the sleigh ride and the corn maze?"

"And the logo. And the mugs." Dana wrinkled her nose. "He complained about everything Ted did."

"Dana."

"Well, he *did*. He didn't appreciate you."

Evan surveyed the remaining crowd. "Profits must be up. You can't tell me he didn't appreciate that."

Ted grinned and shook his head to imply that Uncle Ned had to be experienced to be believed. "He said it was the principal of the thing." Ted's smile faded. "It's so unreal." He took a deep breath and let it out. "I guess it will really hit me tomorrow morning at six a.m."

Evan nodded. "Delayed shock. Why specifically six a.m.?"

"Because that's when I'll start working under a new boss."

Evan got a sinking feeling in his chest. "A new boss?"

"When I come to work tomorrow morning, Mark will own twenty-five percent of the family business. Ned divided his shares—fifty percent ownership of the farm—between me, Tim, and Mark, with half to go toward each sister's kids. Tim and I will have to split our twenty-five percent." He grinned. "I wonder if he'll make me call him sir?"

"He better not," Dana said. "You're the one with all the knowledge."

The woman dressed as an elf, the one who had been helping Santa, came through the swinging kitchen door and headed straight for Ted. She'd removed her pointed cap. Up close, she was in her middle fifties with a face freckled and lined from the sun. Her blonde hair was losing the battle with gray. "Why didn't you take Dana home?"

"The deputies told us all to stay here."

Dana placed a hand on her arm. "It's alright, Mom."

The woman blew out a huff of breath. "Nothing's alright. Won't be for a long time." She gave them a quick smile. "Thank you both for holding the fort out here. We don't want our guests to feel abandoned."

"Of course," Dana said.

Evan held out his hand in greeting. "You must be Linda. How is Ma Friendly holding up?"

The elf ignored the gesture. "How do you think?"

"Mom!" Ted apologized to Evan. "Naturally, she's under a lot of stress right now."

"You don't have to be nice to him. He's not a guest. He's a reporter."

Evan protested. "I came to buy a tree. I even went through the maze. In fact, I'm sorry to say that I found Ned."

All three of them paled, and Linda reached out for the counter to steady herself.

Dana sucked in a breath. "You shouldn't have said that."

"It's the truth."

Linda shot him a quick glance and then looked away. "Did he say anything before he died? Was he in any pain?"

"I'm afraid I was too late for last words. I've been told his death was quick. He didn't suffer. I'm sorry for your loss."

After that lie, because Evan had no idea if the man had lingered or suffered, he left them.

Mark now had a motive and opportunity. All he needed was means. Would Sheila really blame him if Simms arrested the man? It wasn't fair. She was just starting to speak to him again. Was it his fault she chose to date a man determined to be Simms' best suspect?

He pulled himself up. *Stop whining, Evan.* He had a job to do. If he worked at it, he might find another good suspect for Simms. That's all the detective really needed. Someone to take the spotlight off Mark.

As he turned away from the counter, he noticed a deputy step out from a recess in the wall on the far side of the kitchen. There was something different here. He stood still and concentrated, pulling up the interior of the barn from his childhood memories. The picnic tables and circular stands loaded with product faded along with the platform and Santa display. In this memory, sunlight slipped through the cracks between the slats that made up the barn walls, reflecting off dust that floated in the air. The place smelled of wet hay and sawdust, not spiced cider and candy canes. The counter, a wooden plank laid across rain barrels, had a black manual cash register and scale in one corner along with stacks of butcher's paper for wrapping up purchases.

The kitchen—was there a kitchen? He remembered bins with old-fashioned candy and useful odds-and-ends. There must have been a stove, because there had been warm cider donuts, fresh from the oven. To the right of the counter, past where the kitchen was now…a ladder! The ladder leading up to the hay loft, an off-limits space young Evan desperately wanted to explore. A ladder that now led to Ned's loft apartment.

He kept his movements casual as he crossed the room,

and once there, he checked on the Friendly family. Ted's mother had returned to the kitchen, and he and his wife had their heads close together in conference. Slowly, he backed into the recess. Instead of a ladder, he found a wooden staircase. A sign reading *No entry* hung from a chain between two metal posts.

Once he made certain no one was looking in his direction, Evan slipped past the sign and up the stairs, careful to tread lightly in case there should be deputies scouring the belongings of the late Ned Roper. There weren't. The staircase opened at the top into a large, living space decorated for Christmas.

The room didn't have a lowered ceiling, but insulation had been pressed into the barn roof to block out the cold. Several faded print area rugs covered the wooden floors, and the only source of heat seemed to come from three space heaters placed around the room.

The apartment had been divided into the necessary areas for comfort. A kitchen table sat next to a counter crowded with a toaster oven, an electric kettle, and an electric burner with a small refrigerator tucked under the counter. Across the room from the stairs stood a dresser, and next to that was a double bed piled high with quilts. In the center of the room, a recliner, end table and lamp faced a television set on a stand. On closer examination, the rugs hid a tangle of extension cords necessary to provide Ned with the basic amenities.

His clothes hung from a standing rack, as there wasn't an armoire. Evan searched the pockets of the pants and jackets but only found a used tissue. He wiped his fingers on his jeans in disgust and took a last look around the room. Either Ned had kept all his paperwork with his sister, or the deputies had taken it with them.

He felt sudden pity for the man. In his late sixties or

early seventies, all he had to show for his life was a barren room above a barn. Evan shook the feeling off. The man had family. He had a place to live and call his own. He had friends. A pretty rich man after all. And he must have been happy, because he had taken the time to decorate the small tree next to the television set. Evan smiled, wondering if Ned got a family discount.

Cheap silver tinsel hung from the branches, and a gold star tilted at the top. It looked as if Ma Friendly had been baking. Real gingerbread men edged in royal icing and decorated with candies hung from several branches. He squatted down to get a better look at the few presents under the tree. Ned had purchased gifts for his sisters. The nephews were out of luck. The only other present, decorated in blue paper with white ribbon, was addressed to Lucky.

"I wonder."

He reached for the present.

A rustle of fabric was the only warning Evan had before the blow came. It caught him on the back of the head and sent him to his knees. Too dazed to put up a fight, he fell to the floor and covered his head with his arms to protect himself should there be a second blow. It never came. When he opened his eyes, he was alone. He pushed off the floor with his hand to get to his knees, but the room swam, so he sat back on his heels with one hand on the floor to steady himself until his vision cleared and then took his time getting to his feet. Lucky's present was gone.

He made it back down to the ground floor by holding tight to the bannister and taking one step at a time. When he got to the bottom, he scanned the room. Everyone seemed natural, and no one noticed him standing in the corner. When he felt sure of his footing, he headed straight to the popcorn stand.

"Did you see anyone go upstairs?"

"The deputies."

"Anyone else? Just a few minutes ago?"

Tim, leaning against the wall, looked up from his cell phone screen. "Nope."

Evan swore under his breath. Because of cell phones, criminals could raze an entire city without one witness. The kid looked surprised at his language, so Evan thanked him as nicely as he could and made his way back to the table where his neighbors were gathered.

Mark was still the center of attention, and his gossip-hungry admirers, trying to impress the recently minted farmhand, were sharing reminiscences of their own experience with the simpler, country life. Like most conversations with that group, it had turned into a competition.

"I *love* fresh milk with the cream on top," Frederick announced.

Samuel jumped in. "Oh, sweetie, it's the best." It wasn't clear if he was referring to Frederick as sweetie, or if the endearment was for the object of all their attention, if not affection.

"I heard one young person call it *that scum on top of the milk.*" Frederick snickered, as if sharing a joke about the peasants with the elite. "The younger generation has been spoon fed processed food all their lives. I don't think they know what a *real* tomato tastes like. They should try one from my garden."

Evan rubbed the back of his head and winced when he found the tender spot.

Gus nodded. "Or a crisp, juicy apple straight from the tree. I've got a small orchard that beats anything in the grocery story. Kids don't know what they're missing."

"Maybe that's because you threaten to shoot anyone who goes near your trees," Evan snapped. Sheila was the only one who acknowledged his tone. She looked up, her brow wrinkled.

Mark didn't seem to notice that Evan's neighbors were falling over themselves to get his attention. "Ned was down-to-earth, that's for sure. And he could be a bonehead." He scooted back on the bench and looked around the barn. "You see all this? You can thank my cousin Ted. A marketing major. He came up with all the ideas, and they really paid off. In fact, he's on a new project."

"Reindeer rides?" Evan mumbled.

Mark nodded, accepting Evan's sarcasm as a legitimate suggestion. "That's not a bad idea. But this would be a year-round attraction." He paused to let the excitement build for his audience. "He wants to spruce things up so we can offer receptions and corporate events." He held up his hands as if his statement had been met by cries of disbelief, which it hadn't. "Now, that means building onto the existing barn and adding a permanent canopy outside for pictures, but think of the business it would bring in."

"And Ned wasn't on board," Evan said.

Mark met his statement with surprise. "He would have come around. After all, he was part owner and would enjoy the profits."

"I imagine your uncle was doing pretty well from the current business."

"I'm sure he made a decent living."

"Then why did he live in the upstairs of a barn? I can't imagine it was comfortable."

Mark's brow furrowed, as if he had been perplexed by the same question. "He said he liked to be close to the business. It meant everything to him. I think it reminded him of when he and grandma were growing up and didn't have much. You know. Up early to milk the cows and all that. And he could be a skinflint. I remember he was babysitting me once. We went to the park, and all the other kids had kites. I begged him to buy me one, and he told me homemade was just as good." He grinned. "We came back to the farm and made a kite. Every time I tried to get it up in the air, it spun and dive bombed straight to the ground. He never spent a penny he didn't have to." Mark jerked up straight in surprise. "I just realized something."

Evan had a bad feeling. "Some things are better left unsaid."

He caught Sheila's gaze and gave his head a barely perceptible shake, and her eyes opened wide.

"Mark, why don't you tell us about that time the bull chased you into your aunt's house?"

"But this is important, Sheila."

"It's such an exciting story," she stressed, urging him on.

"But I've just remembered."

Sheila leaned forward, elbows on the table, trying to draw everyone's attention. "There was Mark, ready to cross the field, when suddenly—"

Simms had approached the table, coming up behind Mark. "What did you remember?"

Mark twisted his neck to see the detective. "I'm Uncle Ned's heir. Well, one of them."

Sheila lost her audience.

"I inherit half of Ned's shares, which is a quarter of Friendly Farm." He sent a pleased grin around the table. "That will make a world of difference to me."

The seniors at the table were quicker to realize the implications of what Mark was saying, and their smiles got tight around the edges. He didn't notice.

"Can you believe I still have college loans? Accounting doesn't pay that well."

"I hear you, brother," Crooked said under his breath.

Sheila rested her forehead on the table, and Frederick leaned his head toward Samuel.

"The really good-looking ones should never open their mouths. It spoils the effect."

Simms mouthed the word *motive* at Evan, who quickly responded. "It's also a motive for Tim and Ted."

Mark jumped up so fast his leg got caught coming out of the bench and he had to hop to regain his balance. "Hey. Who's talking motive?" He stepped away from the table, obviously no longer in favor of sitting down with his back to the detective.

"I was just telling you about something good that's come from this." He gave Evan a chastising glare. "You've got a negative attitude."

"I'm sorry to interrupt." Carla Seavers stood next to Mark with her girls. "Excuse me. I couldn't help but over-hear you're one of the family."

Shelby threw back her head and bounced. "I gotta pee!"

Carla smiled an apology. "I didn't see a sign. It's kind of an emergency."

"The washrooms are in a separate building." Mark held out a hand toward the door. "I can walk you there, if you're nervous."

She thanked him, and he led the way.

Mark to the rescue. Oaf. Evan was angry, and not just at Mark for giving Simms more reasons to suspect him. Someone had crept up on Evan and delivered a blow which left his head throbbing. That was enough to tick him off, but then they had stolen the blue-and-white present just as he was about to get his hands on it.

What if it had been the jewelry? What if Ned had wrapped the stolen merchandise up for his good friend, Lucky? No one would question him handing a gift to his childhood friend. But why would he risk it all for a small cut of an illegal transaction? Ned owned half of Friendly Farm. He might not have had ready cash, especially if it was tied up in improving the farm, but Lozano had told Simms he wasn't in a hurry to get paid back. If that was true, there wasn't any pressure for Ned to help the thieves.

Evan took a deep breath. It wasn't good to jump to conclusions. He had no proof that Ned's murder had anything to do with the Bantam Burglaries or that Ned was involved with the transfer of stolen items. Maybe the present wasn't the jewelry. Maybe Ned had come up with the money to pay Lozano back and had a sense of humor about how he returned it.

Ignoring Sheila when she called his name, Evan crossed the room to where Lozano stood. This time, he declined the offer of a cigarette.

"Having fun?"

Lozano shrugged. "I've had better times."

"You see, I was wondering." Evan glanced around the room. "The sleigh ride, photos with Santa, stale popcorn, they just don't seem to be your thing. A little *Cioccolata Calda* by the fireplace, or a glass of Prosecco and some Panettone with family. That seems more your style. Or even matzo ball soup and brisket for Hanukkah."

Lozano gave him a tolerant smile. "I can't enjoy myself with my friends?"

"But you're not, are you? You've been squirrelled away in this corner all night, except when your friends came to you."

Lozano shrugged. It was a dramatic, Italian gesture. "I'm an observer."

Evan nodded. "That's true, but what are you observing? That's the question. Why are you here? It might have been to speak to Ned, but then why didn't you leave as soon as you talked to him?"

Lozano turned his hands palms up. "Why don't you tell me?"

Evan changed tactics. "How did you like your gift?"

Lozano hesitated before taking a drag off his cigarette. "What gift?"

Although Evan had been wrong twice tonight, he still trusted his instincts. The man knew nothing about the present that had been waiting for him under Ned's tree upstairs.

"Forget it." Evan's lips twitched. "I can't see you sneaking around anyway. I think if you had wanted something from me, you would have punched me in the face, not knocked me on the head when I wasn't looking."

Lozano grinned. "Damn straight. But what is this I'm supposed to want?"

Evan scanned the room for the next possible suspect. "Ned left you a present under his tree."

"A present? Me and Ned don't exchange gifts. Not for holidays; not for birthdays."

"Maybe he was feeling sentimental this year."

Speaking of sentimental... Joseph stood across the room next to Crooked. The teenager didn't look happy, and Evan thought the cause might be more than the inconvenience of murder. The young man's memories of this place had been with his grandmother, and now his only remaining family member had abandoned him for most of the evening to talk with strangers.

Evan had to get his act together.

Sheila met him halfway as he crossed the room to join Joseph to make up for ignoring him. She took Evan's hand and guided him to a quiet spot next to the wall.

"So? Have you found out anything?"

He searched for some fact that might be useful and came up empty. "I know that Carla Seavers' brother runs around their house naked when he's babysitting."

"What?"

"Something the little one blurted out. Something she wasn't supposed to see."

She smiled. "They do like to share. It takes a bit of skillful redirection to stop my students from telling me their parents deepest secrets sometimes." She took a close look at him. "What's wrong with you?" She felt his forehead and he winced, for once not enjoying her touch. "You look pale."

Her concern irritated him, as he knew it was temporary. "I'm fine. Did your boyfriend confess to the crime while I was away?"

Her protest seemed half-hearted. "He's a bit naïve."

"He's dumber than a load of bricks. He might as well have raised his hand and said *Oh, Detective. Don't forget me.* You know he already told Simms about being separated from you for his little joke?"

"Oh, dear. Means and motive. All he needs is a method. Evan, you've got to do something. Ma Friendly would just die if one of her grandsons was accused of murdering her brother. She's already had one shock, and a second upset might do her serious damage."

"Does that apply to all of her grandsons? Because Ted had an opportunity. He and his wife were separated in the maze. That puts him in the same category as Mark."

"What's his motive?"

"You heard Mark. Ned wasn't thrilled about the improvements Ted was making, and he might have wanted them stopped."

"And Tim?"

Evan laughed. "Unless he could kill Ned by cell phone, I think he's out of it."

She bit her cuticle, a nervous gesture Evan hadn't seen since they were in grade school. It made him want to kiss her.

She shook her head. "None of them could have had anything to do with it."

"The idea is distasteful." Evan looked across the room at Dana. "Of course, there's another possibility. What if the wife didn't want Ned standing in the way of the success of her one true love? She seems very enthusiastic about his success."

"But to murder someone? Don't be silly."

"Sheila be reasonable. The usual motives are love, money, and revenge. I don't think Santa was having a torrid affair with anyone's wife. If someone wanted revenge for a past injury, we won't find out about it tonight. That leaves money, and you want to eliminate everyone who would have gained from Ned's death."

Although, there was still the possibility Ned's death was related to the Bantam Burglaries. Simms thought so, and that would let off all those family members and please Sheila.

"Let's say Ned was going to pass the stolen jewelry tonight."

"Stolen jewelry?"

Evan shushed her. "The best opportunity would be through the gifts. Someone attacked me to get their hands on Lucky's gift—"

"You were attacked?"

Evan shushed her again.

"So, maybe Ned didn't intend to pass the gift off until late tonight. Otherwise, why not have it with the other gifts? Or is that why Lucky's been hanging around?" He tapped on his lower lip. "No, Lozano was genuinely surprised about the present. And the obvious choice for the recipient had a package of fluorescent slime to show for her present. But where were the criminals getting their information? They were well-informed on the movements of each victim."

Sheila tugged on his arm. "Evan, you're not making sense. And if you shush me one more time, I'll scream."

There was something Sheila had said that might explain everything.

He held out his hand. "Give me your cell phone."

Taking this as a rebuff, her tone became snippy. "A please would be nice."

"Do you want your boyfriend cleared or not?"

She pulled her phone from her back pocket and handed it to him. Friendly Farm had Wi-Fi access, and once Evan was in his cloud storage, he looked through his notes on the Bantam Burglaries. He scanned the names of the victims and handed her phone back.

"Thanks."

"Are you going to explain—"

"Not now."

He moved to Bill Seavers' table and asked to join him. Once he was seated, he gave him a friendly smile. "You said you're a teacher at the elementary school." He nodded at Sheila, who was watching them. "We were talking about the families we know in the area, the ones who have kids, and I was wondering if the Mitchell family's youngest is in your class."

Bill frowned. "Tony Mitchell is, but I don't think he's the youngest."

"Little buggers are hard to keep track of, aren't they? Especially when you know several people with multiple children, and they all get together for the holidays. For instance, the Mitchell's are great friends with the Shimecks, aren't they?"

Bill Seavers' brow wrinkled. "The adults might be, but Tony and Felix don't really get along. And Felix doesn't have any brothers or sisters."

Evan shook his head. "My mistake. I must be thinking of the Kohlers."

Bill laughed. "Tony and Freida are friends, alright. If I don't watch them every chance I get, they're into trouble. Not bad trouble, you understand. Kid stuff, like drawing a mustache on the poster of Einstein. That kind of thing. You know."

"I don't have children, so I'm afraid I don't know." Evan said this in a tone of regret, a deliberate move intended to generate empathy from a man who voluntarily surrounded himself with children five days a week. To his surprise, the feigned emotion felt real.

He studied Bill Seavers. The epitome of average. Average shade of brown hair. Average height. Average build. The only time his features seemed to wake up was when he was talking to or about children. "Do you like your job?"

"Love it. Kids are so honest and open. When you're around them, you see the world through fresh eyes. Their eyes. That dark cloud over the playground isn't just a sign of rain. It's the mop of an angel sent to wash things clean. The butterfly in front of them is the most beautiful butterfly ever. Dandelions are kingly flowers instead of weeds. And when their eyes light up because they've understood something you've worked hard to teach them, it's an incredible feeling." He looked over at his returning wife and daughters. Shelby threw herself on him and he scooped her up. "Carla, I was just telling—I'm sorry. I don't know your name."

"It's Evan Miller, isn't it? I read your coverage of the Robinson—" she glanced at her children, "*thing* in *The Signal*. And I'm sure I've seen your column."

In his life before Settlers Ridge, Evan's column had been syndicated in smaller papers around the country and online. He'd been proud of his work back then, until he'd made an emotional breakthrough and realized most of it was tripe.

"Wow." Bill grinned. "Talking to a celebrity and I didn't even know it."

"What's a 'lebrity?" Shelby asked.

"Someone who's overrated for their work." Evan glanced at his watch. "It's getting late. I don't suppose we'll get our tree. At least we got to try the corn maze. I haven't been in one of those since I was a teenager. I understand that you were in the maze when *it* happened."

Bill's eyebrows shot up. "I hadn't thought of that. I suppose we were." His mouth dropped open. "I just realized—" He looked up at his wife. "You could have been killed."

She met her eldest daughter's concerned gaze and then sent her husband a warning glance. "Don't be silly. You love to exaggerate."

"My wife left her wallet in here. She came back to get it."

Her warning glance turned into a scowl. "You try keeping track of potty pants and pretzel snacks and sippy cups."

He held up his hands to ward off the attack. "I wasn't criticizing."

"What time was this?" Evan asked.

Carla wasn't over her snit. "I'm supposed to keep track of the time, too?"

"Did you see Ned sitting on his bench? He would have been smoking a cigar."

"I didn't see anyone sitting down. I was too focused on my wallet. I've had my identity stolen before, and I was afraid it would happen again." She rubbed her fingers against her brow. "It took so long to clean up the mess. Years."

"It sounds like a nightmare." Evan frowned, as if an idea had just occurred to him. "You didn't see, or even hear anything on your way back to your family?"

"Like what?"

"A struggle. The sound of someone falling."

"Santa fell," Shelby announced. Her eyes grew wide. "Did you see the elves?"

"I'm afraid I didn't stick around long enough. Sorry."

Shelby sighed and leaned her head back against her father's chest. "They forgot him."

Bill bounced her on his knee. "That would be pretty silly. How can they deliver presents without Santa? He's the only one who knows how to get down the chimney, and he's the only one Rudolph will listen to."

Carla picked her daughter up, and kept her back to Evan. The move was a dismissal, so he wished them a Merry Christmas and moved on. This time, when he found Lozano, the man was alone. He hadn't moved from his position behind Santa's platform and backdrop.

"I have an idea that I'd like to share with you."

"Be my guest. It's a free country."

"Ned owed you money."

"I already said that."

"Did you arrange to wave the debt if he did you a favor?"

"What kind of favor?"

"I think you were in charge of transferring the stolen jewelry from the latest Bantam Burglary."

Lozano smiled at him, and it was the kind of smile that made Evan wish it wasn't directed at him.

"Are you calling me a crook?"

"You misunderstand me. I don't think you stole the jewelry. I think you were playing a management role. Making sure the goods were delivered. I think you used your friend Ned to make the delivery and offered to wave the loan if he played along."

"I don't suppose you'd believe me if I told you how wrong you were."

"Why don't you try me?"

"Why should I? I don't know you from Adam. Just because you have an honest face—"

"Do I?"

Their conversation was interrupted by a scream.

"Stay away from me!"

Both men turned their heads toward the trashcan in the corner where Mark Weathers stood holding what looked like a filthy kitchen knife. His brow was wrinkled, and his lips frowned in an expression that was half puzzled and half incensed. The expression on Carla Seavers' face was one of pure fright.

"Who threw this away?" Mark demanded.

Evan clenched his teeth. "Is that man a moron?"

Lozano nodded. "Hardly seems real."

Simms jogged across the room with his hands in the air. "Hold it. Don't move." The deputies followed, weapons drawn.

Sheila joined Evan as he moved toward the—well, it wasn't exactly a standoff. Mark pointed the knife at the trashcan.

"Someone just tossed it on top of the trash. That's

dangerous." He held the knife up for inspection. "And there doesn't seem to be anything wrong with it. Except it's dirty."

Carla looked around at all of them. "I just came over to throw away a napkin and he suddenly started waving a knife around."

Evan didn't have any evidence, only a theory, but if he didn't act now, Mark Weathers was going to jail. He decided to take Lucky Lozano at his word, that he wasn't involved. As far as Evan could see, that left one other option.

"Simms. Hold up."

The detective continued to focus on Mark. "Mr. Weathers, put the knife on the floor, slowly."

"Do what he says, Mark." Sheila smiled and nodded to encourage him.

Mark finally noticed all the unfriendly attention he had attracted from the deputies. "Sure. Whatever you say." He took his time crouching and set the kitchen knife on the cement floor, then straightened up with his hands held out to his sides.

"Now step back, please."

He followed Simms' instructions, and a deputy holstered her weapon and moved to retrieve the weapon.

Bill Seavers jogged up to his wife, and she turned to him and sobbed on his chest. He glanced at Mark. "What the hell is wrong with this place?"

"You can cut the act." Evan said this quietly, but everyone present heard him, and they all turned to stare at Bill Seavers, even Simms. "Three of the four burglaries happened in households with third graders. Third graders in your classroom."

Bill frowned. "So?"

"I never asked you. Do the Mazza family have a child

in your class? Mazza is the latest family to be burglarized, isn't it?"

Seavers paled and blinked a few times, and that was answer enough.

Simms narrowed his eyes at Evan, not ready to accept his word after the gift-unwrapping failure. "But he wasn't ever alone. His kids were with him the entire time his wife retrieved her wallet."

"Kids will lie for their parents."

As if on cue, the deputies all took a step closer, and Bill let go of his wife, his eyes open wide with panic. "B-but they *were* with me the whole time. This is a horrible coincidence!"

Evan held up a hand. "Mr. Lozano. Could you come here, please?"

Settlers Ridge's claim to criminal fame crossed the room. His hands were in his jacket pockets, and Evan shook off an image of a well-dressed mobster pulling out a handgun and executing his own, personal revenge for the death of his friend.

"You need to come clean on why you're here tonight."

"I'm enjoying the festivities." There wasn't any joy in Lozano's smile.

"Ned's dead. It can't hurt him."

He glanced toward the closed kitchen doors. "There are other considerations."

Evan followed his gaze. "Don't you think Ma Friendly would prefer to have Ned's killer come to justice?"

Simms walked up and stood nose to nose with Lozano. "If you know something about this murder, you better say so now, before I get impatient."

Lozano held Evan's gaze over the detective's shoulder. "I hope you know what you're doing." He sighed. "Ned came to me and said he had a way to pay me back. He was approached by someone—and I don't know who, so don't ask. This guy said he'd clear Ned's loan if he would do him a favor. All he had to do was give a certain present to a certain person."

"Who?" Simms demanded.

"Again, I don't know who. I didn't want to know. I told Ned we were good, and he could pay me back any time. I told him not to be stupid, because he couldn't pay me back if he was in jail. He finally listened to reason, and tonight he told me he changed his mind. He'd give the goods back and call off the deal."

Simms growled. "Quite the friend. And then you stood back and let him get killed."

Lozano controlled himself, but he pulled his hands from his pockets and clenched them into fists. "I shoulda followed him into the maze, but he said he wanted to think, which meant he wanted to be alone. If you can't honor your friend's wishes, then you aren't much of a friend. I hung around in case he needed me. Then, when I found out he was dead, I hung around so I could find the no-good son-of-a—"

"Children are present," Sheila called out in her best schoolmarm voice.

Evan picked up the story. "Ned went out into the maze. He passed Crooked and me without our knowledge because we were diverted down a dead-end. He went to a bench and pulled out a cigar. Then, for some reason, he went into the closest dead end in enough of a hurry he dropped his cigar. I think he heard the killer coming." He looked at Bill. "Your children would have hindered a stealthy approach."

"You're crazy! You think I killed him in front of my kids?"

"No, but you could have seen Ned and told them to wait for you. Maybe you made a game out of it."

"Th—That's insane." Bill Seavers searched the faces that were staring at him for support, but he was disappointed. "I'm not saying another thing until I talk to an attorney."

"What about me?" Frederick asked, pointing at Bill. "I don't even know that man, but I was attacked." He raised his brows. "Unless I was practice?"

"You were dressed like Santa, red shirt and black pants, and in the dim lighting, he mistook you for Ned."

"Why not just stab the guy?" one deputy called out, nodding at Frederick.

Evan considered the question. "He probably felt the need to render his victim helpless first." He looked at Bill Seavers thoughtfully. "But you're bigger than Ned. Of course, you may have wanted to avoid a struggle, especially with your kids nearby." Evan's tone betrayed his dislike of that idea. In fact, the more he talked it through, the more certain he was that he had made a mistake. However, it was too late to stop now. If he was going to make a fool of himself, he might as well go all the way. Then another thought occurred to him.

"He said his wife came back to the barn for her wallet." He raised his eyebrows at Simms.

"We verified it with one of the kitchen ladies."

Evan turned a hand to show his palm. "But she was back with her family by the time they came upon us kneeling next to Ned's body, which means she came *back* through the maze."

"What are you saying?" Bill demanded. His voice cracked.

"That your wife carries that big backpack with her everywhere, and I'm wondering what's in it."

Simms jerked his head, and two deputies approached Carla Seavers. She took a step back.

"I know my rights. You can't just search me. This is outrageous. Bill, do something!"

At that moment, a cell phone rang out. It played the early 70s hit, *Popcorn*.

"That's it!" Frederick got to his feet. "The sound I heard right after someone hit me." He shook his finger at his friends. "And you thought I was crazy. I knew something reminded me of popcorn."

Simms nodded. "Would you like to answer your phone, Mrs. Seavers?"

"I—I—"

Bill Seavers stepped away from his wife, an unconscious move that wasn't very flattering. "Carla! What's going on?"

She reached out for his hands. "I didn't do anything wrong. I mean, maybe I broke some unwritten rule about gossiping, but that's all I did. I didn't know what he was going to do with the information."

Simms jumped on it. "Who is *he*?"

Evan bent his head toward Sheila and murmured, "I think we're about to see the defense argument."

Carla Seavers performed a first-year drama student's version of angst. She put the back of her hand to her forehead.

"Oh, dear." Then she spread her hands open. "I'm sure he didn't know what he was doing. It was those friends of his, leading him on."

Simms grunted to show he didn't give a hoot. "A name, please."

Her entire body drooped with her dejected sigh. "Jimmy. My brother Jimmy."

"She rolled over on her *brother?*" Sheila blurted out,

much louder than she intended, and the responses varied from shushing noises to mutters from people who agreed with her.

"Let me get this straight," the detective said. "Your husband came home from work and told you all the cute things the kids said during class—including their parent's plans for the night—and you passed that onto your brother, Jimmy, so he and his friends could rob them. Nice family."

Simms made a motion, and two deputies moved to Carla Seavers and pulled her hands behind her back.

"Do you have to do that?" Bill Seavers asked. "She made a mistake. An easy one to make."

"Hello!" Samuel called out, pointing at Frederick. "She attacked an innocent man. That's *not* a mistake. Well, technically it was a mistake since he wasn't Ned..." He made a noise of frustration. "You don't *accidentally* hit someone!"

Simms finished the thought on all their minds. "And Ned's murder was no accident."

Shelby streaked across the room to her mother, but Bill caught hold of her before she made it and lifted her into his arms. Katelin walked up next to him and took his hand all the while staring at her mother as the deputies cuffed her.

Simms dumped the contents of her backpack on the closest picnic table. In the middle of a pile of snacks, juice boxes, wipes, a pink stuffed pig, coloring books, crayons, tissues, a plastic bag holding soggy training pants, and sippy cups, sat a wrapped gift that Evan recognized as Lucky's. The detective poked at the present with a pen and flipped it over to show the label. "You want to make a claim on this, Lozano?"

"It's like I told your friend. Me and Ned never exchanged gifts."

Simms nodded, satisfied. "I want fingerprints taken yesterday so I can get this baby open."

One of the deputies left for the maze to retrieve the appropriate person.

He studied the pile again, cocked his head and hooked his pen through one of the handles on the larger stainless-steel sippy cup, but the cup was too heavy and slipped off the pen. "Is this what you used on Frederick?"

"It packs a wallop," Evan muttered.

Simms looked at him, surprised, and the reporter felt his face grow warm with embarrassment. "I was upstairs when I spotted Lucky's gift. I wasn't quick enough."

"Must have hurt. This thing weighs a ton."

"Why?" Bill struggled to keep his voice level. "Why would you do it?"

Carla pressed her lips together into a tight line. "Do you have any idea how sick I am of hearing about Anna's Paw Patrol pajamas and Tiffany's L.O.L. doll and Nina's flip shirt and *why can't I have one*? Well? Why shouldn't Katelin have those things?" She took a deep breath, and her voice lowered to a growl. "Do you have any idea how much a Barbie costs unless you buy one naked and home-less?" Her upper lip curled in a sneer. "Why couldn't you have been a plumber?"

Bill hesitated. "What's a flip shirt?"

But Carla was in the zone. "And all I had to do for some extra spending money was pass on a few bits of stupid information blurted out by kids in your classroom. That's all. For all I knew, the kids didn't know what they were talking about and nothing would happen. No harm done."

"Then why kill Ned?" Simms asked. "Why not just write it off?"

"All he had to do was hand me a lousy present. That's

all. When I opened that package and saw the fluorescent slime, I lost it. My cut was—this was going to be the Christmas of Christmases." She took in a shaky breath. "A 2019 Mercedes electric car with an entertainment system, leather seats, rubber tires," she sobbed, "in cherry red."

Evan gaped. "That's a child's toy?"

Carla mumbled. "Ages three to six."

Simms blew out a breath. "I can see the insanity plea coming now."

"I'll call an attorney." Bill gave his wife a half-hearted smile. "Don't worry, honey."

Carla grit her teeth. "On what they pay you, I look forward to meeting the public defender."

The deputies escorted Ned's murderer out, with Bill staring after her, helpless. Sheila moved next to him and stroked Katelin's hair. "I'll watch the girls for you, Bill, until you make arrangements for someone to pick them up."

"It's so embarrassing," he said, tears in his eyes. "I thought I was lucky. That my wife was interested in my work, and all the time she was looking for opportunities to rob people."

"Technically, they were burglarized," Evan said without thinking, his mind already at work on his article.

Sheila swatted his arm and then smiled at Bill. "It's not your fault. How could you have known? No one could possibly hold you responsible."

"I'm finished." The teacher blinked several times as it sunk in. "No one will ever trust me with their kids again."

Sheila looked to Evan. "We'll do whatever we can to help you."

"Sure," Evan said, rewriting the first draft of the story in his head to stress Bill's innocence and the inadequate pay of teachers.

Simms joined them after Bill left, and the detective gave Lozano an unfriendly glare. "So, you knew all along who killed your friend? And you did nothing?"

Lozano clenched his jaw. Evan could see the muscles pulsing. "I didn't *know* anything. I thought maybe the sellers were here to observe, and maybe *they* killed Ned when he didn't go through with it. Since I didn't know who they were, I kept my eyes open."

The detective snorted. "Not very well, or your friend might not be dead."

A rumbling growl came from Lozano. "And all the time that *woman*…a *mother* for the love of—"

Evan didn't see it coming, and before he knew what hit him, he was sitting on the floor looking up at Lozano. The man's hands were back in his pockets, and Simms had hold of his elbow.

Without any signs of anger, Lozano said, "Sorry about that. I had to relieve my feelings, and I couldn't hit a woman." He slid a mean glare at Simms. "Or a cop."

Crooked and Joseph helped him to his feet, and Simms, with something bordering on pleasure, asked him if he wanted to press charges. Evan rubbed his jaw and moved it gently. Over Simms' shoulder, his geriatric neighbors were holding their breath, waiting for his answer.

"Doesn't seem to be any major damage. I'd rather just forget it."

His neighbors surged forward and surrounded Lozano.

"It's not your fault." Dot rubbed Lozano's back. "You have every right to be angry." She led him away, and the geriatric gang, never ones to miss out on gossip, followed.

"That was pretty clever, Miller," Simms said. "The way you made us all think you were after the husband."

"That's me. Clever to the core." No need to mention he thought Bill Seavers *was* the killer. At least at first.

Joseph took him by the arm. "Come on, Uncle Evan. You should sit down. That was some punch for an old guy."

Evan protested when the teen led him back to the same table as Mark, but Joseph insisted he didn't want to miss anything. The seniors were all gathered around, eagerly soaking up the details of the accountant turned farmhand's experience as the accused.

"It must have been frightening," Dot said to Mark. Evan noticed that she and Lucky Lozano held hands under the table.

"Yes, it was, ma'am."

"Did you have any thoughts about your last meal?" Tildy asked. "I'd have a difficult time choosing, because I have so many favorites. Chocolate? No. I think I would prefer to go out with a savory."

Mark gaped and then glanced around the table for confirmation that the woman was a lunatic, but Evan's neighbors were busy nodding and agreeing.

"No, ma'am," he said, his voice weak. "I didn't think that far ahead."

"You know what I'd do," Gus said. "I'd pick something hard to get hold of, like rhinoceros."

Frederick narrowed one eye. "Aren't they endangered?"

Gus grinned. "I think so. The jailers would have to wait for one to die, and that would give me more time."

"Well," Dot said with a sigh, "this wasn't a nice way to begin your new life in Settlers Ridge. Your grandmother said she was happy you decided to join them on the farm." She held out her hand. "Welcome back."

Mark grinned and shook with her.

"*Begin* your new life?" When Evan blurted this out, they all stared. "How long ago was Ted's wedding?"

"Last weekend. You missed a great party. Once I got

here, I fell in love again with the laid-back pace and the country air. I cancelled my return flight and called my mom to explain. She's happy for me. Of course, I'll have to go back and collect my things."

"Last weekend?" Evan repeated, stunned. A week wasn't enough time to form a relationship with Sheila Baker.

"What's the matter with you?" Gus demanded. "You keep repeating everything, like a parrot."

Evan raised his brows at the old fart. "Repeating everything?"

He didn't hear the reply, because he was headed to the corner table where Sheila worked to keep the children amused. Joseph and Crooked caught up with him.

Evan shot his best friend a narrow glance. "I thought you said Mark was quite a catch. How would you know?"

"He's one of the Friendly family. Good stock." Crooked said this as if it were reasonable. "And you have to admit he's a good-looking guy."

"You said it to irritate me." Evan couldn't infuse his words with anger, because he was too pleased at the outcome. Sheila had been trying to make him jealous with a man she hardly knew.

"Naturally."

"More important," Joseph said to change the direction of the conversation, "is the outcome of the race. Technically, I made it to the center of the maze before you."

Evan barked out a laugh. "You cheated."

The teen looked to Crooked for a ruling.

"You didn't specifically say *no cheating* when you set down the rules," Crooked advised.

Evan made a scoffing noise. "I said we were on our honor. It's implied."

Seeing the argument was lost, Joseph changed course.

"Do you think this place will be open tomorrow? We still need our tree."

Evan stopped walking. "Are you serious?"

"I *know* they won't have Santa Claus, but it's a short season, and they *have* to keep going if they want to make money, right? So, we'll be helping them out. And there are *other* family members that can help cover, ones that weren't so close to Mr. Roper. And besides. You guys keep saying how much Mr. Roper loved the farm, so he wouldn't want them to go out of business because of him."

Evan stared, but Crooked cackled with delight and clapped his friend on the shoulder. "The reasoning power of a child." At Joseph's scowl, he quickly amended his statement. "Of the younger generation. Now you'll be able to sympathize with me when I complain to you about my twins."

Joseph still waited for his answer, so Evan said, "Why don't we discuss it when we get home?"

The teen had to settle for that.

Mommy's unusual departure did not seem to have affected the three-year-old, who was giggling over a game of hide-n-seek that was limited to Sheila ducking sideways in her seat. The older daughter ignored them all to concentrate on her drawing.

Crooked took over the game, and Sheila stood up and came to Evan. "Bill's mom is on her way to pick them up." She glanced over her shoulder with concern. "I can't get Katelin to talk to me."

"Maybe her grandmother will have better luck."

"I hope so." She smiled. "Evan, thank you for helping Mark."

"Well, seeing as how you have your heart set on him..." Evan looked at the subject of their conversation, who was listening to Tildy with a dazed expression on his handsome features. "He's quite the catch."

"Yes. Well. Thanks."

"Sheila."

"Yes, Evan?"

He bent forward to put his mouth next to her ear and spoke softly. "How could you kiss a guy you've known less than a week?"

She jerked her head back. "*I* didn't kiss him. I told Ma Friendly I would look out for him, that's all, but he misinterpreted the situation and—" She suddenly realized he was grinning and pressed her lips together. "None of your business."

She returned to the children, and Evan said under his breath, "One of these days, it will be my business. One of these days."

Someone tugged on his elbow and he turned to find Tildy, flanked by Gus, Samuel, Frederick, Dot, and Lucky.

"We wanted to apologize," the old woman said.

He sent a questioning glance around.

Samuel stepped forward. "We should have invited you to come with us tonight, but—"

"Having fun doesn't seem like your thing," Gus said.

Frederick glowered at him. "That's *not* what Samuel was going to say. I, for one, think Evan is probably grateful he's been spared your company for the evening."

Tildy placed a hand on Gus's shoulder, perhaps to restrain him from further outbursts. "We should have invited you and let you decide if you wanted to come or not."

"We apologize for our thoughtlessness," Dot said from the back of the group.

Lucky's gaze met his. "What? I'm not part of this."

Dot, her arm through his, gave her friend a gentle shake. "Not yet."

They waited with expectant looks on their wrinkled faces. Evan cleared his throat. "That's very nice of you, but there's no need for an apology." He coughed. "I'm having a—" Having a Christmas party? No. That sounded too childish. "I was planning to invite you, that is, I *am* inviting you over for drinks and, um, there will be music, at least Joseph said there should be, and—" He was *not* going to encourage them to dance. "It's nothing fancy, you know. Not a big deal." He felt like an idiot.

They continued to stare and he had an unexpected desire for them to say yes. It was like waiting to see if you were going to be picked for the team in gym class. If they rejected him, he'd have to start sneaking out of his house by the back alley.

Tildy suddenly beamed at him. "He's having a Christmas party!"

"Oh, fun." Dot looked up at Lucky. "You'll come, won't you?"

"Are you kidding? He said there'll be drinks."

"You have to let us all bring something," Samuel said. "My barbequed bacon-wrapped water chestnuts are a favorite, I've been told."

"And I can get the word out." Frederick paused. "Unless this is an intimate, sit-down affair?"

"No! Not intimate." Evan almost shouted his response. Now that the invitation was out, he wanted a crowd big enough to hide in. Maybe later, years and years later, he would feel comfortable enough to sit around a table chatting with a select few neighbors for an hour or so, but not yet. He let out a sigh. "That's settled then."

As they filed for the door, Dot started singing *Deck the Halls* in a husky alto, and the others joined in. Even Lucky.

Mid *fa-la-la-la-la*, Frederick turned back to return Evan's jacket.

"Thanks. It helped."

Evan slipped the jacket on. "While you're spreading the word—"

Frederick gave him a bawdy wink. "I'll make sure a certain schoolteacher knows about it."

Evan planned to be subtle about his request, but what the heck. "Thanks."

The old man nudged him in the ribs. "You're one of us now. We have to look out for each other." He caught up to Samuel, who gave him a questioning look, and Frederick leaned his head in and whispered. Samuel looked back at Evan with delight.

As the group exited the side door, Evan stared after them with an unfamiliar warmth in his chest. *One of them.* It was a new experience. A little scary. And horrifying, especially if they considered him a contemporary. Still, he thought he could live with it.

He motioned to Joseph and Crooked, and they joined him at the door.

"That was exhausting," Crooked said. "All that waiting around was worse than a workout."

"I'm pretty tired, too." Joseph sounded surprised. "Let's go home."

Home. Evan had a place to call home, something more than a sparsely furnished apartment in an anonymous neighborhood in Los Angeles. If what Frederick said was true, he had friends, albeit more friends than he wanted. He glanced at Joseph. And family, which was something he never thought he'd want again.

The Evan Miller who left Friendly Farm that night felt he was a pretty rich man after all.

Also by Jacqueline Vick

Frankie Chandler Mysteries

Barking Mad at Murder

A Bird's Eye View of Murder

An Almost Purrfect Murder

What the Cluck? It's Murder

A Scaly Tail of Murder

A Scape Goat for Murder

Some Like Murder Hot

Harlow Brother Mysteries

Civility Rules

Bad Behavior

Deadly Decorum

Standalone Novels

The Body Guy

An Unhealthy Attachment

Family Matters

Short Story Collections

Binky's Boss and Other Short Mysteries

About the Author

Jacqueline Vick spent her childhood plotting ways to murder her Barbie doll. Mystery writing proved a more productive outlet.

While researching an article for *Fido Friendly Magazine* (Calling All Canine Clairvoyants), she came up with the character of Frankie Chandler, pet psychic. She also writes the Harlow Brothers mysteries and numerous standalones, short stories, and novellas. Her books are known for satirical humor and engaging characters who are desperate to keep their secrets. She currently resides in Southern California with her husband.

You can find her books and sign up for her newsletter at www.jacquelinevick.com.

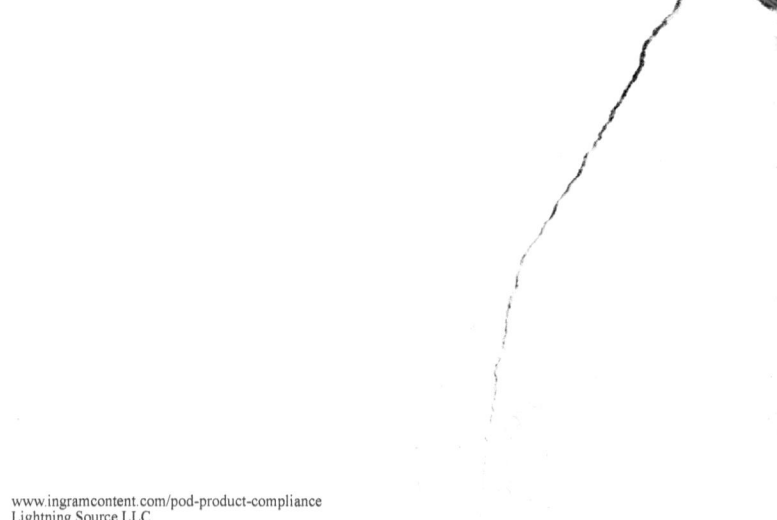